THE WHICH WAY TREE

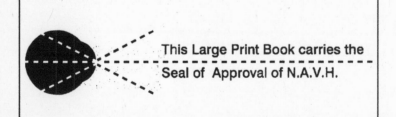

THE WHICH WAY TREE

ELIZABETH CROOK

WHEELER PUBLISHING
A part of Gale, a Cengage Company

GALE
A Cengage Company

Farmington Hills, Mich • San Francisco • New York • Waterville, Maine
Meriden, Conn • Mason, Ohio • Chicago

**LIBRARY OF CONGRESS CIP DATA ON FILE.
CATALOGUING IN PUBLICATION FOR THIS BOOK
IS AVAILABLE FROM THE LIBRARY OF CONGRESS**

ISBN-13: 978-1-4328-5279-5 (hardcover)

Published in 2018 by arrangement with Little, Brown and Company, a division of Hachette Book Group, Inc.

Printed in Mexico
1 2 3 4 5 6 7 22 21 20 19 18

*For my grandparents
Howard Edward Butt (1895–1991) and
Mary Elizabeth Holdsworth Butt
(1903–1993)*

TESTIMONY OF
BENJAMIN SHREVE

Before Grand Jury of Fifteen
Home of Izac Wronski
Judge E. Carlton Presiding
18th District
County of Bandera
State of Texas
April 25, 1866
As Recorded by Alfred R. Pittman

Having been duly sworn, state your name.

Benjamin Shreve.

State your age.

Seventeen years, sir.

Where do you live, Benjamin?

Over on Verde Creek. Near Camp Verde.

All right. You may stand there. It's crowded in here; I apologize for that. My name is Judge Edward Carlton, and this is Alfred R. Pittman. He'll be writing down what you say before the grand jury today. Speak clearly. If he asks you to repeat something, then repeat it.

Yes sir.

You can hang your hat there by the door.

I prefer to hold it, sir.

All right, then. Do you know why you've been called here?

On account of the men I found dead on Julian Creek.

That's correct. We believe you were the first to see the bodies and that you may have seen one of the men who hanged those gentlemen. We realize this happened three years ago and justice has had to wait out the war. So your memory on the particulars might not be clear. Simply recall what you can. Don't make anything up. If you don't remember, say you don't remember.

8

I will remember, sir.

Very well. Now, the basic facts of the murders have already been established, but we're trying to verify the names of those who took part.

I can tell you Clarence Hanlin was one that did, sir.

I'm not looking for your opinion, Benjamin. I'm looking for your testimony. That means what you saw, not what you think. Answer only the questions I ask you. Now. What were you doing on Julian Creek that morning when you discovered the bodies?

Hunting, sir.

Julian Creek is quite a few miles from Camp Verde. Why were you not hunting closer to home?

There was no game closer to home. The Sesesh soldiers at Camp Verde had killed it all off for theirselves and their prisoners down in the canyon.

How did you get to the Julian that morning?

9

Horseback, sir.

Were you alone?

Yes sir.

What time did you leave your home?

I suppose about a hour or so before daylight. I recall I rode in the moonlight.

And your intention was to hunt on Julian Creek?

My intention was to kill the first game I come across. It was a deer near the Julian. I fired and missed it.

What happened after that?

I pitched a fit, sir. Dismounted and cursed, and then right away wished I weren't behaving in such a manner.

For fear you would scare off game?

For fear of Indians and Sesesh and bush-whackers and vigilantes and whatnot. It was loud and dangerous behavior, sir.

Benjamin, the men in this room, some of whom you probably know, are of various persuasions on the late war. You would do well to refrain from name-calling.

Yes sir, I know one . . . two . . . three . . . four . . . five of them here that me and my father sold shingles to. That one by the door there —

Don't bring politics into this.

No sir, I won't. But it was Sesesh that done in the men I found dead.

It is true that Confederate major William J. Alexander from Camp Verde, whereabouts unknown, is currently under indictment for murder and highway robbery. We're trying to ascertain which of his men took part in the hanging of the eight travelers you found dead.

Clarence Hanlin was one, sir.

I know that's your testimony. But if it's true, we have to get to it in a logical way. Simply answer my questions.

Yes sir.

11

So you fired at the deer, and missed, and pitched a fit. What happened next?

I heard coyotes yipping and I thought it was Comanches. I tied my mare in the brush and went a distance off and laid down flat where nobody could've seen me in the grass. But the longer I laid there and listened, the more I thought, "That is not Indians, that is actual coyotes." I figured maybe I'd shot the deer and wounded it, and it had run off and gone down and now the coyotes was closed in and devouring it. So I thought to go and investigate and see what they was up to. I went on my belly on the chance it was Comanches in fact and not coyotes. And that was when I come across what I seen.

As precisely as you can, describe what you saw.

Clarence Hanlin and a pack of coyotes under a clump of scrub oaks, sir. Some ways from the creek. They was in dusky light of the morning, amid prickly pear, on rocky ground, and the coyotes was lighting out because Clarence Hanlin was waving a stick and yipping at them with a yip like he was one of them. He was spooking them out. It was a puzzle to me why he did not shoot them if they was bothering him. He had a gun. But it appeared that he —

You had not, at that time, ever seen Mr. Hanlin before — is that correct?

Not exactly correct, sir. I'd seen soldiers coming and going on the roads near Camp Verde, and I believe I'd seen Clarence Hanlin amongst them, as I'd noticed he had a eye that drooped. He had a distinctive look, sir. It was not a pleasant look. He was not homely, but his looks was against him and not right.

Gentlemen, can we please have no snickering? Alfred, I hope you're getting everything down. I want the details recorded. All right, Benjamin, you saw a pack of coyotes and a man, whom you thought you might recognize as one of the Confederate soldiers stationed at Camp Verde, but whom you did not, at that time, know by name and with whom you had never conversed, waving a stick at the coyotes in the apparent effort to scare them off. Is that right?

Yes sir. And yipping at them, sir. It was a odd thing, to my thinking. There was a dog-like thing about it, sir.

Are you casting aspersions?

If you mean am I insulting the man, no sir. I guess you could say he sounded a bit like a pig, too, sir, if you wanted to cast what you said. A aspersion. It would not be off the mark. I will put it this way. It was a weird noise he made to fuss at them coyotes. Rather spooked me. Then I seen him squat down like he was fixing to pluck up firewood or some such. There was plenty of broken limbs laying about. But what he plucked up was not firewood, it was a arm. And then I seen that it was attached to a body. And then I seen other bodies.

Pause there. Where were the bodies?

All about at his feet, sir. Scattered, I would say. Maybe a dozen of them.

For the record, there were eight bodies.

They looked like more than eight to me, the way they was strewn. But eight's on the mark if you say so. I was twenty yards off, or more. The light was feeble, on account of the sun was not full up. And now that I think on it, I suppose my first idea was the bodies was logs and branches, and nothing amiss. So how many of them there was, I did not contemplate on at that time.

There were eight dead, precisely. We have their names. Some of these men here in this room were called out from town to help bury them. Now continue. What did you do when you saw the bodies?

I tried to figure it out like this: here is these bodies and these coyotes and Clarence Hanlin with his stick and his yipping. So —

Clarence Hanlin, whom you did not yet know to be Clarence Hanlin, but with whom you would later, I take it, have some familiarity?

That's right, sir. At that time I known him for a man with a droopy eye, in a Sesesh outfit, who I thought I might have seen before on the road near Camp Verde. So I figured the coyotes was trying to feast on the bodies, and Mr. Hanlin, the Sesesh,

15

was scaring them off. That's how I seen it, the best I could figure. But then it come to me that I had more to figure, because what was the bodies doing there? I figured maybe Comanches was there and killed the men the coyotes was trying to feast on, and this Sesesh come along, and though he was not friendly to look at, he was protecting the bodies. But hold it there, I thought. Because then I seen him take a object from the jacket of one of them on the ground. He took from one, and rose a step, and poked at another with his stick, and squatted and took a object from that one, too. He was looting the dead, sir. He was taking what he could find. He went from pocket to pocket, searching for valuables to pinch and pilfer. He had a satchel strapped to his side, and he put things in that. I was fearful to breathe, sir. I figured if he should see me witness him, he would come after me. I did not so much as twitch. He turned my direction at one time and did not see me, but I got a good look at him. His gaze was oddly fixed, sir. He had a harsh stare. When I seen that, I rose to my feet and took to my heels in a hurry. I made my way to my mare and rode as fast as she would take me back to my home.

And why did you not report the crime you had witnessed?

It was not easy to know what was a crime, and what was not, with so much mischief afoot.

I understand your parents are deceased?

Yes sir.

For some time now?

Yes sir. I live alone with my sister.

Very well. Now. About your subsequent encounters with this man. Tell me about those.

Well, that's a long story. He wanted to do me in. Me and my sister both.

He wanted to kill you? Because of what you had witnessed?

No sir. Because of a thing that happened. I'd rather not be made to speak of it, if that's a option.

It is not an option, Benjamin. Why did he

want to kill you?

Well, sir. I guess it was on account of my sister had shot his finger.

Shot his finger?
Shot it off, sir.

You're saying she shot off one of his fingers?

One and a portion, sir.

Gentlemen, hold your amusement. The boy will explain. Benjamin, will you recount the circumstances?

Some time after what I seen on the Julian, my sister and me was sitting in a tree with a goat staked out on the ground to entice a panther. It was my sister's wish to kill the panther but Mr. Hanlin got hisself in her aim.

She shot him by accident?

No. He provoked her, sir. He was hollering and advancing so she shot at him, and rightly so, if you ask me, although I did not think so at the time.

Can I assume he had a reason to be hollering and advancing?

I suppose, sir. She was hollering at him.

I see. Benjamin, I have at least a dozen other people I need to question today, so I don't have time for digressions. But if Clarence Hanlin is a man prone to committing violent acts without provocation, that would be helpful to know. Would you say that's the case?

I would say there was some provocation by my sister only if hollering is provocation. But before her provocation he was provoking of her by the needless act of stabbing a camel, sir.

One of the camels stationed at Camp Verde, I presume.

Yes sir. So I would say the first provoking act was on the side of Mr. Hanlin, done by him. The camel was decrepit and broke down, and Mr. Hanlin jabbed it a fair number of times in the hump as it was not moving as fast as he wished it to. It made loud and fearful noises whilst being stabbed, sir, and fell to its knees — a monstrous end for a beast come all the way from Egypt. My sister would not sit for it, and being as she was in the tree and had a pistol, and the panther had not come hisself to get hisself shot, it was a poor time and place for Mr. Hanlin to be stabbing the creature in such a way. I will give you the short of it if that is what you want. My sister —

I'm afraid I don't have time even for the short of it at the moment. I need information specific to Mr. Hanlin's guilt or innocence in murder and his current whereabouts. How many times did you have contact with him after seeing him on the Julian?

It was ongoing, sir, after what my sister done to his finger. He was tracking us for two full days and a portion of another. On occasion he gave chase. There was words spoken. There was shots fired.

I'm uncertain if you're providing a deficit of information or a surplus, son, but I'm getting no closer to what I want to know. Can you stick close to the point?

Clarence Hanlin was one that done in the

men on the Julian, sir. Hanged and robbed them. He told me by admission of the hanging and I witnessed the robbing. If that's what you're in search of, then there it is, sir. The very, very short of it, sir. You have my word on it.

He told you of the hanging?

Yes sir. In some detail, when he caught up with us. He told me he'd string me up, too. Said he'd string up my sister right alongside and watch our necks pop. He was a terrible pest, sir.

And your sister heard this confession and threat also?

Yes, she did. It led to a great deal of conflict. She is a person of uncommon temper.

I will need to have her testify.

She won't do that, sir. She's cat-marked and poor to look at. Also mulatto. Her mother was a Negro. She won't come.

I'm to understand she had a different mother from yours?

Quite different from mine, sir. However, both passed. Alike in that respect, sir.

How old is she?

Younger than me by two years. Fifteen at the present time. Twelve when she done what she done about the finger.

I see. Can you read and write?

Efficiently. I have twice read the whole of The Whale, about Moby Dick. I have read Malaeska: The Indian Wife of the White Hunter. And I have read two novels of the Waverley brand. They was all given to me by the Yankee prisoners down in the canyon. I tossed them a ear of corn and up come The Whale. Fell at my feet. And next day I —

Do you post and receive mail?

No sir. I have not in the past. The Camp Verde post office is shut down now. That whole place is a shambles and looted. I could receive mail at the post office in Dr. Ganahl's home at Zanzenburg, which is not far off from my home. However, he was Sesesh, and remained so, and has fled to Mexico, and I do not know if —

We'll settle on the post office at Comfort. I want you to write a full account of every encounter you've had with Clarence Hanlin. Write in detail and be frank. I'll be back in Bandera in three months and at that time I'll need to render my recommendation to this grand jury. I will be questioning others about this case in the meantime. But because you have had personal interactions with Mr. Hanlin your statements are essential. It's our job to make sure justice is done in these crimes of Confederate soldiers against civilians of Union sentiment. A big part of that job will be yours. I want you to write a clear statement of who you are, who your parents were, who your sister is, and describe every brush you've had with the individual you know as Clarence Hanlin. Remember that this is a testament and you are under oath to be truthful. Then I want you to deliver your report to the Comfort post office. The postmaster will see that it finds me. If I have further questions I'll put them to you in writing and send them to Comfort. Do you often go there?

Yes sir, I do on occasion, to sell furniture I make.

All right. Before you leave now, let me be clear on one thing. I presume you have not seen the man you refer to as Clarence Hanlin in the three years since the encounters we've discussed?

No sir.

And where, exactly, was he when you last saw him?

The Medina, sir. Somewhat north of here. He went round a bend. Swept away.

Swept away?

In a gullywasher. Off he went in the gullywasher and I've not seen hide nor hair of the man since that time.

This is unexpected. Do you presume him dead?

I'd be spooked if he was not dead, sir. It would be unnatural.

This is certainly news. We may finish with

Mr. Hanlin sooner than I thought. You are certain it was he?

None other but him, sir.

I see. Well. This only increases the importance of your job. Evidence is our bulwark against chaos. If Clarence Hanlin is guilty and living, he has to be found and convicted. If he's deceased, he has to be proved so. He can't simply be presumed so and allowed to go free when eight men traveling to Mexico were captured, robbed, and hanged. I want you to write the account I asked for and deliver it to Comfort as I said. I want all the details on record.

Sir? I have no pens and papers.

Izac, can you spare Benjamin quill and paper and a pot of ink?

Yes, Your Honor. I can.

Benjamin, I assume you're heading home on horseback?

Yes sir.

You're aware the Comanches have been

raiding over in Blanco County?

Yes sir, I'm much aware of it. And Mr. Berry Buckalew killed on the Seco. My father and me once cut shingles with him. And Mr. Hines, that lived at the Mormon camp, done for at Tarpley's Crossing. I know of it all. The troubles with Kickapoos, too. I'm well aware, sir.

Is your sister alone at your home?

Yes sir.

Take care on the road, will you?

Thank you. I always do, sir.

Dear Judge,
Here is my statements to what you asked. However, it is not all of them as there is more. I will send more later.

Yours kindly,
Benjamin Shreve

My Testament

Who I Am
I am Benjamin Shreve.

Who My Parents Was
My father was Alton Shreve. My mother was Millie. I guess her name was Millie Shreve after she married my father. I don't know what it was before that. My father always just called her your mother. I did not know her personally as she died shortly after my birth, which event took place in the winter of 1849. I have been told by oth-

ers she was a good woman and pretty to look at if a tad bit flat in the face. Before I was born, she and my father come here from Duck Hill Mississippi and my father built a house and was making acceptable money in shingles which at that time was starting to be a good living in these parts, if hard work. When I was born and my mother passed, my father had a impossible time taking care of me and cutting shingles and making hauls to market. I was left to squall much of the time, what choice did he have in the matter. I suppose there was nights he wished the Comanches would hear and come take me.

Who My Sister Is

My sister is Samantha Shreve. You asked me to be frank so I will tell you she is my half sister, as her mother was a Negro and mine was white. On occasion I call her Sam, which I think she prefers though I have no reason to know so, as she has never said so. She is fifteen years old, scarred in the face by a panther that killed her mother when she was six. She is scrawny and nothing to look at.

Her mother was named Juda. The way my father met Juda was on the road to San Antonio. I was one year old at that time, lashed to the wagon seat so I would not tumble off. The wagon had a issue at Slide Off Pass with the wheel coming loose and the logs on the top sliding off the back like they are wont to do on that extreme incline. My father had to take me down and strap me to a tree so I would not toddle off. He was retrieving the spilled logs, and had about had all the good times he could stand, when along come a wagon driven by a man with a poorly looking woman beside him and a sturdy Negro woman in the back.

The man called out, Do you need some help with them logs.

My father, not being a man of much pride, I guess, said, I need some help with my whole life. And with that he commenced to weep like a baby — so he told me on the occasion that he recounted the story. He was not a delicate man nor a pessimist but he broke down and let her rip. I have not ever thought less of him for that particular moment. He had got hisself a sorry life, a bunch of logs going their own way, a broken down wagon, a hogback horse that given up, a chance of Indians coming along, and a terrible little baby boy strapped to a tree and making a racket.

The man in the wagon climbed down and helped him out. In the course of this, in some way a deal was struck that the man could take possession of the logs, which he was in need of as he was new to the place and expecting to build, and in exchange the Negro woman Juda would be borrowed to my father for a month to clean up his house, wash his laundry, and otherwise do the work of a wife minus the conjugal — there was to be none of that.

My father, being a man of his word, did not come near Juda during that time I don't think. However, love was in the air, from his part, as I understand. I am not too sure what Juda thought of him. She must of liked him well enough, for when the time was up she did not return to them that owned her, and more deals was struck and finally after a while she and my father was together for good. You want me to be frank. I do not know of any wedding. I do not suppose there could of been one. But Samantha come along.

The only problem was, Juda was mean. She used to about do me in. I believe she might of hated me, but I am not sure. She was a hard worker, and determined, and kept the house in good order, but she could whip the daylight out of a bad little boy. Being as I was the only one of those around, I got more than my share of that.

I was a mere two years old at the time Samantha was born, but when I got my footing in life, and learned to say my piece and have a sense of what was going on about me, I recall taking my fists to Juda when she talked rough to the baby. We surely had our fights, and I would do nothing she said.

One particular time I recall, if not perfectly, it was a hot day and she kept me in the house, sweltering, and made me tend the cookfire, which I felt was women's work, whilst I preferred to go out and help my father. I was about five years old and big enough to help him some.

Stir the pot, she told me.

She was hanging nappies at the hearth, and the whole place smelled bad, of nappies and sweat, and blazing hot, and I said, No, I ain't going to stir it, I am going outside.

Stir it, said she.

I said, I won't. You ain't my boss. My daddy is my boss and you ain't.

She boiled up with fierce anger in her head and her face. She was a sturdy woman. She had a fierce jaw, and skin that was pale for a Negro, and hair cut short to her scalp. She continued to tell me to stir the pot, and I continued to not do so, and the argument got loud, and I thought to make a break for the door, but she got me by the hair and dragged me back and said, I'll snatch you bald.

Her hold on me, as I recall, hurt me quite a bit. She did not let go. I screeched like a caught varmint, and Samantha caterwauled in her crib, creating a further ruckus. When finally I broke loose of Juda I was fed up. I took up the poker out of the fire and thrashed it about and proclaimed in a pitch wail, I will leave my mark on you, I will! I do not like you, and I will leave my mark!

She ceased her hollering, ceased moving altogether, and the look in her eyes become murderous, and she said, in a slow voice, like she was talking to a slow witted person, You think I ain't never faced down a hot poker before.

Then she undone her buttons and dropped her dress to the ground, and stood before me without a stitch on, and I seen a bunch of stripes on her body, darker than her skin.

Agape, I stood. God all mighty, Juda, who done that to you, I asked her.

His name ain't important, said she. But I will tell you one thing. A poker ain't going to get you your way. You stir the pot, you hear me.

I was inclined to stir it then, but my eyes was stuck on her, and my father come in and seen her stark naked, and he looked dismayed at the fearful sight, and rather doleful, and said, Juda, he don't need to see that.

And she said, Yes, by God, he do.

After that, she put her clothes on, and I stirred the pot.

That was the most I ever seen of Juda, other than her meanness.

The fact that she was so hard on me and on Samantha makes it all the more curious the way she laid her life down, in such a bloody fashion, in defense of Samantha, the day a panther come calling.

Dear Judge,

To explain about Clarence Hanlin I have to explain about the panther. Those are of a piece. So this further report I am about to send to you is direct to the point although you might not know it. I have yet to get to what I have to say about Clarence Hanlin but I will make another report after this one. They take time for me to write, as I work at the shingle camp down from here when it's not pouring rain. I have to write these reports mostly at night or early. Also I make furniture in what time I have.

Also the quill is hard to manage.

Here is the facts of what the panther done to Juda on a cold blue morning before the sun come up.

Yours kindly,
Benjamin Shreve

I was eight years old at the time it happened. On the night previous my father brought home with him a man he met in the shingle camp downriver. The man was to stay the night with us, as he did not yet have him a home of his own and it was exceeding cold out. His name was Luke. He had with him a buffalo skin to sleep on. Juda did not like the dirty condition that it was in. She liked things tidy and clean to a fault — you could not track even a piece of grass into the house without having to hear about it from her. She was not quite right in the head about that.

The man had a odd way of twitching his head and had scurf in his hair. Juda had words to say to my father about bringing him home, as she did not want him around. However, she did finally allow him to come in with his buffalo skin, to eat corn bread, and to sleep on the floor. She would not give him any meat.

He did not kill it nor skin it, she said, and he ain't going to eat it.

I will give him a portion of mine, my father said.

But Juda said, No, he can't have any.

She did not turn her back whilst we ate. She kept her eye on my father to see he did not give up any meat. This was unfriendly, as there was no shortage then.

Me and Samantha slept in the same bed at that time, whilst Juda and my father slept in the other. The man spread his skin before the fire and commenced to snore. I had trouble getting to sleep, as I could feel how mad Juda was to have the man there, and how sorry my father felt, and how little caring the stranger had about any of it at all — I do not think he cared about meat, he only wanted the warmth of the fire, and there was plenty of that.

Some time before the sun come up I seen Juda get out of the bed. She wore her dress, other than her gown, on account of the stranger was in the house. She stirred up the coals and nursed up a flame. Then she knelt by the side of the man and set to searching his head. She did not touch it, but only got very close. I knew what she was up to. She had a aversion to lice and was forever at the ready for them. The man's hair smelled bad and I suppose she was suspicious of it.

In a short time she stood up and give him a kick in the side. Get out, she told him. Get going.

He roused with a start, and let out a yell.

My father awoke to the noise. The man

looked to him, as I guess he could not believe my father would let a Negro act like that.

What have you done, my father asked Juda.

I want him gone, she said. I want him gone now.

As if that might of escaped my father's notice.

You get him out, she said. She said the twitch he had got was not natural but on account of the itch.

My father tried to get her to put a sock in it but she would not.

The man said, I ain't going. I don't know the way to the road.

It's yonder, she told him. You can find it. Only a fool can't find a road.

My father said, He is not a fool. It's dark out.

They had words about it.

After some time of this, my father raised his voice and said, Goddamn, I'm going with him. Daylight or not, it's time to go. Hell or high water, it's time to go.

He did not often curse in such a manner.

He and the stranger went to the shed and saddled their horses and left.

That did not satisfy Juda well enough. She had it in her mind that we had all got lice in our hair on account of the man having been in our midst and because they can sneak. This was a terrible thought for her to suffer, as she hated the creatures, and all creatures that was not under her say-so. In a angry manner she swept the floor and got out her ridding comb and dumped kerosene into a bowl and combed it into her hair.

She told me to take off my shirt and to sit at the table. I knew how this would go, as we had done it before. I did not see any use to put up a fight. I would of preferred to ride off with my father and the stranger, but unlike them I did not have a horse. She slathered the kerosene onto my hair and combed in a vigorous manner. I figured I'd have to go out and dunk my head in the creek, and this was a unwelcome thought on account of how cold it was out. I did state once, I have got no bugs. She continued to scrape my head and splash the kerosene over my hair. It burned a great deal on my scalp.

I seen Samantha was awake now and alert to us from the bed. So as to pretend she did not see us, she did not sit up nor fully open her eyes. I knew there would be some difficulty with her. She had a hatred to having a comb in her hair, which was trouble to manage, as it was Negro hair and she had a good bit of it.

Without giving us warning, she bolted out of the bed and run out into the dark. One minute she was in the bed and the next she was out the door and left it open. The night was cold and the sky black with a partial scoop of the moon to see by. Through the door I seen her light out for the creek. I do not know where she thought she would get to, but I had a idea about that. A huge old sow roamed with the notch-eared hogs down in the creek bottom, and Samantha was fond of that sow. It had taken a hatred to Juda, who had beat it out of the house on occasions it dared to wander in, but Samantha had always treated it right and there was affection between them. It might be she was heading down to the creek to hide out with the fat sow. I have never seen fit to ask her if this was the case, as I think the question would trouble her, given what happened on account of her taking off in the manner she did.

She run in her white gown with her arms flapping alongside. She was six years old at that time, and puny for that, racing as fast as she could to the trees and the creek. I might of laughed out loud at the sight if not for the fact that Juda would of let loose on me for doing that. You run, I thought to myself. Hide out where Juda can't find you.

And then I seen a creature low to the ground and moving so fast I could not make out what it was. It went directly at Samantha from off to the right where we kept eight goats in a pen. It come into my line of sight in a flash of yellow-brown color, with a long tail, crossing our bare patch of yard, just under the scoop of the moon. I had no time to think of what it might be before it was on Samantha. It was bigger than I can even say. It covered her fully up. One minute her shape was there in the dark, and the next it was not to be seen. All I made out was the long shape of the beast, as if it had swallowed her up. It did not make a sound, nor did Samantha. In the midst of the quiet it come to me what sort of beast this must be, although I was not thinking much about what to call it.

I got to my feet in haste and was out the door. I do not recall what I thought I would do, but the question arose in me as I drew closer. I would like to tell you I leapt on the cat and forestalled it, and yet it was not me that done so, but Juda. She run faster and past me.

What happened next was loud. Juda threw herself down on top of the cat like she was a rug laid over it. She was plenty big, but

45

the cat was bigger. It yowled and roared. Juda latched herself on to it and swung at it with a hatchet she had got from by the door. It was not a big hatchet. It was a chicken chopper. She shrieked in a manner that I did not know she could, laying it on the panther. But the panther was hard to keep hold of. Juda got her arms around its throat and tried to drag it off Samantha. I thought if she did not hack it to death then she was bound to strangle the creature. It made fierce noises, and the struggle was such a frenzy of twisting and turning I could not tell what was Juda and what was the cat. I was not sure Samantha was still a part of the picture as she was flat on the ground and could not be seen. After a time of terrible struggle Juda flipped the cat on its back and Samantha rose up and run for a tree close by.

I have heard that when a cat has got its eyes on a prey it will settle for nothing else, it wants only to kill what it has set its heart on. In this case that was Samantha. Juda hung on to its neck and all but rode on its back, but it continued after Samantha. The tree Samantha climbed was a old pecan tree. The panther got halfway up after her whilst Juda hacked and pulled at its hind end and chopped at its paws. Juda's screaming was a racket. I run to the house to get my father's rifle. I can't actually swear I had a intention of fetching the rifle, as it is likely I just wanted shed of the fright. But when I got to the house I did think of the rifle. It was a old caplock with a short stock and it took me a minute to load it and get back out the door.

When I was out there I seen the panther had ceased going up the tree and was on the ground on top of Juda. She was on her back and the panther's teeth was sunk in her throat. Its jaws was squeezing down hard. This was a terrible sight to behold, as you could see the death coming over her. She had nearly lost her hold on the hatchet but was trying to hit the panther with it. But a hatchet used to chop up chickens was not handy against a beast such as that which had got her pinned down.

I fired, but did not hit the panther. It did not so much as look about for the sound. Juda made fearsome noises and then she moved no more. The panther got off her and sunk its claws in the trunk of the tree and headed for Samantha again. Samantha screeched at me, Shoot it, shoot it! But I had already spent the ball and could not do so. Therefore I advanced and took a whack at the cat with the butt of the rifle and hit it

47

squarely on the back with a thud as it went up the tree. I jabbed at it with the barrel. It hissed and yowled and swiped at me but kept on going after Samantha. Its hair stood on end. I seen Juda there at my feet, her dress tore up, her skin ripped up, her throat a terrible mess, one of her eyes hanging out of the socket. I had to watch out for fear I would tread on her body. Juda had done a good bit of damage to the cat. Two toes of the hind right paw was chopped clean off and missing. I struck with the rifle, and Samantha jabbed with a stick until the panther backed down the tree, at which time I thought we might win the fight yet.

However, the panther did not flee. When it was on the ground it turned and looked at me straight on with the shine of its yellow eyes. The smell of it was mixed up with how the kerosene smelled in my hair. The panther's whole face went up in a snarl and I seen the fangs. Its whiskers was long and spread out and its ears was flat to its head. Its head looked twice or more the size of my own.

I thought I was done for, but it turned its notice to Juda. It give her a sniff and got its jaws on her throat and commenced to drag her away. Being as she was sturdy, it did not drag her with ease. I was scared it would turn and pounce on me and I was inclined to let it take her. Samantha kept on screaming at me to shoot it. I had on nothing but breeches, as I had taken my shirt off inside the house for Juda to rid the lice. There I stood, half naked, holding a unloaded gun, and I did not have the will to start whacking that cat just to get Juda's body. I figured since Juda was passed and I was not yet, then I should get the prejudice in my favor. It was not as if I had much lingering thought on the matter, it was more my inward opinion.

Samantha however was of a different opinion. She started in hollering at the panther as well as at me. She grabbed pecans out of the tree and chucked them down at the cat as it labored to drag off Juda. She tore small branches and threw them down and screeched at it. Her whole head was covered in blood from where the panther had bit into her skull when it first jumped on her. The blood was slick on her face and in splotches all over her gown. The morning was not yet light but I seen the glisten of all that blood in the blue before dawn.

She screamed at the panther. You turn my mama loose!

The pecans startled the cat and pestered

49

it whilst it was tugging at Juda. She was sturdy, as I have said. It dragged her in fits and starts.

I begged Samantha to stop provoking the creature, as I thought it would turn around and come after me.

You are a coward if you don't shoot it! she screamed at me.

I can't shoot it, I told her. I have spent the ball! I already fired and missed! What would you have me do!

Go after it! Whack it! she cried.

I did not want to provoke it further. You hush, I warned her. It'll come after us!

But what was I to say to my father if I was to stand by and watch the panther lug Juda into the brush. We would have to hunt what was left of her. I could not be a coward like that.

I backed my way to the house, keeping a eye on Samantha up in the tree and watching the panther drag Juda. My feet was bare, so it was one bare foot in back of the other the whole way across the yard. We had our eyes on each other — the panther, Samantha, and me.

Samantha screamed at me, Where are you going! Don't leave me up here by myself!

I am going to re-load the gun, I told her.

I went backwards into the house. It was

hard not to bolt the door and stay there, as I would of preferred to do that. I put another ball in the rifle and come out and made ready to shoot the panther as best I could in what small light there was. It was almost into the line of brush at the slope down to the creek, pulling Juda along. The manner in which it took her was awful. She was a heap of dinner to it, and not Juda at all. I could not help but think of the ways I knew her. The particular ways she was. And now her legs was dragging along in the dirt. Samantha called for her a number of times but could not raise her.

When I seen a clear shot of the panther I fired and missed it, or maybe nicked it. It went off into the brush, but I did not think it was gone. I loaded another ball.

You come on down, I told Samantha. I'll shoot it if it goes for you.

You'll miss it! she yelled at me. You've missed it two times already!

No, I'll hit it! I yelled at her.

You're a liar, she told me.

You think that panther can't climb, I asked her.

I ain't leaving this tree! she kept hollering. You can't shoot worth nothing!

It was not easy to listen to that, as there was more truth in it than I would of liked

51

to admit to. So there the three of us was. At times I seen the terrible eyes of the panther watching us from the brush nearby Juda's body. I seen the yellow-brown of its pelt as it moved about. I am sure it wanted to crawl out and drag Juda farther off but would not do so, as I had shown we would fight.

Morning begun to come on. The light arose from behind the pecan tree where Samantha was holding tight to the bare branches with her scrawny arms. It was a fearsome standoff. I do not know how long it went on. It was full light by the time the old sow come up from the creek and put a end to the situation in a way I had not expected. She come shambling up from the bottoms and sniffed out Juda's body and nosed it about. I am sorry to say it, however I think she intended to eat it. She commenced in a rough way to drag it a bit. I thought the panther would jump on her, but it did not show itself. It had been some time since I'd seen it. I guess by now it had gone off nursing its wounds, as there was plenty of those. Or it might of been hiding, awaiting another chance at us. There was a instant I thought that Juda had returned to life, as parts of her moved as if by her own free will. As if she'd had enough of that sow for one last time and was coming around.

But the movement was on account of the old sow pushing and nibbling at her.

I believe that Samantha, up in that tree, must of been scared out of her wits. But for her whimpering, she had got quiet by now.

Hold on to them branches, I called up to her. Don't think about nothing but holding on.

I sure wished my father would hurry and get home, and yet I knew that was not likely to happen. He would not be home until dark, as he would be at the camp all day. Therefore we had the day to get through. I could not see how it was any more noble to let the old sow feast on Juda as to let the panther do it, so at long last I dared to venture over and shoo the sow away. I think Samantha was fearful for me whilst I done so. She did not say much that I could make out. It was like she become a whimpering statue up there in that tree. I thought any moment the cat would come flying at me from out of the brush if it was still there, but the presence of the old sow give me courage. I figured she might stand up for me.

Get, I told the sow, and give her a whack with the gun to fend her off Juda. She did not like it, however she moved aside.

Juda was face up on the ground and she

was a fearsome sight to behold, tore nearly to pieces. Her face was ripped by the claws and her throat was mush. The eye I seen hanging out of the socket was now not to be found. I don't know if it dropped off or if the cat ate it. I could not hunt for it, as I had to look out for the cat.

I tried to raise Juda into my arms but that was a hopeless effort. I turned her about and took hold under her arms to pull her, but her head flopped back with her throat open and I had to put her down on account of I had to vomit. After that I resolved again to get Juda into the house. I told Samantha she was to come down slow and take my gun and shoot the panther if it should jump out of the bushes at me, but that I thought it was gone. I figured it could not of been feeling too good after the beating me and Juda give it, and lacking the two toes Juda hacked off.

For once Samantha done as I told her. She got down out of the tree, with some trouble, on account of how hurt she was. I give her the gun and she took aim toward the bushes. She was a bloody mess. The cat had sought to crush her skull in its jaws. It created a good deal of blood. Her face was fairly ripped open. I worried that she would have trouble seeing the cat if it showed itself, as a good deal of blood was in her eyes. Also the gun was heavy for her, as she was puny and also weak from being up in that tree in the cold and hanging on for so long. She was scared and looking about for the cat, but she was game for the work.

I commenced to pull Juda by her ankles whilst Samantha followed along beside, walking backwards, like me, so as to keep her aim at the bushes. The sow went with us, but it was going frontways. We did not tarry. Juda was barefoot but had big feet, so there was no risk of me loosing my grip. Her tore up dress dragged up and tangled about her neck. It was awful how her head bumped over the ground, but what could I do about it. I kept my eyes on the bushes.

Shoot if you see it, I told Samantha a number of times.

What else would I do, she told me. I could hardly make out what she said, on account of the blood was so thick it had just about sealed her mouth up by that time.

We got Juda into the house, and that was a great relief. The sow tried to come in too, but I swatted her out. Samantha's face looked awful. A chunk of flesh had come loose and was hanging out from her cheek. There was blood all over her head. I tried to get her to let me look at the cuts, but she would not let me touch them. She would not be still to let me put flour on them to stop the bleeding as I had once seen Juda do when my father had cut hisself whilst skinning a deer. We had only one bag of flour. I tried to pour it on her head but she fought me off and screeched at me that there was bugs in it. I did not see any bugs, but I admit it was old flour, as Juda had been saving it for as long as I'd been aware that we had it. I threw a bunch at Samantha in hopes it might stick. She run around to get away but did not have anywhere to go. She looked nearly white. Then she wrapped her whole head in a rag and mostly all I could see was her eyes.

We stayed there all day. We was scared to leave the house. I told Samantha I could go to Camp Verde and bring back help. However, she did not want to be left alone. I was glad of that, as I was not sure I had the courage to walk outside. In fact I doubted it strongly. I eagerly wanted my father to arrive home and yet I felt dread of the moment that he would do so. We tried to clean Juda up so the awful sight of her would not come as quite so much of a shock to him. But we had only a pitcher of water, and I did not want to leave the house and go down to the creek to get more. So it was not a good job of making Juda look right. Her eye was the worst part of the trouble, as it was gone. I tore strips out of a dress she had, and made her a blindfold, and then likewise wrapped her neck and hands and legs and arms and other parts that was tore up. After that, there was not much left of her to look at.

We kept the door shut and the bolt set and the window shuttered. The smell of the blood and kerosene together made me feel sick. I stayed away from the fire for fear it would light up my head. I hauled our bed against the door in case the panther had a mind to come busting through for its supper. I did not know where to keep Juda. It did not seem right to leave her to lay on the floor, but neither did it seem right to put her up on her own bed, as she had always been so particular about keeping that tidy and fresh. Of course what could she say about it now. Still, it did not seem right. And I did not want her on our bed. That did not seem right, neither. We laid her out behind the trunk in the corner, hoping we might have suitable time to explain to my father the matter of what had happened before he laid eyes on her.

We was cold when we run out of wood. I ate what was left from the night before, but

Samantha would have none, on account of her face. The chill come in, and Samantha commenced to shake. Her teeth was clanking together. She was a terrible sight to look upon, as most of her was covered in flour, and the rag around her head and face was soiled with blood that come through — not a clean spot to be seen. Her head looked small, as I was used to her hair sticking out and now it was tied down flat with the rag. There was gashes on her neck but not so deep as on her face. I guess that is lucky, or she would of been dead. She kept looking out of the chinks to see if the cat was out there. She went from one chink to the other and then started over again. I told her to stop, but she wouldn't. I told her to sit, but she wouldn't do that, neither. From chink to chink she went all day. Her feet left tracks in the flour that was all over the house. She would not let me look under the rag, or tie a clean one, or even get anywhere near her.

That is the end of what the panther done.

Dear Judge,

I have used the pages Mr Wronski give me at his house that day and have not even hardly laid the tracks in front of the train. The report I am sending now is six pages filled up and I am writing small. Mr Hildebrand give me more pages at the post office on account of he is generous and would like to see justice get done. He is a thoughtful gentleman and talkative for a German. I had not talked with him on many occasions before, as I had not had cause to send letters.

Mrs Hildebrand is in charge of the store whilst Mr Hildebrand is in charge of the post office within it. When I was there she give me a pastry called strudel. I never had it before. I found it the best thing I ever ate.

I am sorry it took me near a week to write these pages but I have been busy making a coffin for a woman in Comfort who passed. Chairs is my specialty, but coffins is what people mostly want.

Also a goat run off and Samantha and me had to hunt for it all yesterday. We thought the Kickapoos took it, as our neighbor down the way said they was through here. Or we thought maybe he took it hisself. He is known to do that. But these was false accusations, as we found it alive in one piece.

There is still more to write after this.

Yours kindly,
Benjamin Shreve

MY TESTAMENT

My father come home late in the afternoon and found us as I have told you. Juda was in disarray behind the trunk in the corner, wrapped in a number of rags and passed. Samantha was scuttling around in the house. She smelled bad, like raw blood. Her teeth was clanking together. There was flour everywhere all over her and everything in the house.

My father was taken aback by the terrible sights and shocked to the bone and sick to his stomach. I had a time telling him what had taken place. He got Samantha into his arms and made a attempt to look at her face but it was tied up in the rag and she would not let him take that off. He fell on his knees and undid the blindfold off Juda in haste as if he thought she might still be alive under there, despite that Samantha and me both sought to explain she was passed. When he seen her face and that her eyeball was gone he was not in charge of hisself for a minute and I thought he would choke as he did not breathe freely for some time. Her other eye still had a lid on it so he closed that one. I think he was trying to sort things out in his mind but there was too much to take in. Maybe he recollected the night before and pondered that the guest and the lice was responsible for the trouble. But truly I can't fathom much of what he might of been thinking, or if he placed blame, or not, or who on, or what for, as it was never discussed at that time nor any time after. Maybe he figured, like I did, that Juda's bad temper had done herself in.

He said, Benjamin, we need to get water and clean her up.

I told him, I ain't going outside even with you.

He said, I need your help, son.

Samantha commenced to whimper. I

63

think her feelings was starting to cut loose. My father and me went outside and each taken a yoke and buckets and made our way to the creek. I tried to bear up as expected in times of need. Our aim was to get the water and return to the house and do what we could to set things right, though I already knew for sure they could not be set so. I had hoped when my father got home he would fix the matter somehow, but that was not the case. What good would water do. It can wash away blood but not things that has happened. I know it is said it can wash away sins, but I believe those are a done deal too.

There was daylight left, and that was a great relief. Nevertheless I could not help looking about me and fearing the panther would jump on me out of the trees or come flying out of the brush. I could not feel free of the panther no matter that it was nowhere in sight.

My father begun to weep as we walked, so I strove to cheer him up. Juda hacked it up a good bit, I told him.

She was a good, fine, brave woman, he said.

Some of that was news to me, as I had not cared for her a great deal. However, it was not the time to say so.

When we come back to the house with the water, my father took the rag off Samantha's face and head, which was not a easy task, as the blood was dried and it stuck. Samantha done a good bit of hollering. My father spied the terrible condition of her face and commenced to breathe heavy and I thought he might be sick again. I thought I might too. Her condition was very poor. He said I had done right with the flour. I asked what we was to do and he said we was to take her to Camp Verde for help.

How are we to do that, I said. We have only the mare, and I ain't going to stay here alone.

You have no choice in the matter, said he. You have nothing to fear here in the house.

I feared Juda's dead body, for one. I feared her spirit too. I feared any noise I might mistake for the panther. Even a snap of twigs. I feared my very own thoughts. There was nothing I did not fear with night coming on as it was.

My father said Samantha was in desperate need of laudanum.

Can the mare not carry us all, I asked.

You know she can't, son, he said.

He beseeched me to be courageous and I begrudged him of it, as I had proved already

I could be and therefore felt I had earned a right not to be, under the dire circumstances. I was but eight years old and had fought a panther and kept my wits well enough throughout the whole trouble. Therefore I had good proof of my courage.

And yet, it was not a time to argue with him. I tried to get hold of myself and prepare for a long night in the company of a passed woman who hated me even whilst she was present amongst the living, and there was no telling what she thought of me now.

Me and my father then carried in wood and stoked the fire. We carried Juda to the bed that was hers and his and put her on it. She was dirty from when I had drug her along, and she was covered in flour, as it was everywhere in the house. My father did not worry that she had wanted to keep the bed fresh and clean. He said, No matter about that now. He covered her over and I was relieved to see it happen. It was hard enough to have her there without having to look at her too. Or that is what I thought at the time. It would not be long before I thought different about it, being as it is somewhat better to look at a hard thing directly than to know it is in your presence and not know exactly what form it might be in, which is what nobody ever knows of those who has passed.

My father went out and saddled the mare at the shed and rode up to the door, and come in and taken Samantha in his arms, and carried her out and off they went, though not too fast, as she was complaining a good bit about the pain she was in.

And then commenced my long wait of watching that shape there under the blanket. It was a colorful blanket made of squares sewn together. It did not have any holes. And yet it was like my eyes was seeing through it to what was there beneath, which was Juda. I knew where all the cuts and lacerations was on her body. I knew her eye was gone. I knew all them details, and yet questions do set in. I thought she might be in a altered condition under the blanket, as the act of becoming a spirit might involve some adjustment. She might be a puff of air under there, or might be turning white. Her eye might be growing back and be able to see through the bedcovers and look at me. Or the lost parts of her might be trying to sneak in the house to join back up with the rest. I recalled how just that morning she yanked my head around whilst she tugged the ridding comb through my hair. And now what was she in charge of. Not a thing I

67

could think of. She was a lump under the blanket and not moving at all, however I will tell you the firelight at moments made me think she was. I kept thinking she would rise up out of that bed and have at me again. It was hard to believe the days of her shoving me around was over. I did not bank the fire, but kept it stoked, and burned most of the wood and nearly our whole stash of cobs, and kept the house warm, and moved about, and then finally got in my bed and pulled up the blanket over my face. But she had more power over me than ever. It frightened me to my bones. To say it was a long night is to not quite reach the fact of the matter.

When daylight come, my father and Samantha arrived back home on the mare. Samantha had her whole face wrapped up and she was as limp as a water weed in the saddle in front of my father. He was holding her on. His face looked blue, and he was quite weary. It was cold out.

Help her down, he told me.

What did they do, I asked him.

Stitched her up, he said.

Was it terrible, I asked.

Yes, he said.

He would not talk about it.

Did they have laudanum, I asked.

They give her plenty, he said.

I put the mare away and my father seen to Samantha and got her in the bed. Two soldiers from Camp Verde rode out midday to help my father and me dig Juda a grave beside my mother's, not too close to the creek. They was United States soldiers, being as this was before the Sesesh took over. They was stationed there at Camp Verde to watch out for Indians. Afterward we hitched the mare and drove the wagon over the grave a few times to tamp it down, and then we set a pile of stones on it to keep the wolves and coyotes from digging it up. The soldiers was nice enough. However, my father did not want to converse much under the circumstances and they went their way.

We made our peace with Juda's passing and got on with our days. Samantha's face healed up, but it was a mess. The marked side would get your attention. There was stripes from her mouth to her ear where the claws had ripped it, and crisscross marks left behind from the stitches. My father was extra kind to her, and required nothing of her, and acted like she looked fine regardless that she didn't. He was bereft about Juda and had a hard time.

Samantha used to cuss that panther. She got it in her head in a strong way that it would be coming back. She was fixed on this topic and would not be talked out of the notion. She waited day and night for the panther, and I do not mean idle waiting. She was at the ready. It was spooky almost.

It aims to finish off what it started, she said. It aims to be the end of me and you both.

You leave me out of it, I told her.

And here is the piece I can't fully account for. She wanted the panther to come. She tempted it to do so. At times she would get hold of my father's rifle and load it in secret, and sneak out in the night, and run off toward the creek like she done that night when the panther come through the dark in pursuit of her. Me and my father awoke on occasion and seen her go out. We kept a eye on her from the door and seen her stop at the edge of the trees, and swing around in a hurry, and aim the gun like she heard the panther running upon her from behind. A time or two she fired the gun, and my father gone out and told her to come on in. Was it out there, he asked her. Did you see something, honey.

He would not take issue with her, no matter what.

One time, in the dead of winter, about a

70

year after the panther killed Juda, I seen Samantha go out in her nightgown the same as she done that night. She was some taller by now but no bigger around. She got on her hands and knees, like she was prey, right there at the spot where it knocked her down that night. It was like she was waiting for it to jump on her.

I swear on a heap of Bibles it's coming, she told me on many occasions.

We ain't got a heap of Bibles, I said. We ain't got one, even.

She would go on telling the tale of how the panther killed Juda. She would not forget any aspect about it. She could recall the terrible noises the panther had made. On one occasion she said, It come last night whilst you was asleep. I sniffed it on the wind. I heard it yowl from afar.

Why was the goats so quiet, I asked her. Go find remains, and I will believe you.

Remains are yonder, she said. Just yonder.

I went in search of them to prove her wrong, down one side of the creek and across to the other. My hair stood up on end when I about stumbled upon the carcass of a buck stashed under a pile of leaves. Its tongue was ate out and its belly a shambles. I looked for the paw prints near it, and did not find even one. I begun to believe the panther was a banshee.

You find any proof, she asked when I got back.

Nope, I told her. Not a hair.

She called me a liar and said she knew for sure it was coming around to get us.

Dear Judge,

I might of gone on too long in the portion you are about to read which I am sending you now, as I might of got carried away. We have been having a good spell of rain that keeps me and Samantha cooped up in the house and I would rather write to you than have to talk to her. She will talk your ear off if you allow it, and she has got no one else here other than me who is tired of listening.

Also this time is the first I have been asked to write something other than measurements and I am having a good time at it. As I told you in Bandera, I have read books before. I was taught a thing or two by a person named Tom Wellford that my father sent me to learn from who lived down the river near Dr Ganahl and used to teach a few boys.

He used to call me his best student by far. I was sorry he left when the war started.

Whilst I was last in Comfort I bought more paper and quills. I spent my own earned money to purchase them, as I was reluctant to ask Mr Hildebrand to give me five more pages for free. If you would see fit to reimburse me in the future I would appreciate it, as this report is composed at your request, though there may be more to it than you need, in which case a full reimbursement would not be fair nor expected and I will accept that fact without complaining about it, as fair is fair.

They was not cheap.

I hope you are having good travels and keeping yourself safe these days. I hope the reports I posted have found their way to you with no trouble. There has been three of them besides this one. I will need more ink, on account of this pot is about empty. If you could afford me a steel nib pen I would have a easier time of writing and I believe you might have a easier time of reading.

Mr Hildebrand said to tell you hello, on account of he has met you. Mrs Hildebrand give me more strudel. She insisted I have it. It was hot from the oven. She said Tuesdays is when she makes it and it was Tuesday. She give me the piece for free.

Yours kindly,
Benjamin Shreve

MY TESTAMENT

I estimate it was four or five years after Juda passed that the Sesesh begun to rise up against the government and torment the Germans who was of a different opinion. I felt bad for so many Germans getting beat up and set fire to and such things, although they was not always the friendliest people. But my father said, Stay out of it. Neither him nor me had a word to say about any of it. We kept our mouths shut. He was tolerating me to come along to work in the shingle camp, where we went about our business, which was enough work to tire us into not caring much one way or the other about much else. Some time passed that way for us, but when things become hot and the Sesesh taken over Camp Verde they put their Yankee prisoners in the canyon across the way, and those had to be fed. That cost us a lot of our game. We had to ride some distance to hunt.

My father said, Stay away from the canyon, it's dangerous to go near there.

The Sesesh called it Prison Canyon but we called it the canyon, as we had never called it nothing but the canyon.

However, I ventured close and spied prisoners down there and seen they had kept theirselves busy digging holes in the walls and cobbling up shanties of sticks and rocks on both sides of the creek and making a whole town down there that was quite tidy. I heard a good deal about how the prisoners was hungry, but my father said, There is no way to fix the matter. Leave it alone. It is not your business.

I thought, What does he know. Not everything. So I snuck up and threw down a ear of corn to see what might come of that. I heard voices and a harmonica down below. When the corn went tumbling down, the harmonica stopped, but the voices kept on. I could tell they was discussing where the corn might of come from or who might of tossed it.

Soon there was scrabbling noises that went on for some time, and then up comes a book and lands in a big cactus. I picked it out of the cactus and took a look. It was a fat book, and I seen it was called The Whale. It had on it a picture of a whale. I had never laid eyes on one but I knew that one ate

78

Jonah and I figured this was a good chance to learn more. So I took off with the book.

I showed my father when I got home and he said, What in the world was you thinking to go so close with the pickets there.

But he liked the book a good deal. He was not as good of a reader as myself, so at night I read pieces of the story to him and Sam. Do you mind if I call her Sam at times here in this report, as that is what I often call her, and it is extra work to keep writing her name the long way.

We had a tin candle lantern that I could use to read with at night after work was done. Before I knew it, I read the whole thing and it was quite a tale. There was a great deal about rigs and harpoons and whatnot. I have not been to visit a ocean but figured things out and got the gist of it without a great deal of trouble. Also I could see how Ahab acted the way he did about the whale, as I seen how Samantha acted about the panther.

Also I knew what a peg leg was like, as there was a peg legged Mexican who worked at the shingle camp. He was a good horseman. He could mount with his peg leg in the stirrup just as if it was a actual leg.

In the meantime I gone back and tossed another ear, and got me another book, and another. I tossed soap and candles and salt and pepper and other things I figured was needed. There was times I tossed and got nothing. But most times something come up. As I told you in Bandera, I have read four books and that is how I come by them all. They taught me a good deal that I did not know about some places I never went and feel sure I may never go in my lifetime, if they do even exist.

But then my father got the fever and passed, and that was the hardest time of my life. I will not dwell on it here, as I do not care to remember how terrible a time it was. Also, it is not what you asked about, although not much of this is.

It was a hard time, is all I can say. Me and Samantha dug the grave and buried him ourselves. I could not ride down to the shingle camp to get help, as Sam did not want to be left on her own with our father when he was passed. We thought it was not a good idea for her to ride with me for help, as what would we say if somebody said, She is a runaway slave, take her. In times before, we had our father to vouch for her, but that was not the case any longer. We was on our own to vouch for ourselves. This worried us a great deal. She was but eleven years old at this time and I was but thirteen and we was supposed to get on.

I built him a coffin the best I could. We got wore out digging the grave. The ground was nearly froze, as it was winter. We cried the whole time. We dug it between the graves of my mother and Juda, and tromped on it some, and put rocks on it to keep the animals out, the same as we done to Juda's. So there was three mounds of rocks and a rather sorrowful aspect to the whole place, as there was now more dead there than the two of us amongst the living.

When people got wind of the fact my father had passed, I had a offer to live with a family in Fredericksburg who said I could stay with them and work for room and board. But how could I go off and leave Samantha. She had got a sorry hand to play as a half Negro girl orphan. The only Negros we come across on the roads or nearby was slaves, and I did not want her taken for one of them. There was good people down the road and a Mexican family on Privilege Creek that known us and said they would help her out, but when they come to our house she did not want to go with them and did not want to be apart from me. Diphtheria had broke out and done in a bunch of children, and despite that Sam was a older child than most of them that passed of it, I feared her coming down if she was not looked after. She was not a healthy looking girl.

So it was just her and me on the place. We had goats in a pen and chickens and the sow and a few pigs that lived in the creek bottom. We had a garden, but it was not much, and Sam did not tend it in the way she should of. We had a few rows of corn but mostly the varmints ate it. I had my father's mare and his rifle. The mare was a trail pony that had got herself branded by a previous owner and then taken by Comanches and left on the trail half done in with hardly a hide to speak of, as it was whipped off. My father had estrayed her in the proper way and nursed her back to decent health but she was fairly wore out. If I so much as laid a hand on her rump she would swing around and bite a chunk out of any part of me she could get hold of. She was fine for a ride to Comfort or the shingle camp however, so I got around and kept on doing some work at the camp, as the men there was good to me.

I also had a double barrel percussion pistol, smooth bore, that I got in trade for some work. It said Gasquoine and Dyson on the locks and Manchester on the barrel rib. The sidelocks and hammers was engraved with designs. It was a far cry from a six shooter but it could blast a hole in things and it was a nice looking piece. However, powder was hard to come by, on account of the Yankee blockade, and the worth of what we could get was chancy, on account of most of it come from saltpeter made of bat shat dug out of a cave in New Braunfels. I never was sure if it would go off or not.

It was the summer after my father passed that I gone for the hunt where I seen Clarence Hanlin picking the pockets of the eight dead men on the Julian. I come home from that and thought about it a great deal. I heard it was Sesesh out of Camp Verde that done it. I did not talk with Samantha about any of it, because she already thought too much about things, which in her case was mostly the panther. So why trouble her with hanged men.

It was a few months later on from seeing Hanlin on the Julian, when Samantha was twelve years old, and I was fourteen, and winter come on, and the wind was blowing a gale, and dark was a thing we dreaded, that the panther called on us again.

For six years, Sam had been waiting in a way that was eager. It seemed sometimes that all she did was wait, and watch for that panther. There was a kind of a hesitant manner in which she would venture out, with a glance to left and right, and a kind of a sudden way she would swing around, like she heard something coming, and a way she would try out her fears by going out in the night.

Under such circumstances as these you might think the panther's return would be no surprise to either of us when it did come back. To the contrary, it was a shock. It was like death, in that way. A person might have it fixed in his mind that death must call on him sometime, but that time will startle him nonetheless.

That night it was quite windy. Samantha and me was alone in the house. The wind bothered us a great deal. November had begun uncomfortably cold, and the ground outside was wet from a rain that come and gone the night before. We was closed up in the house and had us a fire going, but it was a small fire on account of I did not want Comanches to see the smoke. The wind come down the chimney and messed with the flames, and the noise of it made us uneasy. We felt mischief was afoot. We did not know in what form it might be, if in the fearsome form of Comanches or other assailants, and we did not know who would come to our aid if we was visited by evil.

The Sesesh at Camp Verde was no more than a ten minute ride from our house at a good pace on a good horse, but we did not have a good horse, and I did not trust the Sesesh, as I seen what mischief they done on the Julian. There was many a Sesesh that was good hearted, I hope you will not mistake me on that. But I am sure you know of that gang of thugs called the hangerbande who might hang any fellow sixteen years or older who would not join the cause. They was a harsh, unruly lot, and I feared they might arrive to my door unexpected, and say I was grown enough, and demand I go with them.

Therefore, on that night, Sam and me had our portion of things to fret over. We was not German, but we was not Sesesh neither. Sam prowled about in our house peering from chinks in the daubing so as to see if trouble was on the way.

You can't see nothing but dark, I told her. And what good would it do anyhow. If mischief is coming, we're done for. I ain't got enough powder for a pea shooter, and it's bat shat.

You ain't got enough on account of how you shoot ten times and by then everything's run off, said she. You squander it, that's what.

She was in a foul mood and we was both spooked by the wind. It hooted around the corners and shoved at the bolt on the door.

On account of my father was passed, I had taken to sleeping in his bed. Samantha had the other bed to herself now. After some time, when no mischief come, we retired into those beds. But the whooping sound of the wind was like Comanches moving in, and I had it in my mind that they was out there in the dark about to break out hollering in their bloodthirsty way of it. Or else stuff the chimney and smoke us out.

Sam said, The panther is coming around, I can feel it.

I said, He ain't been here in years, and why would he come now. If we hear something, it's Comanches.

She said, He's out there. I know it. I feel it.

All at once there begun a snuffling and scratching at the door and the latch shook fiercely.

Samantha sat up in her bed. It's him, she said. It's the panther. He's here.

It ain't him, I told her. It's the sow.

But I was not so sure. The sow was in a habit of walking in at her leisure when the door was left open, but it was not her custom to demand entry when it was shut.

The scratching and snuffling and shoving went on for a stretch of time that I figured unnatural, and I begun to think that indeed, it was not the sow at the door. The fire was no more than a scant bit of red from the embers, but it shed enough light to show me how troubled Samantha looked. She commenced to blink and squint her eyes like she has a habit of.

Can she bust the latch, she asked me.

It's a good latch, I said. However, she's a big sow, she could maybe bust the door.

My heart thrashed about in a painful manner. By way of action I hollered out, Who's there. Who's at the door.

The scratching come to a halt, as if whatever caused it attended to what I asked. However, then it took up again. I thought, Hell or high water I am going to see what's out there. I got up and loaded my pistol with what powder I had, bat shat or not, and went down on my hands and knees to look out of a chink low to one side of the door.

What I seen out there was the shape of the big fat sow. Indeed it was her. She must of spied me looking out, as she stuck her nose to mine in the hole and huffed a bit of slime at me before I could pull back.

It's her, I told Sam.

Let her in and give her corn, Sam said.

She shats when she has corn, I said.

If she's chomping on corn we ain't going to hear the wind or nothing else, Sam said. We'll have us a little piece of quiet. Let her in.

So I done so. Hardly had I cracked open the door when the sow shoved her fat self inside and snorted at me and demanded corn. I latched the door back, laid my pistol aside, stoked up the fire, and shook a few fistfuls of kernels around on the boards of the floor. She went about chomping and snorting long enough for Sam to think of other things and get to sleep, whilst I lay there watching them both in the light of the fire and wondering what my life was ever going to amount to. Here I was, trapped in a house with a girl and a big pig, nothing between me and all the world, with whatever it might hold of liberty and undertaking, but a shoddy door and one good latch. But whether I wanted out, or preferred to be in, was hard to say at that moment.

And that was when the screaming commenced.

I cannot hardly describe it except to say it was not plain to me at the start exactly where it come from, or what it might be. It was the goats in the pen, for one thing, and the loud wind for another. But it was also the mare. I heard her loud and clear in the shed. And it was another thing that was like a woman yelling about something. I almost thought — and this was wrongheaded — I almost thought Juda had somehow come back. However, very quickly I surmised that what I heard was the same sounds as I heard the night Juda was killed, and it was not the sound of Juda screaming like she done. It was the caterwaul of the panther.

Samantha and me sat up in our beds in haste and alarm. For a instant we stuck to our beds and stared at what we could see of each other in the feeble light of the embers. If the wind had not been so fierce and steady I think I could of heard my heart. It pounded away at a gallop. I think I could of heard Samantha's too. She was the first of us to open her mouth, but it was only to whisper.

It's come around, she said. It's come back. I told you.

Before I could move a finger, she was out of her bed and had grabbed my pistol from off the table.

You can't go out there, I told her, and got out of bed to argue with her about it. There ain't enough powder in that. It ain't good powder.

Come out there with me, she said. I'm scared to go by myself.

I ain't coming, I told her, and made a effort to wrestle the pistol from her. However, I could not fight her in earnest, as she bent over the pistol and was so determined of keeping her grasp of it I feared she would pull the trigger by accident and shoot herself in the belly, or fire the ball through herself and into me. I thought, This is not a struggle worth doing, and I turned her loose.

Bring a knife and come on, she hollered, or you're a coward!

Juda had her a hatchet and we seen what the panther done to her, I said. I ain't taking it on with a knife.

In all this time, the uproar outside went on. We had one goat in particular that could yell like he was a grown man, and he was doing so without ceasing and louder than I ever thought a goat could yell. The wind was nothing compared to that noise. The other eight goats was chiming in. Two of them was kids less than a year old and I figured it was one of them little ones that the panther had got hold of, as there was some high-pitched bleating. The mare was screaming and knocking her hooves against the shed walls. The chickens was squawking.

Without one other word between us, Sam went for the door.

You asked me to be frank, Judge. I did not care to follow her out. I was barefoot and had nothing to see by, much less shoot with. But what choice did I have. I lit the lantern as quick as I could. Out I went behind Sam into the dark and followed her to the goat pen.

When I got there, she was climbed half up the fence, shrieking her head off. It was a six foot picket fence and she was standing on the crossboards, screaming over the top. I got up beside her with the lantern and seen the panther there in the pen with the goats all making a ruckus and churning around pretty fast. It was hard to make out what was what, as the lantern did not light much.

The panther was bigger than I can tell you, sir. It looked about three times my size, although I know that could not be the case. It had a kid by the throat and was dragging it the way it drug Juda. The kid was still kicking — or so it appeared to me. Its little brother stood there watching it get hauled off and screaming about it.

Sam yelled at the panther to let it go. She

aimed the pistol at it. Let it go! she hollered, let it go! As if it would do so.

Some of the goats was bunched under a roof that my father and me had nailed over a part of the pen for shelter. Others of them was banging theirselves against the fence to get out. I thought they might knock their brains out. One got out by climbing up on another one's back and then up on the shelter, and from there it taken the leap. The big male was yelling. It was a terrible commotion in the dark, and the wind was harsh in our faces and kicking up dust.

Get it from him! Samantha screeched at me about the kid being dragged off. Get it back!

I hollered that she was crazy and to quit acting that way and get down from the fence and back in our house or she would be done for like Juda. Half of me was trying to figure out how the panther was going to get that kid out of the pen, as it is one thing to leap into a pen over a six foot picket fence, and another thing to leap back out of it with a kid in your mouth. The other half of me was trying to figure what Sam had got in her head to do, as she was not doing what I told her.

And then she done the most heedless thing. She climbed the rest of the way over the top and dropped down into the pen. There she stood, barefoot, in her nightshift, holding the pistol. The panther was not more than fifteen feet away. The dust flew around it. The kid sagged out of its mouth, either dead or alive, I did not know which. It was the least of my questions.

Sam did have the good sense to stop squawking at that time. The goats become quieter too, I guess thinking she might of come to their rescue. It seemed to me even the wind laid up a bit, as I was able to speak to Sam in a careful, quiet way and she heard me.

I said, You're done for if you move.

She seemed to of just figured that out, as she looked froze in fear.

I thought, Lord, Sam, how am I to help you. The inside of the fence had no cross-boards nailed to it, it was only the bare pickets, so there was no easy way for her to climb back out. And if I tried to pull her out she would have to turn her back on the panther and scramble and kick around for a foothold, and the panther would get excited. It could drop the kid and drag Sam down in one big leap. She would get slaughtered right then and there in front of my eyes. Also how was I to hold on to the lantern and the fence and her too. But what else could I do except try.

Back up slow, then turn around and take my hand, I told her.

She did not heed me. The panther's eyes was alight from the lantern and fixed on her in a severe manner and it was like she lost the say-so to draw herself away. Its face and head was scarred and one of its ears partly gone, like it was tore off in a fight a while back. It must of known a good number of hard years and asserted itself on a good many creatures, large and small.

Sam aimed the pistol at it and taken a step closer.

I said, Don't.

She said, I can kill it.

I said, It's bat shat powder.

She had enough sense to be frightened, but too little to heed me. I guess she figured if she got close enough, then the bat shat would do.

The panther flicked its tail, and laid its ears flat, and dropped the kid in the dirt like it was no more than a dish rag. It crouched so low its belly was nearly against the ground. It drawn its mouth back, and I seen its fangs, and it let out a terrible hiss.

Sam taken another step closer toward it.

My heart commenced to pound so hard it nearly knocked me off the fence. I thought,

If you go one more step I ain't going to help you.

She had the pistol in both hands and they was shaking so harshly I figured she was just as likely to shoot me who was behind her, as the panther out before her. The panther's snarling got louder and rose up to a fierce yowl. I recalled that awful sound well.

I got down off the fence and run around to the gate. It was a picket gate and I did not have a notion of what the panther might do when I opened it. I stayed to the side, hoping the panther might run out and take off without paying me notice. But when I pulled the gate open, the panther did not come out. So I held the lantern up and taken a few steps in. I seen the panther before me, but not facing me, as it was looking at Sam. It twitched its tail. The kid laid dead before it. The other goats was bunched up in the dark on the far side of the pen. The panther then turned its face to me. Its yellow eyes in the light of my lantern was like two holes showing a fire burning inside the creature's skull.

I had to either go further inside the pen, or out, and you might guess which way I preferred. But I had charge of Samantha and I was all there was of a man on the place. She was my sister, if only half. I could not let her get drug away like her mother. How would I live with myself then.

Sideways was how I made my way over to Sam whilst keeping a eye on the panther and holding the lantern high. I got so scared I almost thought it would be a relief if I laid down and give myself up. I thought I should maybe do that, and allow Samantha to live. Then I thought maybe not. If I was to die she might as well pass on with me, as she was bound to be in a heap of trouble throughout her whole life without me.

The wind was again blowing hard. It tossed the light about and I thought it might put it out. It was a long, long journey across that small pen, I will tell you what. I recall the feel of the goat shat under my bare feet, the wind blowing dust in my eyes, the fickle light of the lantern, and the way the panther kept up a ominous growl.

When I got close to Samantha she had the shakes all over, but she was still aiming the pistol. I figured if she was to pull the trigger the ball would drop like a stream of piss. I thought, If you bet your whole life on bat shat I ain't going to hardly cry for you. I feared talking, except under the wind. I said, Come with me.

She said, I can kill it.

I said, If you try and the powder's bad, it'll pick the puniest of us.

She give that a moment of thought. Her eyes was squinted in the way she was in a habit of doing when she felt scared. She said, Can we get away.

I stepped closer and got hold of her arm and walked her sideways in the direction of the gate, moving as slow as I'd come. We did not take our eyes off the panther. It twitched its tail and hissed and snarled at us. It kept on showing its fangs, as if we might forget what they looked like. I believe it would of jumped on us except it was guarding the dead kid on the ground before it. The nearer we got to the gate, the harder it was not to turn and run.

We was almost out of the pen when the goats started up yelling again. The big male must of seen us taking our leave. He hollered, and the rest chimed in and jumped on each other and shoved each other about. One gone wild and got herself up on top of the shelter, and the boards give in and crashed, and the goat come down on top of the others beneath it.

I did not stay around to watch. Out the gate we went and I latched it shut behind us and taken off with Sam for the house. I could swear we had wings. I am not sure my feet even lighted upon the ground. I expected any moment the panther might jump the fence and be on us from behind and knock us to the ground and be done with us. My only comfort was to keep moving fast.

When we got inside the house I thought my heart might give out. God all mighty, I told Samantha, you are a idiot and a fool.

She said, I could of killed it! What did you go and stop me for!

There she stood, hardly able to catch her breath and shouting at me like she was in the right. I could of smacked her and nearly did.

I ain't talking to you, I told her. I ain't saying nothing to you.

You done me wrong! she said. I could of shot it in the face and killed it once for all! You stole away my chance!

For some time she went on about that, but I declined to listen. Even the sow declined to listen, and laid about. She would not leave and I did not make her. I was busy trying to hear what was going on out in the pens. The goats had got quiet by now.

It's gone now, I said. I believe it to be gone.

It ain't never going to be gone, Samantha answered me.

She sat on her bed and sulked even whilst she was shaking, and I sat on mine, and neither of us said nothing. The wind was still loud but other things had got quiet. I got up and stirred up the fire.

Go on to bed, I told her.

Then all of a sudden the noise commenced all over again — the goats hollering, the chickens squawking, and the horse trying to get out of the shed.

Samantha went for the pistol but I snatched it up first. I backed myself to the door and said, I'll shoot you if you come closer.

She said, You won't neither.

I will, I assured her. I'd rather you die that way than get tore up by a panther. And I ain't going out there again.

She demanded, Give me that pistol and stand aside and let me out the door.

I refused. She sat back on her bed, and I stood at the door, and we listened to all the fearful noises.

She put her hands up over her ears so not to hear the goats yelling. She said, It's killing another. I think it might kill them all.

Then so be it, said I.

I might of loaded the rifle if we had powder, but we did not have it. When things was quiet again, Sam laid down and pulled

99

her blanket up over her head.

I stayed against the door all night in case she might try to take the pistol and get out.

When daylight come, we shoved the sow out and went to figure the damage. The goats was all badly spooked and quite badly bloodied. The one that had leapt the fence was trying to get back in. The panther had carried both wee kids into the night. The mare was all right in the shed, just nicked up and skittish. The coop was worked over but none of the chickens was missing.

The tracks was sure enough those of the panther that done in Juda. The hind right pad lacked the very two toes Juda had hacked off.

What I learned that day looking at them big tracks made by the panther taking our two kids off, was we was small things to such as that cat, and had no say in the matter, nor in much of many matters at all. We was only two kids ourselves, in a shoddy house in the midst of a war, at risk of Comanches and whatnot, short of all things on account of a Yankee blockade, and with nothing but a pea-sized bit of bat shat to shoot with.

However, Sam was not likewise a quick study about such matters as that. She figured the whole thing to be learned was

the panther had to be tracked down and
done in.

Dear Judge,

Mr Hildebrand give me the letter from you. It is the first I ever got. He had read it on account of the seal come loose and he didn't much think you would mind. He said to let you know if you ever need more statements against Clarence Hanlin he will line folks up with no trouble, as it is a well-known fact that Hanlin was oftentimes seen with the hanger-bande, although he was not strictly part of them. Mr Hildebrand said there is a woman in Kerrsville who knows Hanlin's mother over in Bastrop County and says even she would not claim him when he was a boy, he was that rotten, a bad seed from the first, he would torment creatures of all sorts, so it is no wonder he grew up like he did.

However, as to your letter, Judge.

Thank you for saying to tell Mr Hildebrand to pay me back for what I spent and to please give me what paper and ink I need and he could expect to be reimbursed to the full extent of the cost, as from the looks of things it might mount up. Mr Hildebrand was glad to hear it. He is generous and give me a loaf of bread for free as there was no strudel, on account of he said the strudel is gone by Friday and it was Saturday I was there.

I am glad to know you are not traveling alone as I thought, but rather with your friend Mr Pittman. He seemed like a nice gentleman at Mr Wronski's house. He must of wrote pretty fast, and that is a impressive feat to say the least. Please tell him hello for me and to watch out for trouble for you. I am almost scared to think of you reading my reports, for fear Comanches might be sneaking up behind you whilst you do so. Both of you take good care.

I do appreciate that you said I don't have to write in the thorough manner I am doing. However, I will continue, if you don't mind. I know you intend to be considerate of my time, but what need is there for that. I work all day long but have nothing important after dark. All I do at night is sit in a half-dark house with Sam and look out for Comanches. It is not a interesting life. I have read The Whale twice, start to finish, as I might of before told you, and I am not ready to read it again.

However, to speak of the devil. These pages I am sending involve quite a bit about Clarence Hanlin, as they tell of the encounter Sam and me had with him on the morning after the panther took off with our kids, which was not many months after I seen Mr Hanlin on the Julian picking pockets. As I told you already, I had seen him on the roads with other Sesesh on occasion, and I had seen him picking the pockets of the unfortunates hanged. But until the time you are fixing to read of, I had not spoken a word to him, nor had any cause to do so. Nor had he taken any notice of me.

I do wish I had a steel nib pen in place of quills. A pen would improve my writing a good deal. Mr Hildebrand showed me a advertisement for one that was made in New Jersey. It had a holder with it. I would not need a holder.

Yours kindly,
Benjamin Shreve

As I before stated, I slept all night against the door to hold Sam from going out, and in the morning we took a look around our place and seen that our two kids was missing and the panther had spooked every living creature and left the place with a feel of trespass hanging about in the air. Sam and me was unsettled and in a quandary of what to do next. Sam was of a mind to track the panther, but how were we to do that. I told her to let the whole thing alone and the panther would not be back for a good long while. It took him all those years the last time before he come back for a visit. But what Sam felt was it was not a issue of worrying over our livestock or ourselves or any other practical thing, it was a issue of revenge. The panther had spoilt her face and slain her mother, and now it had run off with the two little kids, leaving the other goats perplexed, and leaving us feeling stole from.

I told her we did not have the means to track it, but she said we would build us a trap and capture it and do it in that way. She went on about it. She had big plans, all hogwash, about digging holes and carving spears out of sticks, and other such nonsense. I hoped she would not light upon the idea of searching out the remains of them kids and laying in wait for the panther to come back for his breakfast, being as we did not have a reliable way to dispatch him even if we was to lay eyes on him.

To my dismay she did hit upon that idea, or the like of it. She was but twelve years old, as I have said, yet she is a tireless thinker, and now and then she will wear you down until you begin to think she has struck upon a idea that will suit. I suppose I would not be writing any of this to you, and would not of ever even known of you, nor you of me, if she had not come up with a plan I thought to be workable if not entirely sensible. She said the panther could not of ate both kids in one night, and if we was to find what was left of one of them we could hide out in a tree overhead for the panther to come back and feast on it. Then we would have us a easy shot at him.

Have you forgot we have no good powder, I asked her.

If we fire down, the ball will go, said she.

How is a ball going to kill a panther by falling on it, I said. And how can you reason the panther won't see us and think it has found three full meals instead of the one.

She had a plan for that, of loading up water buckets with rocks and hauling them up in the tree, and strapping a kitchen knife to the end of the rifle to make a spear, and tying a rope for a lasso. I told her it would not work. She said she would see that it did, and if I would not help her she would do it herself, as she was not my slave, she was nobody's, and had a free will of her own, and could do as she liked.

You will pardon me, Judge, but after a good amount of discussion and frustration with her I allowed myself to think this plan was a feasible undertaking. I was but fourteen years of age myself, and not as smart as I would of liked to of been. Also, she called me a coward. She is fearsome to face down when she is scornful. Her features is not right, on account of what the panther done to her. Her mouth is stretched up on one side and she appears to grin at you even whilst her eyes is looking disgusted. And even whilst you look at her and see very well that she is puny and mulatto and a girl and not too good to gaze upon, you will figure she has all the say-so over you, though you will not know how she got it.

So there we was, with a plan. However, I was not so rash as to volunteer to make it work. I said, You can look for the kids yourself. I ain't helping you with that. And if you do not find one of them under a tree that's big, you can leave me out of the whole shebang. I am not going to wait in a small tree for a panther. I want a good station.

So she gone hunting for the kids and found one by noontime and dragged me off to see it. It was not far from the house, although out of sight of it due to a incline. The kid laid cold dead at the base of a bur oak that stood nearly ninety feet tall by my estimation. It was half covered with sticks and leaves, not ate in the least but messed up at the throat.

There was plenty of things about the setup that did not strike me as right. For one, why did the panther just happen to pick the biggest tree to stash the remains under. And how come the sticks and leaves looked like they was piled on top of the kid, not scratched up over it.

I said, You did not find the kid here. You found it elsewhere and carried it over here on account of it's a big tree and you know I ain't going to sit in a small one.

I did no such thing, she said.

We had words about that.

At last she said, all right, so I done it. I carried it here from just over yonder. What difference is it. The panther can sniff it from there.

She had a further idea too. We was to

111

bring the nanny out and tie her under the tree, she said. We was to leave her there through the night whilst we sat in the tree. She would bleat on account of she would not want to be there with her dead kid, and the noise would draw the panther and we would get a shot at it.

Or else wolves or coyotes will be drawn, I said. Did you not think of that.

I did not, she owned, but I aim to chance it.

I took stock of the tree. It was not a bad tree she had picked. The limbs was fairly high up and that was a good thing. The leaves was turned and falling but there was plenty to hide in. The trunk was wide. I got somewhat shook up thinking of how it would be to tussle with the panther if he was clawing his way up the trunk and we was up there with nothing but rocks and a unloaded rifle with a knife strapped on the end of it and a rope and one ball in a pistol loaded with bat shat. However, I was not ready to be called a coward once more. I could fairly see the word on her lips.

We will get ourselves in the tree before dark, said she. Now help me gather up rocks.

It is not saying a lot, as she is not a hard worker, but she did work that day. She set about gathering up rocks of every which size. We filled the water buckets and two feed buckets. It was a considerable task getting them four buckets into the tree. I had to use the rope to get up there myself, and then Sam and me had us a time hauling the buckets up on the rope. We stretched the yoke over a couple of branches to hang the water buckets from, but it was a struggle to get them balanced in a way where they wouldn't tump over and dump out the rocks. Sam acted in charge of the undertaking and that was a aggravation.

The nanny goat, when we went to fetch her out of the pen, was in a bad way. Her udders was full to busting and she was missing her kids. We had to milk her to get her satisfied, but at least we got some good milk. She did not care to be led away from the other goats, and she was not too happy to see her young one half buried under sticks and leaves, nor to be staked alongside it. I think she was puzzled about its condition and that it paid her no mind. We waited for her to crank it up and make a fuss the panther might hear, but to the contrary she had nothing to say on the matter for some time. That was unnatural. After we staked her by the kid she got as far from it as the tether would let her get, which was clear

113

around the other side of the tree. She made a few complaints and then become what is called deathly quiet and still as a stone.

I said, I don't know that we need her.

Sam said, You'll see. She will bleat when it's dark. I believe you're scared and don't want the panther to come.

I'd be a fool like you to want it to come, I told her.

We got ourselves settled up in the tree before dark. The branches was good ones and wide enough to settle on, although the bark was enough to torture us and made me wish we could be in a naked Indian tree instead of the one we was in. I figured the acorns was a drawback, on account of they attract bears. However, what trouble was bears compared to the panther that we was alluring.

From where I sat I could see three big old mesquites, not twenty yards off, that stood over a old Comanche grave beside a trace. The grave was said to be that of a chief buried quite a few years before I was born. It had been dug up a good many times by people passing on the trace, so all I ever seen of it was beads and charms and bones nobody wanted and which I would not of touched for a million in specie, for fear of revenge by either the dead or the living. Of

Comanches, I figure both is equally bad. I could not see the bones sticking out of the dirt from up in the tree, but I knew they was there. I had looked them over on many occasions. They appeared mostly like leg bones to me. It was weird how even coyotes and varmints had nothing to do with the bones in all these years. Maybe the tales I heard was true and they was cursed.

The moon come up, no more than a shard of light. When it was overhead we seen it in fits and starts amid the clouds drifting over the branches. I could not make out the stars on account of them being blocked by leaves and clouds. I sat with my back to the trunk and my legs straddling a limb nearly the width of a saddle, my pistol at the ready and my ears trained for the panther. The night grew colder than I had figured it would. A good many leaves dropped out of the tree about me throughout the night. Sam and me had agreed not to do any talking, so she was quiet for once. The nanny goat at times shifted about on the tether and bleated but otherwise was unnaturally quiet.

I believe that Samantha was nearly unhinged on account of she wasn't supposed to talk, and that was a hardship. She was scared, but she did not say so. She sat on a limb on the far side of the trunk as me, a foot or two higher up, where I could not see her from where I was myself. Halfway through the night she commenced to drop acorns down from her perch.

What are you doing, I said.

I want the nanny to bleat, she told me. Is she still even down there. I ain't heard her. I can't see her from here.

Where do you think she could go, I said.

Why don't she make any noise, she asked me.

Would you make noise if you was bait for a panther, I said.

That shut her up for a time.

We heard varmints rustling around, and noisy crickets, and coyotes yammering amongst theirselves off in the hills, and hoot owls having their say. I would of enjoyed the night more if I could of been sure it was not my last. The idea of the panther had me scared.

When the sky begun to get light, and the nanny to complain about wanting to be milked, and the flies commenced to gather about on the dead kid, I said, The panther ain't coming. It's time to go.

Samantha said, I ain't leaving here just yet.

I'll stay half a hour, I told her, no more

than that. I'm tired of sitting here holding this pistol for nothing.

Then let me hold it, she said.

I agreed to that bad idea. I give her the pistol and settled back on my branch for a snooze. I was just about to doze off when Sam said, Somebody's coming.

That woke me up pretty quick. We was used to having people along the trace every now and then, but not so often that it was common. What I seen when I opened my eyes was a fellow on horseback, and what I first noted was the horse. It was a pinto, white on black, a mustang by the look of it but tall for one, about fifteen hands, and it struck me right off as a outstanding creature. It had a way about it. A air of freedom, so that it give the impression there was nobody mounted upon it but rather it was taking a morning stroll on its own. It had no bit, only a hackamore. The way it come walking so lightly along the trace, too early in the morning to cast a shadow, made a vision that got my attention in a powerful way. I had to catch my breath before I could even look from the horse to the rider.

When I did draw my eyes off the horse and look at the man, I seen he was a Mexican. He was finely dressed in a linen shirt and nice pants and a good looking pair of knee-high boots. He appeared past his prime. His boots and hat was black and his hair was gray, nearly white. It hung slightly long. Taken as a whole, his attire was fully black and white, so that he matched his pinto horse in a way I had not seen with a man and beast before, and have not seen since. It was like they was twins. The man was traveling light, having only a pair of saddlebags and a satchel.

Sam said, Who might he be?

I told her to hush, and moved to where I might keep a eye on her. The man was singing a song I did not hear the words of. We seen him look at the nanny tied to the tree but he paid her no special mind. He did not see us, as we was hidden in branches. He come alongside the old chief's grave and paused and dismounted and stood over the grave and scraped at it with his boot. I thought he might be hatching a plan to rob it, however what would he take. There was nothing but old beads and bones. He dropped his reins and stood there, side by side with his horse, both of them eyeing the grave in what I thought was a disdainful posture. I thought it was a pretty good trick that the horse just stood and did what the man did. His mane and tail was mingled black and white, the same as the man's gray hair. After a minute the man commenced to talk rather rough at the grave, like he was having a argument with the old chief. I could hear him well enough, although I could not make out what he said, as it was in Spanish. He went on for a time, and it was a longer argument than I would of thought a person could have with a bunch of bones.

The sun had rose up hastily and the light was busting through the motte of big mesquites over the grave. Sam and me had to squint to keep looking, as we was staring directly into the light.

The Mexican might of gone on even longer with the old chief I suppose, had the pinto not snorted and stomped of a sudden and looked in the direction they was headed before they stopped.

And what do you know, but there's a Sesesh coming along, leading a old decrepit camel and escorting a woman with her hands bound at her back. Travelers on that trace was a fairly rare thing, as I before stated, and still is, so you can imagine my surprise to see in one morning such a odd lot as this — a Mexican, a Sesesh, and a woman captive, and along with them a fine pinto horse and a camel that was complaining a fair amount. I had spied others of the

119

army camels but had not seen this old fellow with the two humps.

The Mexican stood there and waited. The camel was moving slow, although he did not have a load of any kind to carry. He made a good deal of unpleasant noise and I surmised him to be in some pain or else just too ornery by nature to get along with. The Sesesh yanked and tugged his rope. He got behind the camel and prodded him with a stick and beat his flanks with it and was generally impatient, calling him many names I would not think I should repeat in a official report such as the one I am making. But I will tell you his language was coarse. He poked at the woman with the same stick as he poked at the camel with. She seemed to take this better than I would of thought a woman would take such treatment. In all, it was a pitiful sight to behold this Sesesh shoving and cussing at a broken down camel and a husky captive woman. Her dress was wore out and she was poorly looking. That is a kind way to put it. I could not figure what he intended with her.

When the Sesesh arrived eye to eye with the Mexican he said, What's a greaser like you doing with a horse like that.

The Mexican said, What I am doing is standing here with this horse.

His English was very good.

I wager it's stolen, the Sesesh said.

The Mexican was agreeable and said it was perhaps the most stolen horse on this side of the Rio Grande. However, it was never stolen by him, he said. He had purchased the horse in Gillespie County.

The Sesesh took his hat off to wipe his face and it was then I got a good look at him. The droopy eye was the sure giveaway. My pulse got quick when I seen it. I did not know the man's name at this time, as you have pointed out to me, but I seen him picking the pockets of the hanged unfortunates on the Julian, and I surely did know his face.

He spat on the ground. Are you a Texan or a Mexican, he asked the Mexican.

I am a Texan, the Mexican said.

Well then, unless you have got a exemption from the army I'll take you to Camp Verde and see if the major will sign you up, the Sesesh informed him.

I am a shoemaker and exempt, the Mexican said.

Shit you are. Let me see your papers then.

The Mexican went to his saddlebags. Whilst he was busy getting his papers, I got a look at the woman. She stood somewhat behind the Sesesh, who was Clarence Hanlin, as I would later learn his name to be.

Something was not right with her. She had a aggravated posture, and she spat like a man. A rag was tied over her head.

Clarence Hanlin eyed our nanny goat like he might take her. Her bags was full and she was stomping her feet and agitated.

I signaled to Sam to give me the pistol. To her credit she did try to hand it over, but I could not of reached it without scrabbling, and such a commotion would of made us known. So we give up that effort and the pistol remained in her hands, which I would later come to wish was otherwise.

The Mexican's pinto did not like the company. I believe he downright hated the camel. He laid his ears flat and bared his teeth but did not try to run off in spite of the reins was idle.

Clarence Hanlin looked at the papers the Mexican give him. I do not believe he could read them, as he took longer than it would take if you could actually read.

In the midst of this pause I seen what distress the camel was in. He had a good many wounds. It's a odd way that camels will bend their knees, and this one was doing so in a way that I seen he was intending to lay down. One of his humps was bent over. He wore a moccasin on one foot. His hair was patchy, like it was shaved. I could smell him even from where I was. It was the closest I had ever been to a camel and I was surprised how he stank.

Clarence Hanlin give the papers back to the Mexican, cursed at him, which did not seem to bother the Mexican, and then told him to get going. The Mexican mounted his pinto and went on his way. He did not seem in a hurry. There was a cut-through in the brush heading down to the creek, and he took that and was out of our sight.

Clarence Hanlin then commenced to beat the camel in the attempt to make him go on. However, the camel had got it in his head that he had walked enough for one day, and by the look of him maybe for all time. He puffed his throat out, and spat slime at Hanlin, and bawled at him and made general noises of protest whilst the captive woman looked on. He did not go forward at all, even as Hanlin walloped him pretty good. His aggravation increased until he tossed his big head clear around and got hold of Hanlin's arm in his mouth with such a fierce grip that he picked him up and tossed him. This made Hanlin even madder, as you might think it would. He shouted enough to scare away any creature within hearing of the commotion. He cursed and kicked the camel in the chest. The camel made burping and growling noises like a old man clearing out his throat. It was a real fight, but the camel did not seem to have the heart for it. He seemed pretty well done with just about everything including his own life. He did not look like he had any intention to win such a fearsome brawl, but rather like he was making a statement of his distress at the whole situation put to him, having come a long way, against his own will, in what must of been tight quarters on a boat, only to meet with such harsh treatment in a foreign land.

Sam is not a girl with a soft heart, but she has a aversion to meanness and she become agitated at beholding such cruel treatment that was going on. I feared she would give us away. I jammed my fist at my mouth to show her to keep a sock in it, but she would not look at me, as she was busy getting red in the face, or rather as much so as a half Negro can get.

After a severe bit of whacking and biting and kicking and a great deal of shouting and awful groaning, the camel folded his front knees and rocked hisself forward, and rocked back, and the hind legs buckled and he laid there, his legs folded under him and his head up, but barely. He looked like he wanted to roll on his side and be done with it all.

However, Clarence Hanlin seemed like he was just getting started. He was in a state of fury. I thought the captive woman might speak up, but what could she say. Her hands was tied. It also come to my attention about then that she was not actually a woman, but a man in a dress. However, I did not have time to reflect much about that, as things was happening too fast. Hanlin walked off a short ways and then turned and snuck up so not to get bit, and jabbed the camel a couple of times and stuck a big dirk knife in the hump that was not bent over. He stuck it so hard it stayed there. The camel let out a awful bawl. Hanlin could not get close enough to get his knife back without getting bit, so he tried to smack it out of the camel's hump with a branch he got off the ground. He cussed the whole time.

It was about this time that Sam could not take any more of that sorry behavior and yelled, Stop that! I believe she intended to shout louder but must of thought better of that idea, as the noise that come out was puny.

Clarence Hanlin looked about him to see where the sound come from. His eyes lit on the nanny. I suppose he thought it was her that give the yelp. I guess what he thought next was that it was time for breakfast, for when he got his knife knocked out of the camel with a couple more swipes he approached the nanny with it.

Sam let out a whole hearted yell. Don't you touch my goat or I'll shoot you! she said.

He stopped when he heard that. Who goes there, said he.

Sam yelled, We seen what you done! You are a mean son of a bitch and if you touch my goat I'll shoot you! I am heavily armed with a pistol!

He seen us then, and come on toward the nanny. His aim to take her was plain. I commenced to throw rocks at him from our buckets that was full of them. He stepped aside from the rocks and stuck his knife in his belt and pulled his pistol out and aimed at Sam and me, one then the other, back and forth. It was a perilous situation we was in. I thought I might jump out of the tree and take off, but it was a high limb I was on and I was pretty sure I would break a leg if I done so, and then where would that leave me. Down on the ground with a broke leg and the man's pistol aimed at my head, that's where. Also, I could not in good conscience leave Sam in a tree when she had only a pistol loaded with bat shat, though I did figure I had the right to leave her if I should decide to do so, as she was the cause of our troubles from start to finish. We would not of even been in the tree if not for her.

I will say this about Clarence Hanlin. He had some sense. I would of expected a blind charge but he took some caution and come on fairly slow, because what kind of kids have got nerve like that to take on a grown man. Also he had to duck the rocks I was pitching as fast as I could. However, I did not have a clean shot on account of so many branches being in my way.

I believe I knew Sam would pull the trigger even before she done so, as it was her nature to do it. However, I did not know she would do it as fast as she done it. Me and Clarence Hanlin both was taken by surprise when the pistol went off. One minute I was pitching rocks and the next I had my mouth hanging open in wonderment as Clarence Hanlin yelled fiercely. His pistol flew out of his hand. His hand went up in the air and his finger flew off in another direction from the pistol. Where before there was one hand aiming the pistol, now there was three different things — the hand, the pistol, and the finger, all going their own way.

You shot me, you bitch, you shot me! he shouted.

As if that might of escaped her notice.

Sam hollered at me, I could of killed him! I could of shot him in the face!

I figured she meant Clarence Hanlin but then it come to me she was back on the panther and meant she could of killed the panther the night before, had I not doubted the powder and made her hold off.

I thought, We are done for now. We are dead ducks now. We are stuck in this tree and that man is about to shoot us out of it as soon as he gets hold of his gun, no question about that. So right away I took action. I seen where the pistol belonging to Clarence Hanlin had landed when it flew. I seen he was not in search of it as yet. I got hold of a knife and climbed down as fast as I could and grabbed up Hanlin's pistol off the ground.

Hanlin did not take much notice of me at first, as he was bent on figuring out what happened to his finger. It lay in the dirt. He seemed not to know if he should pick it up or just holler at Sam about it. Blood was gushing out everywhere. It got all over him. He kept shouting, You bitch. He stood over his finger and yelled, You shot off my finger!

Sam yelled, I'll shoot you again if you come closer!

He did not know she had spent all the powder and ball she had, so he give some credence to that idle threat.

And then here come the man in the dress, rushing at me. He said, Cut my hands loose. He turned his back so I could do so. I figured he was on our side of the situation, so I done as he said. No sooner had I done it than he snatched the knife out of my hands and tussled with me for the pistol. It come to me he thought he might use it to make his escape alone.

And then here comes Clarence Hanlin too, all bloody, throwing hisself on the both of us and knocking us on the ground. He hit me hard in the head. I don't know what he done to the man in the dress, but he got the pistol back even in spite of the fact he had use of only one hand, on account of the other was missing a finger. He got blood all over me and the man in the dress. Who would of thought a hand would squirt so much blood. Not me. What I know is that Hanlin got his pistol. He did not seem to know which hand he aught to hold it in, as the right one did not have the usual fingers. He kept passing the pistol from one hand to the other. He did not appear to be in his right mind. He backed up and aimed at me and the man in the dress and told us to get up off the ground and put our hands in the air. We done so.

Sam commenced to scramble about in the tree to get higher up, and whilst doing so knocked our bucket of rocks out of the branches. The nanny got all worked up about the rocks tumbling down on her. She bleated like crazy and just about broke her neck yanking against the tether after having nearly nothing to say all night when we needed her to. If she would of seen fit to bleat like that in the night I might of been lucky enough to fight with a panther instead of Clarence Hanlin.

Sam yelled, I'll shoot you if you shoot my brother!

This sounded like a actual threat, as how could he know she had spent her one ball. However, he was not in a mood to care about threats. He was trying to keep a good grip on the pistol. I supposed he would shoot me in the head. I did not care a lot about what he might do to the man in the dress. You asked me to be frank. If not for the man in the dress I would of had the pistol myself and the tables would of been turned the other way around.

The man in the dress and me stood with

our hands in the air like criminals. The camel was making a bunch of dreadful groaning noises and had not got up from where he laid. The nanny was tangled in her tether and went on bleating. Sam was out of sight way up in the branches and giving off the mistaken impression her pistol was a six shooter and fully loaded with plenty to spare.

Hanlin was scared, I think. He was the only one of us with any say-so under the circumstances, but he was weak and wobbly. The blood was still pouring out. He did not seem to know how to behave with only nine fingers and kept on hollering about the one that was laying on the ground.

Sam hollered at him, Pick it up if you miss it so much!

He hollered, You goddamn bitch, I'm going to kill you!

She said, You can't see me but I have a clean shot at you. Move a inch and you're done for! You seen what I done to your finger.

Hanlin yelled at her, You are aiding and abetting a escaped Yankee! You think it's a woman in that dress, but it's a Yankee out of the canyon!

I already seen that's no woman, said she.

There was three of them got out in dresses

from the cooks! he said. We ain't caught the others. I have got to bring this one in. You are aiding the wrong side!

Sam was not taken in. I might aught to give you a little pill out of this pistol! she said.

It was a stand off, and would of remained so if the branch Sam was on had not cracked and dropped her down to the one below it. She caught herself on that one but let go of my pistol when she done so. Down it went and landed under the tree. I can tell you my heart sank. I thought, It's over now. We are three goners.

Clarence Hanlin must of come to the same conclusion about us. He got a smile on his face despite the fact he was looking woozy. He said, Well, well. I shall not forget how he said it with a distasteful satisfaction. He walked over and picked up the pistol and looked it over and said, You was trying to bluff me.

Sam did not answer that.

I thought I might make a dash at Hanlin. The Yankee in the dress had the same idea, I believe, as he give me a look. However, it was not a workable notion. Hanlin would shoot us before we even got near him. There was nothing to do but see what he done. He appeared to consider the choices. It was a terrible moment we spent waiting for him to decide if he was going to shoot us, and which one he might shoot first. I am nearly getting the shakes just thinking about that moment. I could already see Sam shot and tumbling out of that tree like a varmint.

I said, We got off to a bad start but I can explain.

He said, The girl shot my goddamn finger off.

I said, I am sorry she done that, she has a bad temper.

He commenced to spit on the ground.

We could not see Sam in the tree too well but we heard her. She said, I am sorry.

Come down or I'll shoot you down, Hanlin yelled, and quick as lightning he fired a shot at the branches.

I can't say if he meant to hit her or not, or what would of happened. It is beside the point on account of a unexpected event, which was the return of the Mexican. He come from behind the mesquite motte with his pistol at the ready. I seen him, and I seen the Yankee in the dress seen him too, although neither of us let on.

The Mexican moved fast. He did not have his pinto with him but was afoot. He run and snuck up on Clarence Hanlin and said, Toss your gun, gringo, and get your hands in the air. If you turn around you will die at once.

Clarence Hanlin got quite still. After reflection, he tossed his pistol, and mine alongside it, and raised his hands in the air. The one that was short of a finger was a awful sight and weird looking too. The Mexican walked over and got the pistols off the ground. I can't tell you word for word what he said, on account of his English was perfect and mine is not. He asked the Yankee where he hoped to be heading.

The Yankee said he was hoping to get to Mexico.

You won't get there wearing a dress, the Mexican said.

He said to Sam, Ameega in the tree, close your eyes.

She said, Why am I to do that.

He said, Two men are about to undress.

She said, All right then I will.

The Mexican told Clarence Hanlin to toss his knife and to take his boots and his trousers and his jacket off.

Hanlin shouted, I ain't giving my clothes to a Yankee, if that's what you think!

But he has only a dress to wear, the Mexican said. He will never reach Mexico wearing a dress. He'll be better off wearing your clothes.

I can't tell you the rest of all that was said, as I was unsettled and could not give it my full attention. What I remember is that the Mexican was polite. Clarence Hanlin to the contrary was worked up and angry. However, the Mexican had all the pistols, so Hanlin done what he said. He took his boots off. They was jack boots. He took his clothes off. It was none of it easy for him to do, on account of the trouble with his finger, or I should say lack of the finger. He cussed a good deal about the pain. Exchanges was made. Hanlin put on the dress. He tied his hand up with the rag the Yankee had wore on his head. He looked like he was about to pass out. His teeth was clanking together and he sweated a good deal. All he had left of his belongings was a plug of tobacco he hung on to out of his jacket. It was soggy with blood, and I felt sick to my stomach just knowing he had it.

The Yankee did not seem grateful to be getting a Sesesh uniform that was a tight fit and bloody. However, beggars can't be choosers. When he had the uniform on, the Mexican told him to take Hanlin's knife and get going. That was one thing the Yankee done without any complaining. He headed off to the cut-through down to the creek.

The Mexican told him, Not so fast, ombray. My horse is there.

The Yankee replied he would not steal a horse that belonged to a man who had saved his life.

None of us thought that was true. The Mexican made him start off in another direction. It is only a small detour on your way to Mexico, he said. A mere stitch in the seam.

So the man headed off. He went quite fast.

The Mexican told Sam she could open her eyes. He told Clarence Hanlin he could not set him free, as it was too likely he would come back to take revenge on los neenyos — by which he meant Sam and me.

Clarence Hanlin said, You goddamn Mexican.

The Mexican shook his head. He lifted his hat and brushed it off. He said it was hard to be scared of a man whose finger lay in the dirt before him. We will have to keep you with us, he said. Because what are we to do. If we let you go, you will come back.

Hanlin said, I got to tend to this wound. You can't keep me here. I'm a soldier. They'll think I deserted. I can't just be gone a long time.

The Mexican said, If I shoot you, you will be gone even longer.

Sam remained in the tree. I don't want

him around, she said. Send him off from here.

I said, He'll come back as sure as the panther.

Hanlin said, I ain't going nowhere in a dress.

The Mexican said he did not see a way for a man to wear nothing. He went to look at the camel. It was a pitiful creature, laying on its side with flies at its wounds. It slobbered and made noises, though they was not so loud as before. I wondered if it would live, but it was a moot question, as the Mexican shot it.

Dear Judge,

I hope my last report reached you. I had a good time in Comfort the day I went to post it. Mr Hildebrand was not in his office nor anywhere in the store when I got there, so I waited around town and seen a few folks. I don't know if you know Mrs Ottenhoff but I run into her on the street and she asked me to make her a nice chair. She is getting old and it is about time for her to get off her feet. She is German and does not speak a lot of English but we was able to get our ideas across. I told her I could not make cushions but I am a good carpenter. She asked what Samantha does with her time and why she don't make cushions, as it would bring in some money to live on. I told her I would venture to pass that idea on to Samantha. However, I will tell you

141

in private it will not take. Sam will not sew nor do a thing more than what she has to. She is not useful. She aims to get grown enough and take off for somewhere else, and go where she pleases, on account of nobody can mistaken her for a slave now, on account of there is no such thing anymore. I can't think how she might make a living of any sort, as she is not a hard worker. Also I can't think a person would choose to take her in. She is not a joy to look at nor be with. She wears nothing except my outgrown attire and a rope for a belt and will not put on a bonnet nor hat, and prefers to go barefoot. If it's cold she'll wear my old boots or get hold of my current ones if I am not watching out. I am used to her but she does daily irritate me in one way or another.

Me and Mr Hildebrand had a good talk. He is a freethinker and will not entertain a notion unless it can be proved. He does not believe in a all mighty god, on account of there is not a good deal of proof of him. Amongst other things, Mr Hildebrand said I am a lucky young man to be friendly with a person of your stature, as you are known to be a honest judge and a good man.

He said the government in Austin has got a bunch of idiots. That is a exact quote. He said I could tell you he said so. Notwithstanding you were known for a Union man, he said nobody in his right mind of either persuasion would sign up to run against you in the coming up election, as you are well liked and it would be a waste of their time, and nobody these days has time they aught to be wasting, as we have all got work to do. I was glad to hear him say so many good things about you.

I told him I was sorry there was not another letter from you. However, he said it makes sense, as you are a long way off. He showed me a map of counties you was to visit and the route you apprised him of a while back. Also we agreed you might be having all kinds of trouble from Indians and robbers, not even to mention the usual hazards. I hope you are safe, sir.

Whilst on the matter of Indians, I have good news to pass along. You might recall, as it was talked about, what happened to the Gilmore family last year when Mrs Gilmore and her daughter went out in a buggy to call on friends and pick up the mail and was attacked by Indians. If you have not heard about it, I am sorry to tell you it was not a good end they come to. The faithful horse come hauling the buggy back home with the mother and girl in it, though they was passed. The mother had her throat cut ear to ear and the girl's head was cleaved off. The family figured the Indians had hold of it, but after a better look in the buggy they seen it under the seat. That must of been a terrible sight to behold. However, the good news of recent days is that Mr Gilmore has got some revenge at last. He come across Indian tracks and followed them and found three Indians off their mounts and having a rest, and he dispatched them. No matter if the Indians he killed was the very same that murdered his wife and daughter, he said they would do. He is aiming to get more men and hunt down more Indians, as that is his main purpose in life as it now stands. I should probably not tell you that, as you are a judge and Uncle Sam has forbid folks to raise arms on account of the troubles that taken place when folks done so before. So enough about that.

You will see in this report that I have started up where I left off. It was troublesome to write and took up good portions of five days, as I was at it before daylight and after dark whilst I was cramped at a small table and wrote with a quill that is nearly wore out. Sam has been pestering me to read her what I wrote. She is not a good reader herself. I have not taken the time to teach her. What has she ever done for me. If I was to read her my report she would not like things I have said about her. She would deny them and put up a quarrel and then claim she come out the victor. She is unpleasant to deal with. However, that is off the topic at hand.

I hope you are having good travels and bringing justice to lots of folks. I will send this report tomorrow and write more later. I could do so faster with a good pen. However, I have only quills.

Yours kindly,
Benjamin Shreve

My Testament

Clarence Hanlin was a mess to lay eyes on under the big bur oak, wearing that dress he had got on that was lacking the buttons on account of the ill treatment of two men now having wore it. You would not believe all the blood that come out of his finger. It was like the fishes and loaves. He kept try-ing to sop it up with the rag. He tried stick-ing his hand up high and squeezing the finger. However, that just made the blood come pouring down his arm. I was aston-ished he had any left. The squeezing made him holler, as it hurt a great deal. He was barefoot but for his socks. He had got his soggy plug of tobacco stuffed in a pocket of the dress, but who would want it. He did not try to get his gone finger out of the dirt, though I thought he would do so, as he did look at it. He said goddamn it a number of times.

The Mexican told Sam to come down out of the tree, and she done so. When Clarence Hanlin seen her face, he yelled goddamn, she's a goddamn witch. Look at her face.

The Mexican took a good long look at her face. It was a serious look. He said, She is not a witch, she is cat-marked.

Sam didn't pay any mind to Hanlin, on account of she had her pride. She got the nanny goat out of the rope tangle and took her off to the house, as if nothing at all was amiss. I think the nanny was pleased to be shed of the place, as flies was after her teats and her kid stank from being passed.

I asked the Mexican, What would you have me do.

He said, Who is the girl.

I owned that she was my half sister.

He asked if she was on her way to our house.

I told him yes, it was yonder and she was headed that direction.

He said Clarence Hanlin and myself was to follow behind her. We done so. The Mexican followed behind us with the pistols. When we got to the house Sam taken the nanny to the pen and did not look back at us. I think she felt bad about her looks after the fuss Hanlin made, although she did not let on about it. She knew for a fact they was not right looks, but it is one matter to know such a thing and make your peace with it, and another entire matter to be scoffed at by the likes of Clarence Hanlin.

The Mexican told Hanlin and me to enter the house, and he come in after us. He aimed his pistol at Hanlin the whole time. He taken his hat off when he come in. Hanlin did not have a hat, as the prisoner had gone off wearing it.

I had forgotten how bad the house appeared until I seen it from their standpoint. It smelled bad too. Our pots was ate off of and dirty. I can't even think what Juda would say about the bugs and whatnot. We had mice shat all over the place. We had pig shat on the floor and chicken shat on the bed. There was a infestation of scorpions that I thought Hanlin might step on, as he was barefoot but for his socks. However, what did I care.

I told the Mexican, I am sorry about the condition you have found us in. We have not cleaned up in a while.

He asked where our folks was.

I told him they was passed.

Clarence Hanlin said, Goddamn, it's a pigsty.

The Mexican told him to sit down. He done so whilst holding his hurt hand wrapped up in the rag. He said, I am just about a gone case.

He did look woozy. He was pale and his teeth was clanking together although the day had warmed up a good bit already and there was not much chill in the air.

The Mexican told me to get a bucket of water.

I told him I had no more buckets, as they was all outside in the tree and most of them filled with rocks.

He asked what we had thought we might do with rocks in a tree.

I told him they was to throw at a panther we was enticing.

He told me to fill our pitcher.

I gone to the creek and done that. When I come back, the Mexican give me my pistol that was empty of lead. He give me Clarence Hanlin's pistol that was loaded. It was a Colt's forty-four six-shot. He showed me how to use it. On account of I was only fourteen and my hands not fully grown, it was a long reach to the hammer. He give me instructions to aim at Hanlin's head and shoot him if he moved in a way he should not.

I asked if I was actually to shoot him, and the Mexican said I was. I said, What if I miss or don't kill him.

He said, Cock the pistol again. Pull the trigger again.

I said, All right then.

The Mexican removed his shirt so as not to spoil it, and made a attempt to stop Hanlin's hand from spurting out blood. Hanlin was behaving unreasonable. The Mexican had to yell at him to press harder on it with the rag. However, Hanlin yelled all the more about that. It was a foul looking hand. The gone finger left a bit of a nub. The Mexican told me to get something to tie that off with, so I give him some of my fishing string and the Mexican tied it on the nub and poured water on the hand to wash it up. The gone finger was the one next to the smallest. The middle one beside it had a chunk of flesh out of it too. Hanlin cussed the whole time, but done what the Mexican told him.

Whilst undertaking this, the Mexican asked my name.

I said, Benjamin Shreve. What's yours.

He said, Lorenzo Pacheco. What's your sister's name.

Samantha Shreve, I said. She will answer to Sam.

He asked for liniment or ointment and for lint or a bandage.

I told him hog's lard was the best I could do and that I had no bandage. I said we could cut a piece of a dress, as I had done so on occasion for wounds of my own. It was Juda's old dress.

Sam come in from the pen after we cut the dress and she had a fit about that.

The Mexican told her he was sorry. He did, in fact, seem to be.

She had goat's milk and give us some but give none to Hanlin.

He said, To hell with you, bitch. He said he felt sick and did not want it on any account.

She said, I wouldn't give you none if you begged. You was rude to me.

He cursed her looks some more.

I asked her, Do you want me to shoot him.

I was not serious about it.

She thought I was serious and expressed that it might be a good idea. This worried Hanlin a good bit. He said, Don't shoot me.

The Mexican wrapped up his hand.

I thought of saying nothing about what I seen Hanlin do on the Julian, and then I thought better of that. I said, I seen what you done on the Julian.

That stopped his cussing. His eyes was rolling about with pain, but nevertheless he stopped to look me over. After what I seen on the Julian I had hoped I might never lay eyes on the man again, yet now here he sat, in my own home. His look would of froze me with fear, if not for the fact that I had his pistol aimed at his head.

He said, I ain't never been on the Julian.

I said, I seen you there, picking the pockets of them that was hanged.

He said, I know of nobody hanged.

I said, It was a number of them, and they was hanged and had ropes on their necks whilst you was picking their pockets.

Liar, he said. That's a falsehood.

I said, Say you done it, or I'll shoot you.

He said, All right, then, so I done it. But they was deserving of what they got. They was evading conscription. They was traveling without permits.

I figured the Mexican would not know the occasion we was talking about and aught to be told. I told him what I seen that day, how I gone for a hunt, and fired a shot, and missed, and heard coyotes jibbering, and come across such a sight as I had never seen in my life, which was this man here, this same sorry one, picking the pockets of passed men that was hanged and laying on the ground, scattered about.

The Mexican took it all in. I did not know what he might make of that information. When he was done fixing the hand, he washed up and put his shirt back on and thought over what I had told him. He asked Sam what she would have him do with the evil ombray.

She was making herself busy about the fire. Do what you want, said she. I don't care about him. I would like never to see him again, is all. I would like him never to lay eyes on me.

The Mexican give her all his attention whilst she stirred up the fire. He asked if she had coffee to offer. She told him to ask me, as I was the one that mostly done the cooking. He asked me if I had coffee to offer. I told him we had no coffee on account of the Yankee blockade. I said we was accustomed to using ground up acorns. He agreed he would have that.

Sam put on water to boil. She did not usually do a great deal for persons other than herself but I think she did not want Hanlin eyeing her, and therefore kept herself busy.

I got a better look at the Mexican. He had pocks of black powder burned into one side of his face that appeared to of been there a good many years. I already informed you his clothes was all black but for his white shirt. He had hung his hat on the stick by the door where my father used to hang his. It was a wide-brimmed felt affair with a high crown. It was black. His boots was black too. They was good boots, about the best I ever saw. He had no spurs. His holster was black, and there was ferns carved in the leather. He was a person of some pride. He did not look like a shoemaker, as he told Clarence Hanlin at the Indian grave he was. He asked would Sam be so kind as to bring him his pinto that awaited at the cut-through down to the creek.

She said all right, and went off, I think pleased to be gone. I give Hanlin's pistol back to the Mexican, as I did not want it laying around for Hanlin to get whilst I made us coffee. When I had made it, Hanlin and myself and the Mexican sat about and drank it. This might of been a peace-

153

able moment if Hanlin had not bemoaned his finger the whole time and cussed the coffee, as it was acorns. He sat hunched before a bowl that was full to the brim of bloody water that made me feel sick to look at. He could not seem to get over his loss. Also, it was not the end of his troubles, for he laid eyes on cooties that was hunkered down in the dress he wore. He commenced to yell about cooties and cuss the prisoner that worn the dress before him, saying such things as, The goddamn escapee is the ruin of me!

The Mexican told him to get quiet or he would shoot him.

Hanlin asked could he take off the dress.

The Mexican said, If you wish.

Hanlin said, I have nothing to wear.

The Mexican said nothing to that.

Hanlin then spied my father's trousers hanging on a peg and said, What about them trousers.

I said, Those was my father's. You can't have them.

He become irate and shouted at me about having nothing to wear.

That is your situation, not mine, I told him.

The trousers would of fit him, as he was a regular size person like my father. He was not bad looking, neither, if I am to be fair. However, he did have the droopy eye and a spiteful air. His hair was a light color, and kempt, but stuck to his head on account of he was dripping sweat. He had a short beard and a well trimmed mustache. His eyes was blue. If I had not seen what I seen of him, I would of thought him all right. However, I would of still not wanted to give him my father's trousers.

Sam come back in and told the Mexican she had brought his horse and it was out front. He give me back Hanlin's pistol to keep a watch on the man, and went out to check on the horse. He come back in and helped hisself to more coffee. He did not seem to have a idea about what to do with Hanlin.

Hanlin said he felt sick and did not want food, but aught to have it, or he would pass out. He said, What have you got to eat.

I said, Nothing I care to share with you.

He said, I got to have food. It's your fault I lost my hardtack. It was in my jacket.

It's your fault you lost your jacket, I told him. If you had not of come after two kids in a tree that was doing you no harm, you would have your jacket and your hardtack, also your boots and everything else including your finger. Now you have lost it all, on

155

account of your meanness. If you ask me, you are not right in the head.

He said, I aught to kill you.

The Mexican laughed about that, on account of I had Hanlin's pistol, so how was he to do it.

I asked the Mexican if he was hungry. He agreed he could eat. I told him we had corn meal.

He asked did it have weevils. He did not care for weevils.

I told him it had none.

I fried some, and we ate it. We did not give Hanlin a share.

The Mexican taken a good deal of interest in Sam. She is hard to figure, and he tried to figure her. I did not know what his motives might be, but I did not think they was risky, as he treated us fairly. He squatted like a Indian when he ate, by which I mean only the bottoms of his boots was touching the floor. He was a delicate eater and did not get food on his face. He kept near the door on account of the stink in the house. I said, You are not a shoemaker like you said.

He allowed he was not.

I said, What are you then.

He did not say, but inquired of Sam about her cat marks. He called her Neenya, and

156

she took issue, as it was not her name. He explained it meant little girl. He said, Neenya, tell me about the puma.

She said, Do you mean the panther.

He said, Yes.

She did not know what to make of the question. She was not accustomed to being asked that question nor any other. She got on the bed and thought it over. I could see she wished to tell him. She was used to having only me to talk to, who already knew that story.

After consideration she cut loose. She said, My daddy brought home a man that had lice in his hair.

Then she went on to tell it. She become serious and yet excited at the very same time. I believe she forgot how bad her face looked, regardless of that being a main part of the tale. She sat on her bed with the mice and chicken shat and told the story straight-faced, as if it weren't what wrecked her life and her face and done away with her mother. She had every detail just perfect. She told about the cold night, the lice ridding, the way she run and the way the panther come flashing out of the dark.

It come from the side, she said. It made not a noise. I smelled it before I seen it. It was on top of me so fast it knocked me flat on my face on the ground and commenced to bite my head. I tried to turn over but then I got a mouthful of its hair. I felt it growling against me. Its breath was hot on me and its slobber was all over my head. I wanted to yell but it had my whole head in its mouth. I felt the teeth go in, right here where you see them bare patches on account of the hair was ripped out. My mama come from the house and jumped on the panther. She said, You run, you run, you run. That's all she said that I heard. She whacked at it with a hatchet but it was moving a lot so she could not get a good whack. I did run, and climbed up a tree.

The Mexican pulled up a chair and was intent on the story. She told the whole tale.

Hanlin said, So you cost your mama her life.

The Mexican told him that if he was to say such a thing again the vultures would feast on his tongue before the hour was over. That shut him up for a time. The Mexican said, The neenya's mother sacrificed herself because her daughter is a great treasure.

I do not know what Sam made of that. She give it a moment's consideration and then went on telling about me throwing the flour at her, and about our father arriving home to find Juda all tore up on the floor, and passed, and her eyeball gone. She pointed to the corner where Juda had laid. She told of our father taking her to Camp Verde and showed how the doctor sewed up her face. It's a ugly face now, she said.

The Mexican asked what wounds the panther had from the hatchet.

She said, It was cut up a good bit all over.

I said, Two toes was hacked off.

The Mexican then fixed his eyes on me in a powerful manner. They was very black eyes. He said, Deeos meeo, which toes would those be.

I said, Those of the hind right. Why do you ask.

He asked if I was sure they was the hind right toes.

I told him I seen Juda hack them off myself, and if he cared to see two-toed tracks of the hind right he might go outside to the goat pen, and there they would be.

He went out, and when he come back he acted more excited than ever. He put his arms in the air and paced about and said the panther we was telling about was famous. He said, People know of this panther all the way to the border. It is called El Demonio de Dos Dedos.

I said, What does that mean.

He said, The Demon of Two Toes.

Ranchers and others down south, gringos and Tejanos, and also Mexicans over the border around Piedras Negras, had been trying to track and kill the panther for a long time, he said, on account of it was unnatural. Varmints and deer was not satisfactory food for the panther, as it favored farm animals. It has only a taste for creatures touched by man, was the way he said it.

As I have before stated, the Mexican spoke better English than I am able, and I would be unreasonable to try to repeat his words. But I can tell you he said them in ways that would make you take notice. He become determined on what he was saying in a way that made me give credence to it. He said El Demonio de Dos Dedos was known by some as El Demonio and by others as Dos Dedos. He said he knew of no other person that the demon had killed, however there was many goats and calves and even horses that met their fate in his jaws. The demon was known to steal newborn colts out of their stalls, and pull suckling pigs right off their mama's teats, one after the other. He said whoever should kill the grandeesemo panther and present the hide with two toes on the hind right, would earn the respect and gratitude of people in villages all the way to the border and beyond it. They would be famous for killing Dos Dedos. People would write songs about them. Ranchers was known to track the panther through chaparral too dense for horses to pass through and mesquite shrub that would tear you to bits, only to see it disappear and leave nothing but tracks with the hind right missing two toes. Some people had swore Dos Dedos was not a flesh and blood panther, but a terrible spirit called a doowindy that taken the form of one.

Sam got mad when she heard him say that about the doowindy. She jumped up off the bed and hollered, He is not a doowindy. He is a actual panther, and I have got marks on my face to prove it. It is my right and my duty to kill him and I am going to do it, not you or them others! I want to get even, and all you want is songs written about you. I have faced the panther twice, and you have done nothing but hear of his name. All I need is a loaded pistol. You already seen I'm a good shot. I plan to sit in the tree tonight and wait till it comes.

Clarence Hanlin said, I ain't staying here tonight, nor any other nights neither, whilst you sit in a tree. I got to have help. I got to have food. You ain't even shared your corn bread with me.

The Mexican said, It will do no good to sit in the tree. He said the panther would likely not come back for the kid, as it was known to kill for sport and leave the kills to rot on the ground.

Sam said if it would not come back, then she would track it and find it. Either way, I intend to do it in, she said. It is my right. You seen my face. You seen my mama's dress there without my mama in it. I don't care about songs. That panther was on top of me. I want its hide laying right here on my floor to tromp on day and night. I will be on top of it! I will make that happen myself, not you!

I would say her fierce opinion startled the Mexican, but he was not a person to show any sign whatsoever of being startled. So I would say it took him by surprise. He told her she could not track a panther without a panther dog.

She said, Where am I to get one.

He said, They are not common.

She said, What are they.

He told her they was trained to follow the scent and chase the panther into a tree and howl at the base of the tree until the hunter come to shoot it. However, he knew of only one pack of dogs that ever caught up with

Dos Dedos. It was four well trained dogs, and by the time the hunters had got there, the dogs was all four killed by Dos Dedos, who had not got up in the tree like he was supposed to but had hid out and turned on them and done them all in, a skillful piece of work on his part, as he did not get harmed hisself enough even to leave bloody tracks.

I said, There is no possible way he could kill all four.

The Mexican said, And yet he did.

Sam said, Where can I get a panther dog. I need to have one.

The Mexican told her he did not know of any this side of the border.

Hanlin declared, I know of one about a three hour walk from here.

The Mexican said he did not believe him, as they was rare.

Sam said, Where is it.

I will tell you that for a fee, Hanlin said.

His gone finger was giving him a great deal of pain and he was shaking on account of it. He said, Pay me, I'll tell you where the dog is, and then you can turn me loose and I can get to Camp Verde and see to my wound.

How about you tell us where the dog is or we'll shoot you, Sam offered.

Who's going to shoot me, he said. I don't think none of you is going to take me out and shoot me. If you do you won't get the dog.

Sam done a hasty turnabout when she heard that. Then we'll give you the money, she told him. We'll pay you to get us the dog.

I reminded her we had no money.

Why did you go and let on about that to him! she hollered at me.

I think he could figure it out, I told her.

Hanlin said, I wager our shoemaker here, who is not a shoemaker, has got money. Any greaser with a horse like his has got money around. What do you say, Mexican.

The Mexican said, I say it's unwise to call someone a greaser if he has a pistol aimed at you.

Hanlin said, I'll need a hundred dollars. Give me that, and I'll tell you where the dog is. The person who's got him will let you have use of him for a small fee. What's a hundred dollars and a small fee to get a song written about you.

I believe Hanlin meant this for a joke, as he had a smirk on his face. I took it for one, because who has got a hundred dollars.

However, the Mexican had neither a smirk nor a scowl nor any expression at all. I aught to of known at that time what I would come to know later, which was that he was playing a different game from what we was playing. He let on nothing about that, though. He said, I do not care about songs.

Hanlin seen that deals might get made. No money, no dog, he said. I want to lay eyes on the money, and I want this boy's word I can go my own way with it when I tell you where the dog is.

Sam said, All right then, you have my word.

Hanlin said, I don't want your word. I don't trust you and I don't trust the Mexican. I trust this boy.

I did not know what to make of that.

The Mexican offered he would pay fifty dollars. That shut us all up. My jaw about dropped to the floor at the thought of fifty dollars. He said Hanlin would have to take him to the dog and then he could have the money.

Sam said, You ain't going for the dog without taking me along.

The Mexican looked at her a good long minute and seen she would not be denied. You may come if your brother will come, he told her.

I will tell you what. I was not keen on it. I put up a argument with Sam about it, but she come out on top.

The Mexican asked who it was that had the dog.

Hanlin must of figured things was moving in his favor, as he become brash. I ain't saying who's got it, or where it's at, until I see the money and deals is made, he said. And I ain't doing nothing for fifty dollars. It's a hundred dollars or nothing. I have lost my finger on account of this girl. My finger was worth more to me than a hundred dollars, so I am not so much as coming out even. And if you are not fixing to shoot me, which I think you are not, then you are going to have to turn me loose sooner or later, and it might as well be on friendly terms. If I have got a hundred dollars I might feel friendly. If I got fifty, I won't.

I figured this was a bluff, as how could he think the Mexican might pay a hundred dollars. Who has got money like that to carry.

However, the Mexican appeared to think it over.

Sam become impatient and told him to pay the hundred.

I said, Why would he do such a thing. There is nothing in it for him. You want him to pay a hundred dollars he has probably not got to get you a dog to hunt a panther you want to keep the hide of.

The Mexican said, I will pay the hundred.

That surely got our attention.

He said, But if I pay the money and kill the panther, I will need to have the hide.

Sam said, You can't do none of that but pay the hundred! I am going outside to pick us some corn to take along with us, and when I come back, I want it worked out. I want us on our way.

There seemed to be a general agreement amongst the three of us that we did not have to listen to her. She went out, and Hanlin commenced to complain that he was in more pain than we understood, and about done in by it, and he did not intend to set out with us, as the person who owned the dog lived ten miles off and it was too far for him to travel in the condition he was in.

The Mexican would hear none of that. He was not going to give Hanlin the money until he took us to the person with the dog and we was able to come to a agreement with that person about use of the dog.

It was a big argument between them about all these particulars. Hanlin got up out of the chair to take a punch at the Mexican, who remained cool as a cucumber, as they say, and who give him a whack on the head with the pistol that put him back in his seat. Hanlin commenced to bleed from his head as well as his hand.

Sam come back in with six scroungy looking ears of corn. She give Hanlin one to
butter him up and get her way. He ate it
raw with his hand that had all the fingers.
He asked her to cut off a chunk of his
tobacco plug that he had put in the pocket
of the dress. It was bloody, as I before said,
and made me feel sick to look at. Sam
chopped off a chunk and give it to him. I
nearly give up the corn bread I had ate.

I told him, Don't spit on our floor. He
done so regardless, to spite me.

The Mexican went out to his horse to
fetch the money. He come back in with a
hundred dollars that about set my eyes on
fire just to look at. They was Confederate
notes, with a fifty amongst them. There was
one of them I never seen before and the
Mexican let me look it over. It had a lady
wearing a dress that had only one shoulder
to it and showed a good part of her bosom.
She was not a good looking woman in the
face but otherwise she was all right. There
was some sailors on it too. The rest of the
bills was fives. The Mexican would not let
Hanlin touch any of them on account of he
was bloody.

Hanlin said, I don't trust it. There's too
much counterfeit bills afloat. I want specie

or bills from the United States of America.

The Mexican thought that was funny. He said he could not figure how a man could have faith in a country enough to sign up to fight for it, and yet too little to trust its notes.

Hanlin said, There's too many Yanks passing bad ones that has found their way to us. He demanded to look over the bills. He said he would not be agreeable to anything until he done so. The Mexican showed him every bill in front of his eyes. When they was done with that, Hanlin said, All right.

Then the matter of the dress come up again. Hanlin said, You might as well go ahead and pull the trigger as make me walk out of here wearing this. It's bloody and it's got cooties and it's a dress. I want your daddy's trousers and a shirt, or I ain't taking you to the dog.

I said, You can't have them. You ain't fit to wear his trousers.

Sam said, Our daddy would want the panther tracked down and shot for killing my mama. He would give up his trousers to that effort. You know for a fact that is so.

For a rare occasion I come to agree with her, as she had a good point. So I give Hanlin the trousers and my extra shirt. Sam went out whilst he changed. The shirt fit him small and could not be buttoned.

We then talked over measures to take for our journey. The Mexican had his pinto horse and we had the old mare. Hanlin had nothing to ride, and said he could not walk, on account of he was woozy. The Mexican said he would not allow Hanlin on the pinto, but he would allow me and Sam. He said he would take turns switching out with me afoot. Sam declared she would switch out afoot too. We agreed Hanlin could ride the mare and that we might make him switch out afoot, along with the rest of us, if the journey become long.

We fed the goats, turned the chickens loose in the yard to scratch, tossed cobs out for the pigs should they come up from the creek, mounted up, and started off. It was about noon at that time.

Dear Judge,

You are lucky to be hearing from me again, as I nearly stepped on a coiled up rattlesnake I mistook for a pile of cow shat when I was doing a favor. A man come to the shingle camp to tell us he had two yoke of wild beeves to break and they had got out, and could we help him round them up. Three of us said, Sure, we would be happy to do that. Whilst we was searching I seen what I figured was cow shat amongst rocks. It's a good thing I seen it and thought to step to the side. You should of heard the racket that snake made. I am surprised you did not.

Sir, I wish you could help me with Samantha. I do not know what to do about her. She complains she has nothing to do when in fact there is a great deal that aught to be done, as we remain in our same poor quarters and she will not spend a hour a day working about the house or doing things that might be useful but sits about saying she has nothing of interest to do. She chatters all day to the chickens as if they was long time friends. She does not mind wringing their necks when the time comes, but she prefers a conversation. She would do well to have people of her own age to talk with, but we live too far off, and what kind of kids is going to make friends with her regardless. Yellow-colored and cat-marked is not a good mixture for making friends. She is currently fifteen years old, as I told you, and she wants adventure and new sights and I have had a time keeping her from taking off. I have been telling her nobody is going to care to have her around and she is better off staying with me. What is going to happen to somebody like her who is hard to look at and not likely to be useful. She told me, How do you know I won't find something I can do.

I told her, Because you don't try to be helpful.

She said, How do you know I won't find people who might like to have me around. I figure nobody is going to marry me, but there might be a person who does not mind hearing me talk, like you mind it, and who might think a few things I say are a good idea.

Judge, I will tell you what she wants. She wants to boss somebody around. I can't think of a person who might care to be bossed by the likes of her. Do you know of any nice person, who lives not too far off, who might offer to take her in and give her a chance to do some work. It should be a person who is not inclined to stare at her, as she does not like that. It would have to be a patient person. She is not skilled about being respectful but she might learn. If you have any good thoughts of ways to help her be more useful or of any patient person that might have her, please write to me about them. Every day I fear she won't be here when I get home from the camp. I worry about her a great deal.

The pages I am sending now continue with my testament. I have spoke of Mr Pacheco as Mr Pacheco and not the Mexican, on account of we was now better acquainted.

Yours kindly,
Benjamin Shreve

It was a miserable ride to fetch the panther dog. Clarence Hanlin would not let us forget the pain he was in. He shook as if it was freezing out. To the contrary there was only a small nip in the air. His teeth rattled nearly as loud as a rattler. Of course that is a exaggeration but they did rattle. He complained of the fishing string being tied too tight, and took it off. He made a effort to hold his hand that had the gone finger up in the air to stop it spurting more blood, but his arm got wore out, and he complained about that too. We none of us had much sympathy about his situation. I did not like the way he treated the mare. She was not adapted to having a rider holding a arm straight up in the air like that.

The place we was heading was ten miles off in the direction of Kerrsville. We stayed clear of the main road, as we did not want to run into any Sesesh on the way. Hanlin did not want to run into them, neither, despite he was one of them, as he was set on his hundred dollars. Also I guess he did not want to explain that he was wearing regular clothes on account of his uniform was heading to Mexico on a escaped prisoner. Also they might ask about his finger, and I guess it was a embarrassment to him that it had got shot off by a girl.

So we was traveling a trace. Mr Pacheco and myself switched out going afoot and riding his pinto with Sam mounted in back. She went afoot for a short distance but preferred riding, as the pinto was a fine horse and she was proud to be on him. Also it was not easy going afoot, as the trace was hard to make out and the grass high. In places it stood nearly higher than Sam.

I liked riding the pinto a great deal and wished it could be just myself without the others along. I could of taken the main road and headed for the United States to make my own way in the world. Whilst I can't say for sure I would of done it, it would of been a privilege to have a horse like that and a choice in the matter.

I asked Mr Pacheco, What are you if not a shoemaker.

He said his life was a long story.

Indeed it was, as he talked about it nearly the whole way. I believe he liked telling a story nearly as much as Sam did. However, his stories was of more interest and there was more of them.

He said when he was young he worked for a great ranchero as a domador. That's a horse trainer, if you don't know. He could train horses without the use of rough measures or even spurs. He could gentle a caught mustang to the point where you could splice the reins with five hairs of the tail and the horse would still do just as you told it. He fell in love with a already married woman who preferred her own husband to him.

Then he become a smuggler. The way he told it, he would drive mustangs up north to Louisiana without paying the duty. He would sell out the mustangs and other things such as furs for a good price and buy a bunch of Louisiana tobacco leaf that he would haul in bags on mules back to Texas. Then he would sell that in Texas to buy more mustangs and whatnot. His enterprise made him rich but cost the lives of three friends that was killed by Comanches whilst they was working with him. God was yet to forgive him for that, he said, nor did he expect God's forgiveness or even ask for it, as he did not deserve mercy of any kind, on account of it was his own fault his friends was killed. He had taken them on a unknown trace that proved to have the Comanches on it, just so he might avoid paying the duties. He was the only one to get away with his life, as he had the fastest horse.

When the revolution begun in Texas he commenced smuggling weapons for the

Texas army. They was brought on ships into Horse Pass and he would haul them to the army. After the war come to a close the Mexicans in Texas was badly treated even if they was Texans like him that had never set foot south of the Rio Grande. So he struck off and went west. He felt lucky to take his soul along with him, as he had committed deeds that aught to of cost him his soul. He was a young man at that time, but had lived a chancy life to that point, and had regrets enough to burden his mind for the remainder of it.

I asked him, What was those regrets.

He said he would not speak of the regrets.

I said, If I might ask, how did you get the pocked face.

He said he did not talk about that.

I asked about family and he would not say much about that, neither. I said, How come you had any hope left at all when you headed off west, if you was barely with even a soul.

To answer that, he asked if I ever seen a lizard get done in by a jay bird. The jay bird will catch it up, carry it to a branch, pen it down whilst it squirms, and peck it to death. A lizard in that condition, when there should be no hope left, will turn the color of the tree in a effort to disguise itself so

179

not to get caught, despite that it is already caught. Why does a lizard do that, he said. How does the lizard still have hope even whilst it is dying.

I said, Sam and myself had nearly the same luck of the lizard until you come to our rescue when we was in the tree. I need to thank you for that.

I wish I had shot both you kids before the rescue come, Hanlin said from atop the mare.

Mr Pacheco said he come into a good bit of gold out west. However, Mexicans was badly treated there too, as the laws was not in their favor, so he come back to Texas and spent what money he had earned to build up a ranch down south. He was friendly with a famous Mexican bandit named Cortina who had a habit of coming over the border from Mexico with his ombrays and stealing horses and cattle from the ranches in that part of Texas. Then the friendship fell out and Cortina burned his house and took his horses. It was a terrible night when that happened, Mr Pacheco said. The pinto was his favorite. His heart was broke to think of that horse in the hands of them bandits. He rode down to Mexico to see if he could find the pinto, and asked around, and was told by one of the ombrays that the pinto had been sold up here to a man over in Blanco. So he rode up here and bought him back. That was his purpose for being near us and for having cash on him. The pinto was all he had left that he cared about having. I can see why he went in search of that horse. It was the finest I ever knew and a pleasure to ride.

I asked Mr Pacheco what was it he said to the old Indian chief in the grave.

He said he had told the old chief that if his people cared to help theirselves to any more of his horses than the ones they had stole in the past, they could find them with Cortina's ombrays, who was sure to hand them over with no trouble at all.

That joke give Mr Pacheco a good laugh.

Sam would talk of nothing but the panther dog. She bothered Hanlin to tell her about it, but he was not in a talkative mood and cursed her. Mr Pacheco said panther dogs was brave and noble friends of man and lived for but one cause, the cause being to track panthers. Their powers of scent was such that they could smell where a panther's pad had merely grazed the ground. They was devoted to the point that they would track on a cold day until they froze to death, or on a hot day until they perished of thirst, or on rocky ground until the pads of their

181

feet wore down to bone and the black of their nose was scraped off. A panther dog has the soul of a knight, he said.

That satisfied Sam a good bit.

After we traveled a good part of the afternoon Hanlin said the place was nearby and he had just as well tell us it was his uncle who had the dog, as we was about to find that out.

Mr Pacheco reined in and impressed on Hanlin that there had better not be any attempts made.

Hanlin said, My uncle would not help me in the direst of circumstances. He has hated me since I was in nappies. He's a preacher and a pious son of a bitch. He don't care a whit about me.

We none of us found that to be much of a puzzle.

The house when we got there was in the midst of a big corn field. We come from the trees along the side. Sam and me was on the pinto, Mr Pacheco was afoot, and Hanlin was on the mare.

It was a bad looking house for a preacher's. I had expected better. There was three kids in the corn but they run into the house when they seen us coming out of the trees. A ugly dog took us in from the porch as we rode up. He did not set up a howl, but stood there looking at us.

Hanlin said, That's the dog.

Sam said, You're a liar. That ain't it.

Hanlin said, It's the very one.

The dog was not as I had pictured and not sightly. It had a big head and powerful looking jaws, however its hind end was scrawny and its legs was short. It was of a murky, dark color. I would be pressed to say if it was black with brown, or brown with black. It did not look like a young dog.

Mr Pacheco said, That is not a panther dog. You have misled me.

Hanlin said he was not fool enough to attempt to trick a armed man when he was unarmed hisself and short a finger.

We rode up to the house and Hanlin hallooed from atop the mare.

A man past his prime come out on the porch. He was loose boned and scraggy. His hair was like a tassel atop a corn plant. He called out, Welcome, strangers. Then he seen Hanlin in our company and said in a rough voice, I rescind the welcome. My door remains shut to you, nephew. Then he went back in his house.

The kids was looking out the windows and Sam thought they was looking at her face, which she took issue with people looking at. Get away from them windows, she yelled.

I told her to hush.

Hanlin yelled, Uncle Dob, I am hurt! I lost a finger! It has cost me some blood and I need help! Can you help me, please!

We waited, however the preacher did not come back out of the house.

Hanlin commenced to beg in the most unpleasant way. None of us cared a lick about him, and he seemed to think some of us aught to. He said, You would think my family at least would take me in.

Mr Pacheco said he would not think that.

Hanlin commenced to curse at his uncle, although his uncle did not come out to hear it. When he had done with that, he told us, If you want use of the dog you'll have to arrange for it yourselves. I brought you here and shown you the dog. My part is done. I aim to get paid and go my way and get some help. I can't endure the agony any longer.

Mr Pacheco told him he did not intend to pay him, as the arrangement involved our having use of a panther dog, and we did not have that, as the dog did not appear right, and even if it was right, we could not just go and take it. We had not come here to steal the dog.

Hanlin said, Well I can't help you any more than I done.

Mr Pacheco then told us to stay put, and

he gone up to the porch. He taken the saddlebag with the money along on account of he did not want Hanlin to grab it and run off. The dog did not seem to mind him and lay down to snooze.

Sam said, That ain't the dog we come for.

Hanlin hollered at her, That is too the goddamn dog you come for.

Mr Pacheco had Hanlin's pistol as well as his own and set them on the porch rail to show he did not intend any harm to the folks in the house. He knocked at the door and called out in a polite way, as he was a well spoken Mexican. We was close enough to hear what he said. He said he had two children along and was sorry to be in the company of such a man as the preacher's nephew, but he had a favor to ask on behalf of us children, in regards to the dog.

The preacher then opened the door and said we was welcome to come into the house, however his nephew was not.

Sam did not want to go in. She told me, There's kids in there looking at me. She squinted her eyes like she done when she was fretful.

I said I would go in without her, as I was hungry and figured they would offer food.

She said, Don't leave me out here with him.

Hanlin said, Bitch, what would I want with you. You ain't got nothing I'd touch.

Sam and me then remained where we was, on the pinto, and Hanlin atop the mare in a huff.

Mr Pacheco told the preacher he did not want to leave us alone with Hanlin. They commenced to talk on the porch and keep a eye on us. The preacher was not so well spoken as Mr Pacheco. Mr Pacheco explained how we was not associated with Hanlin out of any choice or desire. The preacher was surprised to hear it was true that his nephew had got his finger shot off. He said he had figured Hanlin was lying about that, as he was a known liar.

Hanlin held up his hand and hollered, How does a man lie about having no finger! Either he has got five fingers or he has got less, and I got less! The one shot off is laying under a tree ten miles off!

The preacher told him, You were up to no good. You have never been up to any good.

Hanlin denied he had done any mischief at all. I was waylaid by these kids! he said. They was up in a tree, armed with a pistol, and the girl lit into me for no reason! This greaser come and disarmed me and the three of them held me at gunpoint in a stinking house, where I would still be had I not told them I knew where there was a panther dog they might work a deal to use!

The preacher said, You're a liar, Clarence. Before you could talk you laid in your cradle and thought lies. I was told you was one of them that hanged them innocent travelers on Julian Creek!

Hanlin said, Whoever told you that had not a truthful bone in their body! It was the rest of the boys. I said them men aught to get a proper trial!

I thought I might mention what I had seen of his pocket picking the morning after, but I could not get a word in.

If there was hanging, you was in on it, the preacher said. You would not of missed that fun. I know you, Clarence. And now I have been called on to console some of the grieving widows.

They was sneaking off! said Hanlin. They was cowards going to Mexico, and they deserved a good hanging. If I am guilty, it's of not being one of the boys that give them justice! So help me God, I was not one of them that strung them up. Now can I please get some help. I am badly injured.

The preacher said, It's a ugly fact that God will not allow me to turn you away when you're hurt. But as for your purpose in being here, I do not work deals with my dog. These people are welcome to my hospitality but not to my dog. Do you have any weapons on you, Clarence.

Hanlin hollered, No, I don't. They took my pistol. It's right there on the porch rail with the Mexican's! I got nothing on me. I need help and food!

Sam saw fit to remark to the preacher. You got a mean nephew, she hollered. He is a bad son of a bitch! I have had enough of his company! All we want is to use your dog if it will track a panther!

I said, No, I would like some food also, if you are offering it, sir.

Sam spied the window sheet moving, and squinted a good bit, and shrieked, Get away from them windows, I said! Stop looking at me!

I told her to settle down but she did not heed me. She dismounted faster than I could get hold of her, and commenced to throw rocks at the house.

The preacher come down the steps and shouted, God all mighty, girl! Stop that! His voice was thunderous for a skinny man's and got her attention, and she did stop throwing the rocks.

She said, There is kids in your house looking at me and I don't like it! You make them behave or I'll be done with you all!

I do not know why she thought that was a case to make. The preacher had not asked us there and likely would of liked nothing better than for us to be done with him.

He said, I will see they do not look. He gone into the house and come back out and said, Come on in. Nobody is going to look at you. I have made sure of that.

Sam and me started up the porch and the dog awoke out of his snooze of a sudden and got to his feet. The hair went up on his back, and I seen he was looking at Sam. He had but one eye that appeared any good, but it was doing the work of two.

The preacher gazed upon him and said, Zechariah, what's got into you to act like that. This girl is our guest.

The dog was entirely froze in a stance neither friendly nor unfriendly but something other, like he might know something spooky about her.

He's a odd dog, the preacher said, but he won't hurt you if you don't encourage him to. Come on in.

We went into the house and the dog nosed his way in behind us. He would not stop staring at Sam. As I have said, one of his eyes was bad. The eyeball stuck out and looked like a bird egg. It was mostly white.

The preacher let Hanlin into the house

along with the rest of us on account of he had lost a finger.

The house was no finer inside than out, but there was a nice oil cloth on the floor. The three kids was lined up facing a wall. Two was tow headed and one was black headed and all of them was small. The preacher told them not to turn around, as he had told Sam she would not be looked at. He told us their names, but we was only seeing the backs of their heads. The black headed one stole a glance to the side but the preacher recalled him to face the wall. My eyes was drawn to his bare feet, as they was badly maimed with burn scars, like he had trod on red hot coals. I wondered what had befallen him to cause such wounds.

After the preacher had told us the names, he told the kids to run on and not look at us, and they went back outside.

The preacher said his name was Dobson Beck and folks called him Preacher Dob. He wore spectacles that was lopsided on his face, as one of the arms was a stick tied on with string. His shoes was cowhide with the hair still on them in a fashion I had not seen. One of them was red hide and one was black. I would of thought it was a new fashion, however the shoes was old.

There was also a lady in the house who

was married to the preacher's son. He had gone off to fight for the Sesesh army and left her at his father's home with the two tow headed kids, who was the preacher's grandkids. Her name was Ida and she was a beautiful lady. You asked me to be frank, sir. I had a hard time not looking at her. I was used to mostly looking at Sam, and there was a world of difference.

Sam said, Is the black headed kid a Mexican or Indian, or what is he.

The preacher said the most they knew was he was a Mexican that got stole from his Mexican family by Indians and then run off from them. He had showed up in the corn field a year hence, naked and sick as a dog from helping hisself to green corn, and spoke more Spanish than Indian but did not speak much of neither. He now went by the name Jackson.

Sam said, If he's a Indian he'll do you in when he's grown.

The preacher looked her over, on account of he did not know what to make of her. He said, I'll be dead before he's grown.

I asked him what happened to Jackson's feet, as I could not rid myself of wondering. The preacher said the Indians burnt the soles at night with hot logs to dispirit the boy from running off whilst they had him.

191

That picture got stuck in my head and I give some thought to how it must be to have times you want to forget carved on you to fly at your face every time you look at your feet. I wondered if Sam might notice how Jackson shared a hard thing like that with her, as it was the same with her face. But she give no appearance of doing so.

Ida give Sam and me and Mr Pacheco a invitation to sit at the table and served us food the likes of which I had not had for a good many years if ever. There was buttermilk. There was salt she had got by digging up dirt under the smokehouse and boiling it out. It was brown but salty. There was also cabbage and collards.

She give Hanlin a chunk of willow bark to chew for the pain and a rag to clean up his hand. Her manner to him was not friendly. She wrapped his hand and give him food at the table in a rough manner. The dog would not quit looking at Sam whilst we ate. It was unsettling, the way he stared. You almost would of thought she was a witch or some other untoward being, he showed such interest. She kicked at him when he got too close. Ida put him outside, but he stood on his hind legs and gazed upon Sam through the dirty glass of the window with his one eye.

What does he want, Sam said.

The preacher shooed him away from the window but he come back. The preacher then let him in and ordered him harshly to sit by the fire. He done so but kept his eye on Sam all the while.

The preacher sat at the table with us and struck up a conversation with Mr Pacheco. They figured out they had traveled some of the same places out west. The preacher had hauled freight for trappers and fur traders out in New Mexico in his younger days. He had journeyed along some of the same trails as Mr Pacheco. He said he was born in Tennessee but went west and was a freighter until he come to visit his sister in Texas and got in with the wrong crowd and come near dying in a calamity of bad judgment but survived it. He give up his life of hauling furs and whatnot and married a nice lady and settled near his sister, who was a good woman despite that she had gave birth to a heartless boy such as Clarence. Later on he was changed into a man of God and become a preacher about the area and spread the word of the Lord. In the years since, his wife had passed on.

Now the war has split up the country and folks in it, he said. Even my son, Alfred, has joined the Sesesh. I have my thoughts about that. On the other hand, he's a soldier fighting honorably off in Maryland somewhere, unlike this worthless cousin of his who hangs about tormenting the locals. Innocent folks is not free even to ride about anymore, and those I preached to in years past is headed to Mexico or hiding out in the shrubs from the likes of this miscreant Clarence.

Hanlin made a attempt to speak up for hisself but the preacher said, If you speak against any word I have said in my own house, I will turn you out. If you attempt to make a excuse for yourself it had better be to tell me what happened on the Julian. I would like to know if there's any word I can pass along to the grieving families that might give them some peace. Some of them hanged was men of God, and I would bet they had words for their loved ones before meeting their Maker.

Hanlin said, I told you I did not see them hang. We intercepted them heading to Mexico without permits and told them to surrender their arms and come with us to Camp Verde. They give up their arms and come with us. We stopped on the Julian for the night, and some of the boys took them off and done what they done. I had nothing to do with that mischief.

You was picking their pockets at daybreak, I said. Preacher, you can believe me or not, but I happened upon it. I seen it myself.

The pockets was already picked, Hanlin said. I took nothing. And picking pockets ain't hanging.

The preacher said, You was indeed picking the pockets. I believe this boy. It is just like you to have done such a thing. And you was also in on the hanging. Is there no bottom to your lies. What has possessed you to be this sordid person you have become.

Hanlin attempted to stare him down, but the preacher won out.

The preacher then inquired as to me and Sam's faith and Mr Pacheco's. I told him Sam and me had not seen much of churches nor heard much of camp speeches. Mr Pacheco showed him a cross on a chain out of his pocket that was a rosary, and they had a discussion that was not entirely friendly.

Mr Pacheco said, No matter about that, as we have come on business about the dog.

The preacher said he would entertain none about the dog.

Mr Pacheco asked if he was indeed a panther dog.

The preacher said, He is a famous panther dog.

Mr Pacheco inquired as to how many

panthers he had tracked and the preacher said he had tracked more than fifty. Mr Pacheco then inquired of the dog's talents, as they was not apparent.

The preacher said he did not know of the talents, as he had not hunted with Zechariah hisself. The dog had been his companion for seven years and had not hunted in that time.

Sam said, How do you know he's tracked more than fifty if you ain't been along.

The preacher said he knew it by good authority, as what man would pin a note with a lie to his chest in the moments before he breathes his last. He said, The man who first owned the dog was a known tracker named Percy that lived by hisself over on Sister Creek and come to some of my sermons when I went there to preach. When his time to die come, he sent a neighbor to fetch me, but I got there too late and found him passed. He had pinned a note on his shirt.

The preacher got up and got the note out of a jar to show us. It was hard to make out. It said, Please take care of my dog. He is a good tracker. Has tracked more than fifty panthers. Lost his eye to a panther. Take care of him. It was signed, M Percy. It did not say the dog's name. I suppose when a man is perishing he does not have time for particulars.

Mr Pacheco give thought to the note and the dog.

My own thoughts was thus. I did not think it a good idea to go after the panther with a one-eyed dog that none of us seen hunt. He did not look fit, and he was agitating to Sam.

I said, I think he is not the dog for us.

Hanlin said, Goddamn it, I done my part. I earned my pay. I brought you here. I can't help it if the dog ain't to your liking and don't get along with your sister.

The preacher become puzzled about how Samantha was my sister. I had to explain that my mother had passed and my father had taken up with a Negro named Juda who give birth to Sam and got done in by a panther, the very same cat which come back to our place and took two kids the night before last and which we was wanting to track down.

Hanlin made a attempt to get the preacher to give us the dog, whether we might want it or not. He told him, The Mexican has got money and he will pay for use of the dog.

My dog is not for hire, the preacher held.

Hanlin said, They are giving me a hundred dollars for bringing them here, and they will give you the same.

The preacher then hollered at him about being immoral and good for nothing. He said, Your mother has wept buckets over you and cursed herself for bringing you into the world. Your father would likely shoot you if he was to run across you. You are the worst seed I ever saw. We known it when you drowned them cats for the fun. You are not right. How can you bring your sorry self to take money from these kids.

Hanlin said, It ain't the kids that has it, it's the Mexican. He has got plenty.

The preacher said he did not care who had it, if there was money about, then us kids should end up with it, and not Hanlin. His dog was not for hire to anybody, for any amount. He was not seeking money. The only thing he wanted out of the situation was for Hanlin to get out of his house.

Hanlin begun to yell so loud he spit. He beat the table with his hand that had all the fingers and said, I ain't leaving without my money! If I leave now you'll work a deal and give them use of the dog for free, and I'll get nothing!

The kids outside come to look in the windows when they heard him holler.

Sam taken to screaming, Get away from them windows!

Ida went to the door and told them to get,

and two of them run off. However, Jackson the Mexican Indian boy did not want to get. He kept looking at Sam. His eyes was mournful. Mr Pacheco spoke to him in Spanish through the window. I do not know what it was he said but it sounded kindly. Then Jackson went off.

After that disturbance had calmed down, the preacher repeated that nobody would be allowed use of the dog. He had not parted with the dog as long as he had owned him and would not do so now. The dog was a comfort to him and not a young dog and he would not send him off with strangers on a perilous quest.

I said, We will not take your dog.

Sam said, You are speaking for you and not me. I don't like the dog, but what other chance do I have. I ain't leaving this house without him.

The preacher said, Well then, little girl, take your seat by the fire and be at home.

Mr Pacheco was silent all this time, watching the dog. Finally he said, The dog looks at la neenya as if he knows something. I believe he knows a panther has wounded her, the same as a panther has wounded him. I believe we have misjudged him. Then he shook his head and got up and put his hat on as if it was time we should take our leave. He said, What a shame that the demon will go free.

That got the preacher's solemn attention all of a sudden. Things become so quiet it seemed like I could hear flames licking the pots in the fire. Me and Sam and the preacher and Hanlin was at the table, Ida stood alongside with a rag in her hand, the dog stared at Sam from next to the fire, and Mr Pacheco stood there shaking his head.

The preacher said, What demon do you refer to.

Mr Pacheco said, El Demonio de Dos Dedos. The Demon of Two Toes. The panther we are seeking.

The preacher did not care to be drawn in. He was not a gullible preacher. He said, You are trying to bait me.

Mr Pacheco said, Or perhaps it is God who is trying to bait you. Perhaps God brought us here to pursue the demon.

It was my nephew brought you here, and he is a far cry from the Lord, said the preacher. However, the Lord does make use of unlikely agents. I have two questions for you, Mr Pacheco. Why is the cat called a demon, and why would you offer to put forth money like that to hunt it down. Explain what you are up to. If I sense you are trying to work me, I will be done with you.

Mr Pacheco removed his hat and give us a speech I wish I could write strictly, as it was a powerful speech. He said El Demonio de Dos Dedos was a enormous unnatural cat that preyed on farms and ranches and feasted on livestock, taking whatever was easy and killing creatures for sport. The cat was a terror to people from here to Mexico, and mostly along the border down by Piedras Negras. He said me and Sam was not safe, as the panther was sure to come again and take from where he had taken before, and we could not purchase powder nor lead to defend our animals nor ourselves from it. He said, I look at la neenya's face, and I do not believe God would say she should turn the other cheek to the panther. He said his motives was neither selfish nor pure. His ranch was gone, his horses stole, his vaqueros gone like the wind. He had nothing left to show for his life but a pocked face and gray hair and a good horse and a long past and what money he had in his satchel. He said if he would kill the panther, it might win him favor with God and he was certain someday to need that favor. The cat was worth a hundred dollars to him, and more, which he would gladly give the preacher along with a promise to care for the dog and bring it back in a healthy state if that should be possible. He would ask nothing from us in return but the hide, as he wanted to take it down south to prove to the people that El Demonio was not to be feared any longer.

I thought at this time Sam would cut loose again on the matter about the hide and who should get it, but she was quiet for the time being, and kept her fingers out of that pie, as they say, as I guess she knew it was sticky.

The preacher sat at the table and give considerable thought. He said he did not want money and would not lend the dog. And yet he gone on thinking. After he weighed the matter some more and come up empty of any answer, he turned to the dog and said, Zechariah, what say you.

Judge, I am sworn to be frank. I am telling the truth when I say the dog answered as if he spoke. It was the long squint in his eye. He regarded Sam with a hard stare and then regarded the preacher. We none of us had a question that there was meaning behind the stare. There was a message in it. Then he got up and walked to the door and stood with his nose to it. He all but said he was ready to go.

The preacher said, All right, then. He said,

That's clear. He said, But I won't let the dog go without me along too. Could you do without me a day or two, Ida.

She said, If you'll leave me the double rifle in case of trouble.

The preacher said he would leave her the double and the carbine and take his pistol and the Hawken. He stood up from the table and said, Zechariah and me will be at the Lord's service together. The Lord will deliver the panther or not, according to what he thinks is a good idea. We should pack up now and head to these kids' home and hope Zechariah can pick up a scent.

Hanlin then demanded his money and asked to borrow a horse.

The preacher said he could not spare a horse, as he had only his old gelding that he intended to ride hisself and a mare Ida would need use of.

Is this how a man of God treats a hurt victim! Hanlin shouted. I have been nothing but a help to the situation! I have brought them here for the dog! I have no finger! Do you not understand! I have got no goddamn finger!

Mr Pacheco counted the bills and handed them over.

Hanlin shoved them into a pocket of my father's trousers that he was wearing. He told the preacher, Won't you give me a ride to Camp Verde in the wagon.

The preacher said we did not have the time.

Hanlin said, Ida, won't you.

She said, No. She give him jerked meat to sustain him and he set out afoot.

The preacher then told us we was to bow our heads. We done so. He said, Lord, we are about to depart on a journey. We ask that you might lay the path for us and light the way so we might see it. We ask that you might spare us tragedy and mishaps and poor judgment and revelations we do not want. We ask that you spare us encounters with deadly creatures and Indians of all kinds and other dangers. Please keep these children and this dog safe, and the Mexican too, and myself if you see fit. Amen.

He then commenced to prepare for our journey.

Dear Judge,

I am sorry you have not heard from me lately. The man whose cows I helped capture when I was nearly snakebit hired me to help him build better fences, so I was working double time. There was not time for writing any more of this report. I would of stayed over with him at nights and saved the daily travel time, as my mare is about wore out, however I did not want to leave Sam on her own at night. She is chomping at the bit to take off and I fear might use any excuse.

I am grateful for your letter and suggestions as to her. I took a day and rode over to Bandera and talked with Mrs Callahan as you advised and it was a nice talk. However, she asked if Sam was a orderly person and would do some work. I told her Sam did not do much of anything useful or even otherwise for me but might likely change her ways if she was to have better instruction than I have been in the situation to give her. Mrs Callahan said she would think on the matter, however she figured she had enough trouble with her own kids without taking on a girl such as that.

A different day I went to Sisterdale and talked to Mrs Dieter, the woman you said to talk to. It was not easy, considering she did not speak a lot of English. She showed me the letter you wrote her saying Sam was a smart girl and might do well with instruction. It was a nice letter. Thank you for the compliments about me. My father would be proud to see that letter if he was not passed. Mrs Dieter give me a good meal and showed me her violin that she brought from Germany. She was not a stern German like some, and might of been good to Sam. However, she did not want her.

When I got home from my journeys you can bet I had words with Sam about being so lazy nobody will take her. She told me she would work hard for anybody but me, as she is tired of me bossing her and she is not yet tired of anybody else.

I said, Show me one week of hard work and I will believe you. I need some proof you can do it before I can assure somebody it is in any way likely.

However, she will not give me even a day of hard work. She is about as useless a girl as they come and I can't figure why that would be. Her mama was a hard worker. She was a mean woman but she did work. My first years was spent in a tidy house, and that was thanks to Juda. And now I am left with this girl who is a nuisance to me, as I am compelled to worry about her a great deal. What am I to do. Do you have another person I might pay a visit. I could go as far as New Braunfels if you know anyone over there. My mare is not in a good condition but she would do this for me. She would like to see Samantha gone nearly as much as I would, on account of it is her fault I have to ride to camp and back every day. Otherwise I could stay over some nights and save my mare the trouble.

But as to the matter at hand, which is Clarence Hanlin. When I read your letter I felt sorry that I had muddied the water about his guilt or innocence when I told you he had declared to Preacher

Dob that he took no part in the hanging. The point that I did not make clear enough is that that was a lie. He did later admit to his part in the hanging in a unmistakable way, as you will see. There is no question about the fact that he done it. I was only laying the tracks so you will know the whole story start to finish and declare him guilty although drowned.

Meantime I am glad to know you appreciate my reports. My father used to come home wore out from work and I would tell him about what had gone on that day at home. We would sit before the fire and he would get a big kick out of my stories. So now I am having a good time writing to you, as he has been gone for so long. You have kept me company many nights, sir. However, I could sure do with a good pen.

As to your suggestion that I hold off and send the remainder of my testament all in one piece when it is done, on account of there might be so much of it, the situation about that is this. I would not feel right showing up for a visit and taking free strudel if I had no business with Mr Hildebrand. Do you think it is wrong for me to have the strudel. Mrs

Hildebrand insists that I take it. If it is not wrong I would just as soon have it.

A man named Gus at the camp said he intends on going to Comfort and will take these pages to Mr Hildebrand if I will bring them tomorrow, as I am tied up with work and can't be going there myself for a while. He has not had strudel before and that would be a real treat. He appears a reliable fellow. We agreed to share the strudel if it is offered. He will bring me half.

Yours kindly,
Benjamin Shreve

MY TESTAMENT

We packed up supplies at the preacher's house, watered the horses, saddled up the preacher's old gelding that was not much to look at, said so long to Ida and the three kids, and started back to our place with about three days' supply of food including a jar of pickled cucumbers Ida give me on account of I had admired the salt on the chicken and she knew I would appreciate them, as they was salty.

We could not move at a fast pace. The mare was not fresh, Preacher Dob's gelding had seen better days that was over, and Zechariah was afoot. It was only the pinto that was not jaded, as he was young and feisty. We was light of heart to be shed of Hanlin and to of secured the help of Zechariah, although there was none of us not nagged of doubts about that dog. These doubts was aggravated along the way. The dog got winded whilst traveling, sat down to go no further, and Preacher Dob had to haul him into the saddle and ride double with him for a spell, which the old gelding did not seem to much mind in spite of that he had rheumatism and the extra weight could not of gone unnoticed.

The main trouble with the dog being horseback was that it put him on eye level with Sam. He kept watching her just about the whole way when he was up there. She was on the mare with me, whilst the dog was astraddle Preacher Dob's lap and would shift hisself every which way to get a look at Sam no matter if before, behind, or alongside us.

Sam said, What is he doing it for, I got to know.

Mr Pacheco said he believed the dog had uncommon intelligence and sensed in her the distinctive qualities others might not.

Preacher Dob said, Zechariah knows a fellow sufferer and survivor. He knows what you been through. He has felt a panther's teeth and claws on him same as you done.

Sam said, That is all hog wash. Do the both of you take me for a fool. He is looking at me on account of I'm ugly and he can't figure my face out.

I said, If you know that, why did you ask.

Have you not looked in a mirror, she said to the dog. You ain't nothing to look at yourself. Did you not know that.

He did look abashed to hear it. For a while he quit staring at her but he could not hold back for long, and took it up again until Preacher Dob made him walk.

We crossed a creek and watered the horses and approached our place at sundown as the air got nippy. Mr Pacheco had a poncho in his saddlebag, and he give it to Sam to wear. Zechariah was horseback again by then, asnooze and astraddle Preacher Dob's lap. We seen a gang of buzzards circling about the bur oak we had sat in all night, so we rode over to study the situation as best we could in the scant light. The pigs had come up from the creek and was pestering the shot camel and scuffling over the dead kid. We thought we might spy the gone finger laying upon the ground, so we put up a hunt for that. But it was gone from there too. We figured one of the pigs had ate it. Mr Pacheco said he believed one of the buzzards had ate it, and it was now aloft. This give him a good laugh to think about the soaring finger.

Preacher Dob asked how Sam got to be such a good shot as to shoot off a man's finger. Did your brother teach you how to shoot like that, he said.

She said, My brother can't shoot worth squat.

I did take offense at that. I said, It was luck that you had a good shot.

She said, I took aim. I shot that pistol out of his hand. It was not luck.

When we give up looking for the finger, we rode up to the house, thinking to stay the night, as we could not track in the dark. We figured to rise early, make ready, show Zechariah the places we knew the panther had walked, and hope he might pick up a scent.

The trouble commenced when the preacher dismounted and pulled Zechariah out of the saddle. He was fixing to leash him, but before the dog even settled upon the ground he tossed his head up, become alert, sniffed the air, and took off. He run first to the goat pen and just about went crazy sniffing around there. I never seen such energy in a dog. He was all a-tremble with every sniff, and then on to the next.

He run off down by the creek, his nose stuck to the ground the whole way. He did not lift his head even to look around. Sam and me and Preacher Dob run after and yelled at him to hold up, but he was on the go and would not be got hold of for anything. Mr Pacheco stayed on the pinto and took it all in.

The dog was hard to follow, on account of he was of a mottled color and the light was pretty well gone. He come upon the dead kid that we had not found before, which was the brother to the one yonder under the bur oak that the pigs was having a meal of. The panther had broke the neck and partaken of the organs.

Hardly did the dog give it even a sniff before taking off back to the pens. He must of been making his way exactly as the panther done when he dragged off one kid and went back for another. We tried heading the dog off to get hold of him, but he run past us and sniffed at the pens and took off to the place out in the field where Sam had found the other dead kid. It was not to the bur oak but to a hideout by a big rock where the panther had left the kid before Sam moved it to the bur oak in the effort to trick me into thinking that was the place she had found it. The dog was no more fooled by the bur oak than I had been at the time, and did not even give it a glance but lit out in a southeasterly direction that I suppose was how the panther gone.

It was plain the dog did not intend to wait for us but would keep on going. Sam kept after him afoot, although I hollered at her to come back. She was nearly as fast as Zechariah and was not wasting her strength by yelling at him to stop. She was going wherever the dog was going. I was glad to see Mr Pacheco come running by on the pinto, hot on her trail.

Me and Preacher Dob run back to the house to get our horses. They was both tired and old and not yet fed, and they was not happy to have us mount and head off into the dark on rocky terrain on a unmarked route full of thorny bee bush and cactus and following the sound of the dog. I hollered at Sam to hold up and wait, but she did not answer me, so I give up on that, for fear Comanches or Sesesh might hear us.

It was then the dog begun to cut loose with the most peculiar bawling noise I ever heard out of a dog. I have heard dogs on a trail, but I have never, before nor since, heard a sound like this panther dog let loose on the night. I thought Comanches had hold of him and was doing him in by a gruesome fashion. Then it become plain the sound was moving in a orderly direction, and I understood the dog was now on the track in a serious way. Wherever that dog was headed, Sam was headed too, lacking even a pistol with bat shat on this occasion, as she was unarmed. The chill had set in, the night was clear, and the sound sang through the air like the songs of the mermaids in The Whale, enticing Sam to follow along no matter what danger might befall.

It was a wild run, I will tell you what. Mr Pacheco caught up with Sam before Preacher Dob and myself did, as he had a head start and not to mention a better horse. Sam did not put up a fuss but jumped right up behind him on the pinto and off they went after the wailing dog.

Preacher Dob and me rode hard to keep up. It was dark, it was chilly, we was hungry, our horses was not happy, and we was not moving along any known path but through a bunch of brush and scrub trees that scraped us up pretty good. We had to skirt large patches of prickly pear and catclaw and possumhaw and pick our way through cedar breaks, but luckily our horses could see better than we could in the dark and was willing. Preacher Dob's gelding lacked shoes. He had rock feet but it must of been a rough ride for that old boy. My mare picked up a stone and slowed us down, as I had to stop and dig it out. One minute I would think we was gaining on the dog, and the next he was up higher on a bluff, wailing away, or lower in a ravine, and it would be hard to tell if we was closer or farther or maybe even going the wrong direction. I was mostly following Mr Pacheco, and Preacher Dob was mostly following me. There was cussing going on, I think even the preacher had a few words to say. We was all struck by branches. We dropped down through a steep canyon header and had to slow to a walk to get through a cedar break when we come up the other side. Sam was the luckiest amongst us, as she was tucked in behind Mr Pacheco and wearing his poncho and therefore well shielded from the worst of what we was riding through.

It was a good thing the moon come up. It was the right size moon, not Comanche. A Comanche moon would of done me in with fright considering the stir we made. The one that come up was no more than a shard but give us enough light so we was not plunging off cliffs into thick dark. I am not sure how long we rode or how far we traveled, maybe only three miles, maybe four, as it was slow going in places, all up and down, but I can tell you we did not stop until we heard the dog barking from a fixed position and halted to catch our breath and consider a plan.

Preacher Dob said, I think he's got the panther treed. I don't think he would stop otherwise. I worry the cat will jump him if we don't get there fast.

We concluded to ride in as quick and quiet as we could so the cat would not take a leap and lead us off on another chase.

My pistol and rifle was back at the house, on account of Sam had used what ball and bat shat we owned to fire on Clarence Hanlin, and they was useless to us. I had Hanlin's pistol, but Sam had none, and she demanded me to give it to her on account of her aim was better.

I said no. I had not shot a Colt's before and was eager to do so.

She jumped down from the back of the pinto and rushed at me to seize the Colt's out of my belt. I thought we might have a considerable fight, as I was not about to let her take it.

However, Preacher Dob said, Hold up. He said, I think Sam aught to have a shot at the panther, and she can use my pistol. It's a good luck one.

It was a Sharps four-shot breech loading pepperbox just her size, and Preacher Dob said it was given him by a gambler who heard the Lord's word and swore he would gamble no more.

Sam said, I want the rifle instead.

You can't have the rifle, said he. It fires a big heavy ball and chews down too hard. It would knock you off your feet.

She said, If it does, I'll get up again.

Still he refused her the rifle. He loaded the pistol and give it to her and told her just to aim, cock, and shoot. She would have four shots, he said, but he bet she would knock that panther out of the tree with the first out of the barrel. Any girl that can shoot a finger off a man can shoot a cat out of a tree, he said.

Mr Pacheco said Sam aught to have the first shot, and if she was to miss and the panther to flee, then we would back her up.

She declared she would not miss. She said, And I want all four shots before any one of you pulls any one of them triggers.

We started in the direction of the fixed barking and struck a shallow ravine with a small stream where we allowed the horses a hasty drink and filled our gourds. The water was mucky on account of we was low on rain that year, as you know, so we did not drink our fill and was thirsty yet. We had not gone much past the ravine when the fixed barking changed to the bawling again and it become clear the dog was on the trail once more.

The cat must of jumped the tree, Preacher Dob said. He's took off.

We followed a ways, and then the noise ceased of a sudden and left only the chirping of crickets and other expected sounds of the night in our ears. We halted and listened, and none of us for a minute said one word.

Then Preacher Dob said, He'll start up again if we wait.

However, he did not. Zechariah had said all he intended to say on the matter, and had gone mute.

Mr Pacheco said we should follow in the direction we last heard him, and we would come across him.

We started out, but soon we disagreed on the direction we was to be going. Preacher Dob thought we aught to veer off a bit to the north and Mr Pacheco thought to the east. Sam stated a number of sundry ideas about it. I had no opinion on the matter, as I had no sense of where we was, other than we had seemed to go somewhat south then east, but not along any path, and had passed through a header of a canyon I did not know of. I had thought I knew my way around, but there was more to the land than I had figured and a greater number of canyons. The canyons was mostly shallow ravines and dry washes, but nevertheless they was trouble to get into and out of. There was wilderness north, south, east, and west. We was at the mercy of whoever might happen upon us, and of course Indians was foremost in my thoughts, as the Comanches was active in weeks past and busy doing their mischief.

I said, Do you think we should turn back.

Sam said, I ain't turning back.

Preacher Dob said, I am not leaving my dog.

I said, It was only a idle notion.

To tell you the truth, I did not know which way back might be. I figured I could give the mare the bridle and she would take me, but I was not inclined to head off without the others.

Mr Pacheco said we aught to go back as far as the creek, make camp, and wait for the dog to strike up again.

That was the counsel we followed. We made our way back and scouted a tolerable place not more than ten feet from the water and under a persimmon tree. We unsaddled the horses, hobbled the gelding and ground tied the mare where they was able to graze on a oak tree overhead, and left the pinto to his own, with neither saddle nor bridle, as he would not wander off far without Mr Pacheco.

Whilst we was making a fire Preacher Dob bemoaned the possible fate of Zechariah. He said, Zechariah has been my companion for seven years. I hope I have not turned him loose to his demise. He does not see much. He has only got the one eye. I hope he did not try to take on the panther hisself.

Mr Pacheco said it was more likely the dog had lost the panther's scent and was out there searching for it.

Preacher Dob said the panther could of took a long leap into a tree and pounced on Zechariah whilst he searched for it.

We pondered on how this might be so.

Preacher Dob said, I can think of nothing good that would happen that would shut him up. He first treed the panther, then he trailed it again, then he ceased to trail it and was silent. Wherefore is the silence.

We settled in by the fire and nursed our scratches. We ate most of what Ida had packed, however I saved my pickled cucumbers, which I figured I would be glad of later. Mr Pacheco showed us how to clear muck out of the water by slicing portions of prickly pear and dropping the flesh in the cook pot. I had not seen that trick before, nor had Preacher Dob. It drew all the muck to the bottom.

Sam and me was tired out from having sat all night the night before in the tree and rode all day. We made a bed on the poncho and Preacher Dob kindly give us his blanket, as the cold was starting to bite and he was dressed warmer than us. Sam hogged it until I give it to her.

Preacher Dob was so disheartened, on account of Zechariah was missing, that he did not have a cheery word to share. He poked at the fire and recounted tales about folks that lived sorry lives of deceit and died with regrets, such as a horse thief that got shot and passed whilst confessing his sins to Preacher Dob but would not state his name, as he did not want his kids to know what he become.

Preacher Dob said, There's times I can't fathom the ways of the Lord. I am a preacher, and I am supposed to explain these things which I can't. I was once set to join a couple over on Tow Head Creek in matrimony, and the bride flew the tracks a hour before the wedding and left her intended standing forlorn in a suit on his front porch with nothing to do but feed the hogs.

What was I to say to him. The very next day I learned he had gone for a hunt to steady his nerves and shot his own mule by accident when it was tied to a tree. And what was I to say to that. There is no words to make it all right when you shoot your own mule. Other terrible things has happened too. Kids falling off the backs of wagons and getting run over. Indians depredating. My poor boy Jackson getting stole by them from the Mexican family that likely loved him. The hangerbande stringing up innocent folks. Terrible things has happened in my own life as well. As a youngster I set out west on my own and got no farther than Arkansas when a gang of bandits come out of nowhere and beat my head in with rifle butts and left me for dead by the road. If you look here, you can see the dent in my skull.

Preacher Dob and Mr Pacheco then commenced to reveal their scars and talk of their injuries and discuss how the years was wearing them out. Preacher Dob went on for some time about a cousin of his that come down with atonic gout and other things that added up to a awful demise. He took off his shirt and showed us a hole in his arm where he had got a vaccination that ate a chunk of flesh out of it. Mr Pacheco showed us a rib that stuck out three inches, and a hole in his knee where he had hammered a horseshoe nail in it by accident, and not to mention the powder pocks on his face, which he did not talk about. He said there was a time when he was young and boastful and put on spurs with four inch rowels to impress a girl, and got drunk and sat back on his heels and now had rowel holes in him for the rest of his life, which we was not allowed to look at.

It give him a good laugh to tell that story, and yet you could see a ruefulness to the tale, which bespoke of time moving along and things having passed. It was not any of it a inspiration for living your life.

Mr Pacheco then asked Preacher Dob to tell us how he come to be a preacher.

Preacher Dob said more than twenty years back he taken a respite from hauling furs and come to Texas to see his sister. On account of imprudence he fell in with a bunch of troublemakers younger than him that was going to Mexico to take over some Mexican towns and get horses and cattle and plunder and whatnot. It sounded like a lark, so he signed on. They went down there and got caught and was put in prison, and escaped, and wandered about in the mountains, lost like Moses, looking for the Rio Grande, until some of them perished of thirst and the rest was caught again. Preacher Dob was not a preacher nor even devout at that time, but was just Dobson Beck. They was all marched back to prison, he said, and lined up and told to draw beans out of a pot, and them that drew black beans rather than white ones was to be executed.

Judge, you are a man of the law and can likely imagine the consternation of knowing your fate depended on such a thing.

I will make a long story a short one, on account of Preacher Dob give us many details of the men that behaved in a brave manner and made jokes upon drawing a black bean, saying, The jig is up for me, boys, and of them that was overcome with dread of the black beans and could not command their shaking hands as they was blindfolded and prodded into their turn.

Preacher Dob spoke in a slow and doleful manner as he told us about it, and paused amongst his words as if it was hard to speak them. It was a cloudy day it happened, he said, cold and windy in the prison yard, and I was the next to last in line to draw. Whilst I awaited my turn I thought how my mother had wanted better for me than how I turned out. I recalled how I run off in my youth and went out west and drove furs, and fought Indians, and spent time with the women, and drank more than I aught to of. And what good had it done anybody. Here I was, in dirty rags, nearly forty years of age, nearly starved to death, my sins on my head and my head crawling with vermin, and God was about to decide my result when I reached into that pot. I had made the worst waste of my life.

But whilst he mused thus, he said, and watched the other men draw their beans, one after another, he noted the fact the black beans was a touch smaller. And when the blindfold was put on, and he reached his hand in, there was but two beans left, one for him and one for the man behind him, who was hardly more than a boy. He got hold of the small one first, and felt of it, and feared it, and let go of it, and felt of the bigger one, and took it.

And the blindfold was pulled off and there he stood, looking at a bean as white as a baby's tooth betwixt his thumb and finger.

He told us of this in the most somber way, and I will not forget his face in the light of that fire, and how his words seemed now and then to stick in his throat. There was moments he paused so long that we just sat there listening to frogs croaking. He said, The boy behind me drew the bean that should of been mine, and sure enough, it was black, as I had known it would be. Those of us with the white beans was made to lay down and was told if any of us should lift our heads we would all, every one, be shot. Therefore I had my face in the dirt as the Mexicans marched off half of them ill fated ones, and we heard volleys of musketry, and then they come and taken the rest.

These was all men I knew well. We had fought together, and wandered together, and despaired together. We had faced our chances together. And now seventeen of us was gone off on pale horses, and I knew, for sure I knew, I aught to of been one amongst them.

I stayed a prisoner in Mexico for a while after that, and when I got free and crossed back over the river, I was finished with adventure. I got married and settled down and had my son and tended my farm. But I never felt right with myself. I could hear the sound of them volleys blasting in my head. And one day my wife was pouring beans from a bag into a pot to cook for supper, and something in me turned on myself. I took a look at the beans, and a look at my wife and my young son, and a look at my house around me, and the guilt of what I done come boiling out of me like a storm. I broke down. It all come pouring out. I fell on my knees and told my wife what I done. I repented to God and prayed for my salvation and for the salvation of that boy holding that bean I might as well of just handed him, and the fate I give him with it. The shame was too much to shoulder. I had won my life with a cheat, and my life had to prove worth it. It's a hard task to make your life count when you stole the life of another. All I could figure to do was to rise every morning, and try. So I taken to traveling and sharing the gospel.

When he had done telling us this we was consumed by silence, and deep in thought, and reflected upon the flames licking at the dark.

After some time Mr Pacheco shook his head, and stood up, and walked a pace off, and walked back, and stoked up the fire, and sat before the flames again. He said, I, too, am a sinner. I have sinned against the three of you in not telling you something that I know. There is a bounty of two thousand dollars on the hide of El Demonio de Dos Dedos.

Sir, I do not need to tell you it was sure a surprise to hear that. Sam and me had never heard speak of two thousand dollars before, and we sat there dumb as stones.

Mr Pacheco said the allcallday, which was the mayor, in Piedras Negras had money he had got together from a lot of people and it was to be given to any person who would bring in the hide of Dos Dedos with the hind right attached. There was to be two toes only on the hind right, and the gone two toes was to of been gone a long time, in other words healed up, on account of there was a man afoot killing panthers and cutting the toes off the hides and bringing the hides in and saying they was the hide of Dos Dedos, when they was of panthers that was impostors. There was nobody going to fall for that.

He said when he learned we was after the panther he give consideration to going ahead of us and killing the panther hisself and taking the hide. He had built up his ranch out of years of hard work, and Cortina and his bandits had rode in and taken his horses and burnt the place to stubble, and two thousand dollars would give him a good start to building it back. However, if he was to take the hide for hisself, he would forfeit his favor with God. He would be a cabrone without vergwenza, which he said meant a goat without shame. Therefore his conscience had took over and he was now being truthful with us and would share two thousand dollars amongst us, a third for me and Sam, a third for Preacher Dob, and a third for hisself.

You might think I would pounce on information such as that. To the contrary, it took me a minute to figure out what to say, and how much a third might be.

However, Sam did not give a thought to any of that. I don't care about money, she said. The hide ain't going to Piedras Negras, it is staying in my house with me.

That arose a heated conversation that went on for a good while. Mr Pacheco said the hide would have to go to Piedras Negras for the bounty. However, he would bring it back to us and she could have it and keep it in the house.

Sam was set that he could not take it at all, as she intended to have it the whole time.

I told her, Can you see no farther than the nose on your face. Can you not see how we could use the money.

Preacher Dob said he did not need the money to do the Lord's work, but if there was to be money, he could see how his family could use it.

Mr Pacheco offered that Sam and myself could ride with him to Piedras Negras and he would see we got back safe with the hide and our money. He would bring us back.

Sam would hear none of it. She stood up and said, This panther has killed my mama. It has spoilt my face. It has robbed us of our kids. If I shoot it, then I will skin it, and dry out the hide and walk on it for the rest of my life, and never, ever, ever let nobody take it down to Mexico where it might not come back from! Look at me! All of you look at me! You want songs, you want money, but I want payback. And I own the say-so! I own the right! I own all the right!

Preacher Dob said, Vengeance belongs to the Lord, Samantha.

She said, Only if he can beat me to it.

Preacher Dob said, The people down on the border need peace of mind about the panther same as you do. Are you not thinking of them.

She said, I am thinking of my mama.

We none of us knew what to say about that. We sat there some more, and give it more thought.

Mr Pacheco talked of how he had chose to do what was right, and how she was going to cost him his chances, and cost us all our chances, just on account of she wanted the hide.

I said, You might as well be a dog barking at the wind, Mr Pacheco.

Sam laid down on the poncho and put Preacher Dob's blanket over her head and gone to sleep.

The rest of us was too stumped to sleep. We was perplexed. We sat close to the fire. I remarked that I was sorry she was so stubborn.

Preacher Dob said I was not to blame myself.

Mr Pacheco said he believed she might come around.

I said, She won't come around.

We walked a pace off out of her hearing, and whispered about if there might be a honorable way to trick her, but none of us come up with one.

Preacher Dob said perhaps we was better off without the money, on account of money was the root of all kinds of evil and could lead us away from the Lord and pierce us with many pangs. He said, I am more worried about my dog. Poor old half blind fellow. Where could he be.

Mr Pacheco had cigars he called pulkee puros. He said they was made in Mexico where they was soaked in pulkee. He give one of them to me and one to Preacher Dob and one to hisself, and we smoked them. We was careful not to wake Sam, on account of we did not want to hear any more out of her.

The night was cold, so we kept up the fire. However, it was not a hearty one, as we did not want to attract Comanches. Mr Pacheco stretched out and commenced to snore, but me and Preacher Dob did not sleep, although we was tired out. We had things on our minds. Preacher Dob offered up a prayer for Zechariah and I asked him to offer one for my chickens, which was not used to being left out of their coop and prey to coons and coyotes overnight. He done so, and our minds was more at ease after that.

He commenced to talk about the beauty of the stars streaking in the sky over the branches, and I said, I don't see those, where are they.

He pointed out a number of them, and there was moments I did catch a blur, but no more. After a bit he said, Try these, and took off his spectacles and handed them over.

They was tricky to put on, on account of one arm was a stick, but Judge, I will tell you what. It brought tears to my eyes to see so many stars. I had never seen so many, nor even known they was there. It was like a bunch of them had been added. They was indeed beautiful. I sat up and looked about me, and I am telling you, it was a different world I saw. I seen the branches of the persimmon overhead lit by the shine of the fire, every leaf as red as the fire itself and a separate thing from the others, and the yellow of nearby sycamores dangling leaves that was each on their own. I seen the sparks rising up to the sky. I seen the eyes of a possum off in the brush and the swish of my mare's tail. And I known then why I was such a poor shot at things, and why I nearly stepped on the rattlesnake when I was looking for the cows. I known a lot of things in that moment that I did not know before, about me and the world and about many things hard to put into words.

Preacher Dob said, You wear those a while if you want to. Maybe we'll get you a pair one day. He planned to turn in, and asked me to keep a watch out and listen for Zechariah.

I was happy to keep a watch out. I could of sat there just watching for years.

I was on guard for maybe two hours and had commenced to ponder what Sam and myself might do with a third of two thousand dollars, when I got a small whiff of skunk. It was only faint at that time, but then slowly become worse, as if advancing along the floor of the canyon at a pace. I roused up the others to see if they thought we should get out of the way, as it was a terrible smell and we had got the wind of it.

We did not know what it might be attached to. Preacher Dob took back his spectacles so he could look into the dark. I wondered if I aught to get Hanlin's gun ready to shoot whatever was dragging the scent. Then I figured we would be better off to let it pass through than to have it dead in our midst.

It was noisy, whatever it was. Out of the shadows along the floor of the canyon it come. We could not tell at first what it was, as it was nearly on its belly, and then Preacher Dob become excited and said, Here comes Zechariah!

And indeed, here he did. He was gagging and retching. He stank worse than I can even tell you.

I took to my heels and gagged all the way up the side of the canyon. The slope was brushy and rocky but not too steep, and I got to the top pretty quick. Mr Pacheco come running behind me, and the pinto charged up after him, as he was neither tied nor hobbled and followed Mr Pacheco like a dog would. We topped the rim to leave the scent behind us and catch our breaths. We nearly give up our suppers from the smell.

I looked back and made out Sam down

there in the dark hollering up at me for being a coward. Preacher Dob had got hold of the dog and was rolling him in the muddy creek. There was a good bit of splashing and yelping.

Mr Pacheco and me decided we had better go back and help out. We made a headlong descent and got to the bottom and stripped our shoes and boots off and waded into the water.

Preacher Dob hollered, Help me hold him! He thinks I'm trying to drown him! I need clean water to flush his eyes! He's got sprayed in the face!

It might surprise you how Sam took to the chore of fetching the clean water. I myself was surprised at her industry until I figured what she was up to. She did not care a whit about the dog except for it being our hope of catching up with the panther. She grabbed up a knife and the cook pot Ida had packed, and went to hacking pieces of prickly pear and dunking the flesh in the pot the way Mr Pacheco shown us to do it to clear the water. She dumped the water on the dog's face and filled the pot and done the undertaking over again. She got prickly pear spines in her hands and yet did not say boo about that.

That dog was a woeful sight. The smell

was not the least of it, but it was not all of it neither. He was beat up from running through brush. He was already a bad looking dog with a big head and short legs and a scraggy hind end. And now his eyes was swole up. The white one was red as a cardinal. He must of been chasing after the cat and met up with a skunk and got sprayed straight on in the face. He snapped and snarled and bit us pretty good, as we had to dunk him a number of times.

Preacher Dob said, The water ain't helping. We need vinegar.

I said, What about the pickled cucumbers.

He said, Get the jar.

I got it and kept the pickles in but dumped the vinegar over the dog. We rubbed it into his fur. He then smelled of vinegar mixed with skunk, which was worse than just skunk. We rolled him in the water. Mr Pacheco thrown up. It was not a fun time.

Preacher Dob taken Zechariah up to the rim and tied him to a tree. He stank as bad as ever and was shivering. Preacher Dob taken him food. He come back down and said he figured Zechariah was about done hunting panthers for the time being and maybe forever. He said, There is no way he can pick up a scent when he is carrying a odor as strong as that.

Mr Pacheco said he would not yet give up on tracking the panther.

Sam said she would not give up the four-shot pepperbox nor turn back.

I thought, What chance do we have to catch up with the panther without the help of the dog. And what chance do I have to see my share of two thousand dollars, even if we was to do so.

We was cold and did not have dry clothes. We attempted to sleep.

Dear Judge,

I wish you could of seen the look on my face when I got your parcel. It was brought to me by the man who carried the last report I wrote you to Mr Hildebrand. His name is Gus Mapes. I told you about him. Mr Hildebrand give the package to him to bring to me at the camp, and when he give it to me he said, Benjamin, Mr Hildebrand wanted me to tell you how sorry he was not to be around to see your face when you open this, as he thinks he might know what it holds.

Judge, I will tell you what. My hopes was so high upon hearing that, that I believe I might of broke down if the package had contained anything other than this pen. But behold, I opened it up, and found the pen and also the holder for it, which is handy. There was quite a few men at the camp that did not understand why I might make such a fuss about a pen. However, I think they was glad to see me cheerful, as I have been tired out from working hard and they have not seen a smile on my face like that in a long time.

It is the very pen Mr Hildebrand showed me the advertisement of and that I wrote you about and will make my letters a lot easier to read. It is the best gift anyone ever given me. I am not just laying it on thick about that. I will also hang on to your kind note for a long time, or even forever if I can find a good place to put it. It pleased me a great deal. I intend to take your advice and continue to write for a good many years after I am done writing to you.

I could go on about the pen, but I guess you have got other things to do than read more about that. For one thing you have got to make your determination about if Clarence Hanlin is guilty. Pretty soon you will have all of my proof in hand that indeed, he is.

Thank you again, sir, for the generous gift that you give me. I will keep it until my time is up and the reaper should come fetch me.

Yours kindly,
Benjamin Shreve

MY TESTAMENT

We awoke to a cloudy day and the stink hanging over the canyon. My hopes was not high, those of Preacher Dob pretty well gone, Mr Pacheco's wrung out a bit but not yet hung to dry, and Sam's the same as ever, not so passing as to be swept off by a odor, on account of she was bent on killing that panther no matter what misfortune might befall.

Whilst Mr Pacheco stirred up the fire, Preacher Dob gone up to the rim to look after Zechariah and then come down and made coffee in a miserable frame of mind. He said, I am sorry to break the news to you good people, but I see no use in continuing our hunt when we have lost the trail and have no way of finding it again. Zechariah smells too bad hisself to sniff out a panther nor anything else. I could lay a chunk of steak in front of that dog and he would not know it was there. I am not sure how to even get him home, as I don't want him in the saddle with me. I don't think my horse would much appreciate him, neither. He's suffering enough from rheumatism without giving a ride to a smelly dog. So it will not be easy to figure out how, but one way or another, I'm for turning back.

Sam did not appear to listen to any of that. She sat working at prickly pear thorns in her hands and did not make any reply at all. However, I was pretty sure of her thoughts.

I said, Sam, you got to listen to reason.

She commenced to hum some tune she knew. I will tell you what. It was irksome, the way she sat there with her hair sticking out all over her head like a bunch of switch-grass and just worked at her fingers.

I said, That is not a answer, and it ain't polite.

She said, If you want to be woebegone, and cowards, then fine. But I got better things to do than turn back.

I was ashamed having a girl talk to me like that in earshot of others. I pointed out that she had no horse.

I walk fine, she said.

I said, Nobody is going to leave you to follow the panther afoot. You can't out walk a panther.

She neither looked at me nor answered, but hummed her tune.

Mr Pacheco laughed at her being ornery, and I said, It ain't funny.

She is mooee fwairtay, he said.

I asked what that was.

He said, She is a very strong girl.

She was a great deal of trouble was what she was, and I told him so.

But Mr Pacheco was in agreement with her and did not want to turn back. The pinto would not mind a extra passenger no bigger around than a blade of grass, he said, and Sam was welcome to ride with him. Mr Pacheco was of the opinion the dog must of found his way to us by recollecting the way he had followed after the panther and returning by the same route, meaning he had trailed the panther down the very canyon we was sitting in. We could start down the canyon the direction the dog had come from and look for signs.

I have put my dog through too much already, Preacher Dob said. He's had a good time remembering the days of his youth and getting the panther scent in his nose once again. But the party is over for him and me and my horse. The panther will be long gone by now and without a useful panther dog we are more likely to get lost than find it, and this is not a area I want us lost in. There's too much chance of coming across Indians.

I figured we was lost already. I could

hardly tell which direction was forward and which was back and could not so much as see the direction of the sun for the clouds. Even if I had still of been wearing the spectacles, those was not going to show me the way. We was at the bottom of a canyon that looked like any other, in the middle of no place, as far as I could make out. I figured either Preacher Dob or Mr Pacheco could track us backwards and get us home, even if I could not, but none of us was going back without Sam. We was in deadlock.

We paused from argument and ate corn bread Ida had packed and pecans that was dropped, and Preacher Dob went up to get Zechariah and bring him down to wash him again, as he did not want to head in any direction whatsoever with the dog still smelling as bad as he done. We was none of us getting along, and there was a good many tense words when Preacher Dob come back down with that foul smelling dog. Sam and Mr Pacheco was strongly for trailing down the canyon a ways, and Preacher Dob and me was both certain that to do so would only mean traveling further into dangerous territory when we had no chance of catching up with a panther that was likely a hundred miles off by now. No matter how far we went, if we did not have a dog that could track and tree the panther, the cat would keep ahead of us, as they are long walkers.

We pitched in and done our part washing Zechariah again, and the dog put up with us better than the night before, but I was feeling ill treated and wrathful with Sam for making it so clear to everybody that I would have to either leave her behind or hog tie her and take her against her will, when I could not do neither. I might as well of been hog tied myself for all the say-so I had over her.

Me and Preacher Dob and Mr Pacheco stood in our bare feet and time and again filled the pot with cold mucky water, and handed it to Sam to try to clear the water with prickly pear, then dumped it over the dog.

Sam continued to argue her claim, saying, I have my four-shot pepperbox and you won't see me going back.

Preacher Dob said, Little girl, it is my pepperbox and it was only borrowed to you.

She said, It was borrowed to me to shoot the panther. Until I done so it's mine, unless you're a Indian giver.

He said, God opposes the proud but gives grace to the humble.

She said, I favor the hide over grace. I

don't give a snap about grace.

I told Preacher Dob, I am sorry she has no respect for her elders.

Preacher Dob then led Zechariah out of the water and tied him to a low branch of a big sycamore alongside the creek and said, We are at cross purposes here. We have consulted the wishes of all, and fallen to disagreement, and found ourselves at a impasse. There is but one amongst us who has not yet been called on nor heard from, and that is the Lord. We would do well to call upon him.

Preacher Dob then gathered us under the sycamore, and we took our hats off, and bent our heads, all except Sam who did not bend hers, and we heeded the preacher's words, although I feared Sam would not be swayed to the Lord's verdict if it should be other than what she wanted.

What Preacher Dob said went something like this, although I don't claim to recall it by the word. Dear Lord, said he, we call upon you for guidance. We have a judgment to make and would like for you to set us on the path you want us to be on. Mr Lorenzo Pacheco and Miss Samantha Shreve would choose to go in search of a panther that Benjamin Shreve and me both firmly believe to be long gone. They desire to kill the panther as a matter of revenge, a matter of safety, a matter of money, and a matter of humanity toward them that the panther has preyed on by feasting on livestock and tormenting folks with fear. That is their position. It is likely a large tom with about a hundred square miles of territory it thinks is its own. Whilst I can see killing it might be worthy, I fear, as does Benjamin, that the effort might lead us onto a path that would end amongst savages such as Comanches or Apaches, or a unforeseen peril. In following after the panther, we might meet our own doom. I am a old man, as you must know, and Mr Pacheco has also crossed most of the hills of tribulation that he will traverse. The Bible says there is a time appointed to every man, and if this should be mine, and you should want to call us home, then I, for one, will be ready to heed the call. Mr Pacheco strikes me to be of a like disposition. But we have two kids in our midst, and although the boy is verging on being a man, and the girl is tougher than might do her good in the long run, and obstate, and set on what she wants, and fixed in her ways, I am not anxious to lead them into danger. As much as they could make use of the bounty offered for killing the panther, and as much as my family could, and Mr Pacheco could too, a bounty will not buy us a day of life, nor buy our scalps back, if we should run into Indians or other fatal things to encounter. Guide us, therefore, dear Lord, away from the wrong path, whichever way that might be, and set us where you want us to go instead. Amen.

Sam give him a look and said, You did not say it fair.

Preacher Dob said, How would you have me say it, little girl.

Sam said, Fair is to say Lord, let us know if we is to go on, or turn back. Amen. That's what's fair. Saying more is not fair.

Preacher Dob then prayed, Lord, do show us the way.

We stood there with our clothes wet from the splashing we given the dog, our campfire burned to embers nearby and too small to warm us, and the day growing darker instead of more light. There was a wind, as I recall. A cold one. I felt the presence of winter coming, and possibly rain on the way, and a certain dread in my bones with the thought of the long nights before me spent stoking the fire of our broken-down house, and watching the door, and listening to every snap of a twig beyond it, and wondering if the panther might be watching and waiting from the far side.

And a change, ever so slight, come over the way I felt inclined, and I begun to lean more toward the idea of mounting up and moving on down the canyon. I knew what I would find at the end of a ride back home. I would find nothing but back home, and it was a place I had already been in my life, and knew well, and I was not sure it was any more safe than where the canyon might take us. If instead we was to go on down the canyon, and happen across the panther down the way, a third of two thousand dollars would go some distance toward making our home a more decent place and keeping us well fed.

And whilst I was having these thoughts I seen that Preacher Dob's eyes was closed, and Sam's was looking off down the canyon, and Zechariah's, even the bad one, was fixed on Sam as usual when he had a moment to fix them so, and Mr Pacheco's was raised up to the branches overhead dropping their big yellow leaves. And then I seen Mr Pacheco lean his head farther back, like he was looking at something of interest, and I seen his mouth drop open and his eyes squint hard, and I followed where he was looking. And there I seen, hanging limp and bloody over a twisted limb of the sycamore we was standing under, the carcass of a porcupine that I was sure had not got itself into that tree in the half eaten state it was in.

Mr Pacheco then looked straight to the ground, and bent over to look more closely amongst the yellow leaves that laid there. He squatted upon his heels, and moved the leaves about, and raised his gaze to the rest of us, and said, Deeos meeo.

And the rest of us bent to look, and we seen what he seen, and a silent moment fell amongst us, for there in the mud at the creek's edge, filled up with water, was a deep pad track of a panther, a lot bigger than my fist.

Without a word spoke between us we went about doing what any right-minded persons would do. We commenced to search the ground for other tracks. And wouldn't you know, it was Sam who come across one with two toes.

Mr Pacheco said, El Demonio de Dos Dedos has been here.

Preacher Dob agreed it was so, against his own will. He said, The Lord has now spoke. He has told us to complete the journey. He has reminded me that journeys will not often be of my choosing. We stand in a crossways place, and he give us a Which Way tree, the same as he done for Sam Houston at the fork in the road to San Jacinto. He has shown us the way we are to go, and it is onward.

We found more tracks then, and we seen how they doubled back and went forward again, this way and that, and we conferred, and it come to us all whilst eyeing the tracks and thinking how fresh that carcass was in the tree, that the dog had followed the panther down the canyon, and then the panther had followed the dog when he come back this way, and the panther had eyed us in the night, and watched us smoke our pulkee puros, and ate his porcupine dinner whilst we slept not twenty yards from this tree.

The question come to us then as to whether we was tracking the panther or if, by some unknown hand we was dealt, the panther might be tracking us. I am uneasy to wonder at it even now, and I was sure uneasy at that time. I had seen the size of that panther twice. I had beat its hind end as it gone up the tree after Sam on the night it done in Juda. I had seen the lantern light in its yellow eyes in the goat pen. But the thought of them eyes being on me whilst I slept, and watching me in the dark unawares, was a worse thing to think about than meeting face-on with the creature. It give me a frosty feeling in my soul.

There was four good things taking place at this time, however. One was that the panther had not pounced on us in the night. Another was that it had not pounced on Zechariah whilst he slept alone above us, perhaps on account of his foul odor. A third was that we now agreed on where we was to be traveling, as the tracks seemed to be going and coming and going again, headed down the canyon. The fourth was that the Lord had shown us by a sign that we was doing right to go on, so we no longer had that question to argue over. We was now of one purpose.

We packed up, saddled up, and struck out. We led the horses, as we was compelled to start afoot to keep our eyes on the ground for sign and tracks. When Zechariah seen we was going after the panther he again become like a young dog, heedless of his wounds and bleeding feet and the sick stink. There was no more need of a horseback ride for that dog, and it give Preacher Dob a good deal of satisfaction to see him acting so hearty. The dog's own tracks from the night before was jumbled amongst the panther's and confused us at times, as it was not easy on dry soil to tell one from another. But the dog was going by scent and not sight and had a good knowledge of his own odor, so he did not take notice of those tracks nor of tracks from other creatures. There was a good many varmint and coyote tracks and some from a bear. At times Zechariah took hard whiffs on dry land, and sniffed about in circles, and appeared to light upon the scent. However, his nose always taken him back to the mud, where he lost it. There we seen tracks trailing into the water and stood about, scratching our heads.

I kept Hanlin's pistol at the ready and one eye trained on trees overhead and regions of dense brush in case of Indians or the panther. Sam had the pepperbox at the ready and kept saying how she was to have the first shot.

After a while of walking, Preacher Dob come on scat. Further on we seen a pile of dirt and twigs scratched together that was surely sign of a tom marking his territory. Zechariah huffed and chuffed at the pile, and followed the track a ways until it sidled against the water again and he lost it.

Preacher Dob said, That cat is playing with us.

The day got colder the farther we walked. The clouds was thick and dark and we seen from the way they was moving, and the way the high up branches of trees on the rim was behaving, that the wind was picking up speed. We was glad of the wind in spite of that it was cold, as it carried off some of the skunk odor. However, we did not like what it foretold, and we felt ourselves in a hurry. We was certain to lose the tracks as well as the scent if we should have rain.

After some time we come on duck feathers with duck feet laying alongside.

Preacher Dob said, Dos Dedos does not care for duck feet.

That struck me and Mr Pacheco as funny and we laughed about it. However, Sam would not laugh about that or nothing else, as she was too busy looking for panther sign.

About noon Zechariah turned of a sudden and gone straight up the side of the canyon at a dead run with his nose about stuck to the ground. Preacher Dob took off after him, leading his horse in haste up the side of the canyon and yelling for the dog to wait, to no advantage. Both the dog and him gone up over the rim. The rest of us started up after them. It was a rocky slope, but not steep. We topped the rim and found ourselves on a open mesa of Indian grass up nearly chest high. The wind there hit us hard. Preacher Dob was already there. The grass was thick and a lot taller than the dog, so mostly what we saw of him was the commotion he made in it as he went about sniffing for the track.

I now had a better look at the sky and how dark it was to the south. There was a storm heading up from Mexico. The wind was blowing from that direction, laying the grass down in waves as it come. I wished I had been prepared for rain, as I felt sure when it met with the air coming down from the north we was going to have some, and it would not be toasty. It was not winter when we had left our house the day before, only nippy, but now it was downright cold.

Zechariah trailed along the edge of the canyon in the same direction we had been going when we was down in it. The horses wished to graze but we mounted up in haste to keep after the dog.

We had not gone far when the wall of the canyon got steep below us. The panther must of known that canyon well to climb out when he did. Zechariah lost the scent here and there, and run about making a trace in the grass.

We was paused and looking off over the mesa, discussing the dark sky whilst the dog sought out the track, when of a sudden we was taken aback by a voice hollering at us from the far side of the canyon, saying, Stop where you are!

Upon hearing this we was perplexed, on account of two reasons. One was that we was already stopped where we was. Another was that we had neither heard nor seen anyone approach, as we did not have the wind of that side of the canyon and was busy looking the other way.

We turned in consternation and seen three riders reined in across the way with their guns drawn at us. I could not make out much about them, as by my estimate the canyon was sixty yards across, if a inch. All I could make out was one of them was a fat man with a rifle on a good sized gray horse, one was a thin man riding a chestnut and aiming what looked like a bore musket, and the third was of a regular constitution, wearing a Sesesh uniform and mounted upon a dun. He appeared to have a pistol. The sky over on that side was light, not dark like behind us.

Preacher Dob made a attempt to be friendly. He shouted back, Howdy!

The fat man commenced to yell. He said, Lorenzo Pacheco, get your hands up, dismount, and step away from the horse! If you make a move we'll shoot you! Get that girl off the horse too!

It seemed like he meant business. Mr Pacheco told Sam to get down from behind him and move away from the pinto.

She did not at first do so. I told her to do so. Preacher Dob said, Little girl, get off that horse, and she then done so, although in a balky manner.

Mr Pacheco then done the same. He said a few words to the horse in Spanish and stepped away and raised his hands in the air. The pinto stayed where it was.

The fat man hollered, Dobson Beck, you are traveling with a horse thief! Lorenzo Pacheco, you stole that horse from me! I have the law here with me and we intend to get the horse back! If you resist us we'll shoot you! If you run we'll hunt you and hang you!

Mr Pacheco hollered, I paid you for the horse!

You paid me counterfeit! the fat man replied. Confederate counterfeit!

The man in the uniform yelled, And goddamn it, you give me counterfeit, too, Pacheco! Uncle Dob, you are about to get yourself hanged for a accomplice if Pacheco don't turn that horse over and pay me what I earned, that he owes me, in US dollars!

Preacher Dob hollered, Is that you, Clarence!

It seemed like it required a lot of effort to

shout across the canyon into the wind. However, Hanlin done so for a good while at Preacher Dob. The bills Pacheco give me ain't worth their paper! he said. I come across Mr Samuels here at Camp Verde! He was asking about a Mexican horse thief on a good pinto that had paid him counterfeit for the horse! I did not have a question who that might be! We got a member of the state militia here with us who come along to see justice gets done! If the lot of you don't comply then somebody's going to get their head shot off! If Pacheco tries to make a run for it, we'll shoot his horse!

The fat man then yelled something at Hanlin. We could not hear what it was.

Hanlin then yelled at us, What we want is the horse! We don't want to shoot the horse, but we'll shoot any of you that stands in the way!

The fat man then yelled something else at Hanlin.

Hanlin got a earful of that and then told us, We will not shoot the kids but we will shoot Pacheco!

Preacher Dob asked Mr Pacheco, Did you pay them counterfeit.

Mr Pacheco said yes, he did.

Preacher Dob said, Why did you do that.

Mr Pacheco said he had no other kind of

money to pay them. He had got the bills for ten cents on the dollar in Matamoros and they was made in Havana. He said the horse was taken from him by Cortina's ombrays. He said, Would you let that fat man ride your prize horse.

Preacher Dob said, He did purchase it fairly, did he not.

Mr Pacheco allowed Cortina's hombres would not of made a gift of the horse.

The three men on the far side was making plans amongst theirselves.

Hanlin then yelled, Me and Mr Samuels here will be coming around the end of the canyon to get his horse and my hundred US dollars and to get back my gun that Pacheco took from me and give to the boy! Mr Rarick here is a member of the state militia! He is going to stay here and keep you all four in his aim! Uncle Dob, keep a eye on Pacheco! If he tries to run, shoot him!

Preacher Dob yelled over, I am not going to shoot him, Clarence! I am a preacher and a man of God! And Mr Pacheco does not have a hundred dollars! You are a idiot to of ever thought he did!

The man on the chestnut, who was the law, said, Hold up! You said you are a preacher! Is that you, Preacher Dob!

Preacher Dob said, Yes, I am Preacher Dob!

The man said, I did not know that! They said we was looking for Dobson Beck traveling with a Mexican, but I did not know that was you! Do you not remember me! You counseled me on a private matter! It was in Bell County! My name is Tom Rarick!

Preacher Dob said, I recall you well!

The man said, She returned the skillet to the peddler!

Preacher Dob said, I am delighted to hear that, Tom! She has made herself right with the Lord!

The fat man then fired a shot over our heads to show he meant business.

Sam thought he was shooting at us and fired a shot back at him with the pepperbox, but missed.

Mr Pacheco's hands was in the air but when the shots was fired he went for his pistol, ducked in the tall grass, and taken aim at Hanlin. Hanlin jumped off the dun, ducked in the tall grass over there, and taken aim back at Mr Pacheco. I aimed Hanlin's own Colt's at him, as I figured if he was to fire on Mr Pacheco I would have to take action, although I did not know what that might be, as I was reluctant to shoot even so bad a man as Clarence Hanlin that was not shooting at me.

Preacher Dob shouted, Hold up, hold up! Stop everything! There's no reason for folks to get killed!

I wished I could of still been wearing Preacher Dob's spectacles and seen things better. I made out that the fat man had his rifle aimed at Mr Pacheco. He was still seated on his horse and looked quite fat there. The lawman, Mr Tom Rarick, had his musket skyward and was not aiming at anybody. Hanlin was hunkered somewhat down in the grass. I figured his pistol was borrowed, on account I had his. It was in his left hand, I guess on account of his right was done up in a bandage on account of the gone finger. He switched his aim back and forth between Sam and Mr Pacheco and me. The grass was as high over there as it was on our side, so it was hard to see exactly what he was doing, but I could see who he was aiming at.

We fell silent to take stock of our situation.

It was then we heard the dog bawling. The sound come from some distance off and we knew Zechariah was long gone and onto the panther's track once more in a sure way. Sam did not give me a glance, nor hesitate for nothing. Before the sound of the second bawl she had her hands on the reins of the pinto and was pulling herself into the saddle. By the third bawl she was reined about and headed off in a dead charge in the direction of the dog.

Mr Pacheco took off after her afoot.

Hanlin fired a shot at him.

Preacher Dob's horse of a sudden become dead weight and dropped with Preacher Dob still in the saddle. It did not thrash about nor make a sound. One minute the horse was having its breakfast of Indian grass whilst we was hollering over the canyon, and the next it lay on the ground with Preacher Dob seated upon it in a state of surprise as to what had happened.

I looked about me, confounded. Alongside me I seen Preacher Dob seated on the prone horse. Behind me I seen Sam heading off on the pinto into a black sky, and Mr Pacheco making a bee line afoot after her through the tall grass. I seen a flash of lightning. Across the way I seen Hanlin stand up from where he was hunkered down in the grass, as there was no longer a gun aimed at him, except mine, which was his, and I guess he figured I was not going to shoot it.

He hollered, Uncle Dob, I am sorry! Did I shoot your horse! I did not mean to! I was

266

aiming at Pacheco, not your horse! I had to shoot left-handed on account of my right is missing the finger! Is the horse dead! I am sorry!

He did appear regretful.

Preacher Dob got hisself up off the saddle and looked at his horse and found it to be shot in the head. There was no life in the horse at all. The only part of the horse moving was his tail and his mane, which was blown about somewhat by the wind. The Hawken was half under the horse and the stock appeared to be busted clean off.

Preacher Dob and me had to ponder fast. We had a dead horse wearing a good saddle that I was pretty sure Preacher Dob did not want left on the edge of a canyon he was likely not to return to for some time, if ever. We had people across the canyon who was well armed and of intentions that was not to our benefit. We had Sam, the pinto, Mr Pacheco, and Zechariah heading off over the field in pursuit of a panther that might, or might not, be worth a third of two thousand dollars to each of us, depending on if we could get hold of the hide.

My biggest concern was Sam. She was a heap of trouble to me and yet I did care about her. I believe Preacher Dob felt a obligation to take care of her, whether he had a fondness for her or not. He was also worried for his dog. Also, a dead horse is a dead horse and no use at all, no matter that he was a use at one time, and a good horse, and still wearing a saddle.

I mounted the mare in haste. Preacher Dob seized upon what was left of his Hawken from under his horse and run toward me with a evident limp. The fall had done him no good. He did not have a easy time mounting behind me and yet done so in what could be called a jiffy.

We neither of us had a question about which direction to go. The dog was on the trail of the panther, Sam was on the trail of the dog, Mr Pacheco was on the trail of Sam and the pinto, and we was all traveling as fast as we was able in the direction of the bawling. I would of felt a whole lot more at ease if I had not known that the fat man and Hanlin, and maybe the law — though I was not so sure about him anymore — would be chasing after all of us as soon as they come around the end of the canyon, however far off or near that might be, and would have no question which way we was headed, as the bawling was a sure pointer.

I was yet a boy of fourteen years old, not a large one, and Preacher Dob was neither tall nor heavy. Yet I am sure my mare did not have a easy go of it to carry us both. Bless her, she was a good mare, and is a good mare to this day, and I suppose she had never forgot the kindness my father paid her when he found her, left as she was on a trail, and patched up her hind end, and nursed her back to life after Indians used her up and nearly done her in. Other than her bad habit to take a chunk out of whoever might lay a hand on her rump, she is as noble as mares are made.

She carried us straight into the wind at a good speed.

Dear Judge,

I sit here tonight in a slow and rueful frame of mind. It is sweltering hot in here but I don't dare crack the door for air, as who knows what might come in. Sam is sound asleep. As much as I tire of hearing her talk, there is times at night I wish she would wake up and start at it again. It gets lonely with just me and the shadow of my head from the trifling light of this lantern. I recall nights it was Sam and me and my father, and cold out, and we had us a fire going.

I wish you was here in person.

I am almost to the end of the tale. I will miss the tale when I find it over. I will miss writing to you.

Goodnight, sir, to you.

Yours kindly,
Benjamin Shreve

Preacher Dob and me rode at the storm headlong on the mare whilst the storm come headlong at us, the wind whipping our faces hard and the sky before us dark as night but for the lightning streaking top to bottom. I could hardly tell what was the pounding of the mare's hooves under us from what was thunder off before us, as the world was all a rumble. I did not like the cold but was glad for the fresh smell after being all day in the canyon with Zechariah.

Mr Pacheco had a good lead on us afoot. However, the law was in full chase and Mr Pacheco had no horse, as Sam was gone off on his pinto, if it even was his pinto, as it might of belonged to the fat man depending on how you felt about that. So things was stacked against him as he run through the tall yellow grass. He was afoot, he was in trouble, he was likely a horse thief, and even if I was to ride up and give him my mare, he could not go fast enough on her to catch up with Sam on the pinto. However, one thing I should of known about him by then was that he knew how to act in perilous times.

What he done was come to a halt and whistled. I do not know how the pinto heard the whistle, as he did not have the wind of it and he was a good bit ahead of Mr Pacheco. But he come to a full stop from a dead run, and Sam went hastily over his head and onto the ground. However, in haste she was back in the saddle. She commenced to kick and slap at the pinto to encourage him forward, but the horse did not budge. He did not move a peg. It was like his hooves was nailed to the ground. Sam might as well of tried to ride a pile of rocks for all the movement that horse made. Up run Mr Pacheco and got hisself in the saddle behind her, and off they went into the wind before us.

So there the four of us was, on two horses, in a dead charge at the storm and the dog's bawling. I looked behind long enough to see the law was not caught up with us yet, and was nowhere to be seen, as I guess the canyon they was trying to get around was a big one.

We was not even across the field to a line of cedars on the far side when the bawling turned to a fixed barking. Preacher Dob yelled into my ear that I might hear him over the wind, saying, Zechariah has treed something for sure!

Mr Pacheco and Sam was a fair distance ahead of us. I had thought Mr Pacheco might want to strike out in another direction to evade the law that was after him, but I guess he wanted the panther more than he feared the law.

We could not tell the exact place the barking come from on account of the wind tugging the sound. Mr Pacheco and Sam appeared like they was having the same trouble. They turned the pinto this way and that on approaching the trees, which was a thick cedar break. My mare give it her all to catch them but by the time we got to the cedars Mr Pacheco and Sam was already dismounted and leading the pinto through the break and down into a canyon.

We dismounted to follow them. It was not a deep canyon but a rocky one. Preacher Dob sucked his breath and flinched a good bit from the harm done when his horse dropped on his leg. He hung on to what he had of the Hawken although it was no use to him until he might fix it, as who cares to lose their shoulder firing a gun without a stock.

I hollered to Sam and Mr Pacheco to wait for us. I do not believe either of them known Preacher Dob's horse was dead, as they had took off before that happened.

I hollered, Hanlin shot Preacher Dob's horse! It's dead! Preacher Dob's hurt!

I do not think Sam slowed down nor even

so much as looked about when she heard me yell that. She was deep into the cedars and I could not see her to know for sure, but it sounded to me like she just kept on going. You would think she would give some thought to the fact it was Preacher Dob and his dog that had got her thus far on the hunt for the panther. You would think she might feel a obligation to help out. But that was not the case.

If there was any of us with the right to go off and leave Preacher Dob it was Mr Pacheco, on account of him being chased by the law and now having got back his pinto that could outrun it. However, he had two reasons not to run off. One was he wanted the bounty. Another was he was polite and good hearted and not likely to leave a hurt companion behind him, unlike Sam, who was in the act of it.

Mr Pacheco come shoving his way back through the cedars at us and inquired of Preacher Dob if he was in need of help.

Preacher Dob, not being a man of weak disposition nor gutless, said he thought he could walk.

We made our way down into the canyon, leading the horses. We had a good whiff of skunk and was able to hear the dog barking, so we knew we was going right. None of us, nor the horses, was happy to be scratched by so many cedars close about, but there was not a lot of complaining amongst us, as we did not want to make noise if we was approaching the cat.

We did not get free of the cedars until we reached the canyon floor. It was a dry bottom and only about ten yards across. Sam was already down there when we got there. The rain had commenced, although not yet in earnest.

And guess what we laid eyes on. Halfway up on the far side, in full sight, not fifteen yards off, on a branch of a big anacua tree hemmed in by a bunch of scrubby cedars, stood our panther.

Judge, I will tell you what. It was a shock to have such a plain view of that huge cat. It was the first time I had a chance to look at him and breathe at the same time. We could not see Zechariah, as he was at the base of the tree and there was thick cedars around him, but we knew he was there from his fit of barking.

The anacua had three or four wide trunks to it, joined together. The branches mostly grew upward, but there was one that spread nearly straight out, and the panther stood upon that one, amongst the leaves but not much hidden by those, and looking down at

Zechariah. We gazed up at the full length of him. I could not take my eyes away. He was more than eight feet long nose to tail. I had a good view of his round head and sturdy jaw that had squeezed the life out of Juda. He did not appear concerned much about Zechariah who he could pounce on if he wanted to, although he did twitch his long fat tail at the very tip, so I guess he was feeling some agitation at being barked at like that.

He terrified me. Even so, I wished I had Preacher Dob's spectacles to see him better. I thought I might ask to borrow them. However, before I done so, the pepperbox gone off nearly in my ear. I let out a whoop at the noise it made, as it was a shock to me to hear that. The panther taken one look at us and crouched in readiness to leap out of the tree. He did not appear to be hurt but did seem about ready to take his leave of the situation, as I guess he figured it was one thing to wait out a barking dog and another to stand there and be a target for armed people.

I don't recall what I hollered at Sam, but I did holler at her.

Mr Pacheco drew his pistol and took a shot at the panther with the aim to bring him down in haste before he leapt. He likely would of hit him, but Sam jumped at him and shoved his arm as he pulled the trigger, and sent the shot afoul. The ball could of hit one of us or the horses, but Sam did not care about that. She only cared it did not hit the panther, as she wanted to shoot him herself.

We all hollered at her.

Then Zechariah gone up the tree in pursuit of the panther. I do not know what that dog was thinking. Maybe he figured out that the panther was about to leap and that when he done so we was liable to lose him for good, as the rain was falling in earnest now and whatever scent might be picked up was about to get washed off. I guess maybe the dog foresaw that. Or maybe he just figured he had been patient long enough, and we was not acting right, and he was going to have to take care of the matter hisself. Whatever his reasons, he was on his way up the anacua.

Sam tried to squeeze off another shot with the pepperbox, but Preacher Dob got hold of her by the hair and snatched the gun out of her hand. She had proved she could not be trusted, and I guess he thought she might shoot the dog in a rush instead of the panther, which was likely. There was a scuffle between them. In haste me and Mr

Pacheco got her off Preacher Dob and got a good hold of her. Preacher Dob kept the pepperbox high up out of her reach. The panther was further along the branch now and crouched low and the dog was about up to him. Then the panther leapt. He landed amongst the cedars and took off down the canyon. Mr Pacheco fired a shot after him but the cat was moving too fast and no harm was done him.

Sam commenced to screech at us. She said, I hate you, every one of you! I could of got him! I had two more shots left! He aught to be dead! If I could of been left to myself I would of hit him! She yelled at Mr Pacheco that he did not have the right, and at Preacher Dob that he was a Indian giver, and at me for having my head in her way and making her miss. She screamed at Zechariah, What are you doing up in the tree! Why ain't you chasing after the panther! How dumb a dog are you to climb that tree! Are you stuck!

He did appear to be stuck. It is a well known fact that a dog can climb up a tree but can't climb down one. How Zechariah had not learned that, old as he was, is a mystery to me. I guess maybe he just got overexcited and took the chance that come.

I will say this. He did get awfully close to

that panther's tail before the cat leapt. What he would of done if he had got hold of the cat, I don't know, as it was pretty clear which of those two would of come out the better. Now the panther was long gone down the canyon and Zechariah was left stuck on a empty branch, in the rain, with no way to get down. A jump for him would not of been so easy as for the panther nor without serious costs we did not want.

What could we do but go get him down.

Preacher Dob had to favor his hurt leg, therefore the task fell to me and Mr Pacheco. The dog was wet, as the rain was falling full out, and he stank so bad I might of had to give up my lunch if I had even had one. Preacher Dob and Mr Pacheco and me took our shirts off so as not to get soaked. We shoved them under the saddles. I climbed the tree and handed Zechariah down to Mr Pacheco. It was not easy. He was wet and he stank. Sam cussed us the whole time. Zechariah looked embarrassed about the situation, but what could he do.

When we had got him out of the tree he took off down the canyon in the direction the panther had gone. He did not bawl, as the ground was now wet and what dog can pick up a scent on wet ground. However, we give him the benefit of trust and mounted up and followed him at a fast clip, me and Preacher Dob on the mare and Sam and Mr Pacheco on the pinto.

A cold, hard rain pelted us, and thunder rumbled down the canyon, which was narrow and had sloped rocky walls with trees and thick brush. Branches spread over us and give us some protection for a good half hour but then become a soggy mess and no help at all. Sam complained of the fact she had not shot the panther and said it was our fault and now where was the panther.

I said, It's your own fault he got away. You did not take proper aim. Preacher Dob give you a loaded pistol. Mr Pacheco and me give you the first shot. You got excited and did not take aim. You nearly blew my head off from behind me.

You was in the way, she said. You got your head in the way! I could not see around it. You should of moved aside! I could of shot the panther in the head!

Mr Pacheco told her the head was not the right place to of aimed, as panthers' brains is small.

Did you even think to ask what place to aim for, I rebuked her.

Mr Pacheco said she aught to of aimed for behind the front leg to hit near the heart.

She said, Why did none of you think to tell me!

You give none of us time, I said.

But she would not hear reason.

The canyon become steeper and the rain become torrents and commenced to flow down the sides and through the middle. Before long our horses was tramping in water that was heading down canyon. We had to dismount and lead them afoot on the edge of the flow, as the center become too deep and the slopes of the canyon too slick. We was hungry and wet and shivering and I was wore out listening to Sam complain of the size of my head. We passed no shelter but bee caves in the rock walls alongside until after a half hour or so of hard rain we spied a ledge, about twenty feet up, with a entry to a regular cave that did not appear to house bees. Preacher Dob said we aught to try to get up there and take shelter, on account of even if we was to catch up with the panther, our rifle was a gone case and our powder was soaked.

Mr Pacheco agreed. He had some bit of dry powder in his flask, but we had none for the pepperbox nor for Hanlin's pistol.

Sam put up a fuss about that idea, as you might think she would. She would not hear of stopping. She had her head down and the rain dripping off it. Her teeth was chattering. She had on Mr Pacheco's sopping poncho and she walked like she was a hound dog herself, looking neither left nor right, following Zechariah with a purpose we all knew, as she cared for nothing in life but to do in the cat and stomp around on his hide. I think she must of imagined a whole life of being happy just traipsing back and forth on that hide. She walked in a stanchly manner, rain or no rain, thunder nor none, quivering cold nor not. She had just as well got on four legs and stuck her nose to the canyon floor alongside Zechariah.

She said, As long as the dog's going, I'm going along with him.

Preacher Dob said, Little girl, we are stopping here, and my dog is stopping with me whether he likes it or not.

She said, You are not so hard hearted as to stop if I keep on going.

Preacher Dob said, Matthew tells us that whoever is not with me is against me, and whoever does not gather with me, scatters.

She said, I do not know Matthew, I do not care what he says, I will scatter if I want to, it is my choice on account of you are not my boss.

He said, Then you move on, little girl. You

keep on, in the rain, seeing nothing, knowing nothing, having nobody to care a whit about if you have got a scalp on your head, or not. I have seen enough of you.

She did not take her leave.

I said, He has called your bluff.

For once, she had nothing to say.

I volunteered I would climb up and have a look at the cave. It was not a easy climb. I had to haul myself up through cedars growing out of the wall. They was wet and I was shirtless and already scratched up and had tolerated all the fun I wanted.

The ledge when I got up there was partly dry under a overhang, and the cave looked to be big enough for us all, maybe fifteen feet wide and about that deep. I figured the overhang outside would protect the horses if we could get them up to the ledge, which we would have to do, on account of Preacher Dob could not make it up without them taking him. I hollered down to come on.

Sam come up the wall and joined me in a huff. Mr Pacheco and Preacher Dob scouted a route the horses was able to make their way up. Zechariah come with them. We tethered the horses on the ledge outside the cave. They did neither of them like it in spite of it was plenty wide and mostly dry.

The mare yanked against her tether.

Zechariah would not enter the cave with us but remained out with the horses and commenced to bark at us that went in.

Bless his heart, Preacher Dob said. He favors to keep on going. He's a dedicated panther dog all right. Wringing wet, and won't even come in to dry off.

Sam said, How come you like the dog and you don't like me.

He said, I like you a good bit, little girl. I would like you a good bit more if you had some sense.

I could not blame the dog for failing to enter the cave. It was not a very hospitable place, but a gloomy room with a dirt floor and spears of rock hanging down from the top. It smelled rank. You had to watch out not to knock into the spears, as some of them was long. Dark tunnels wound further back in the rock but we could not see much into them. There was remains of a old fire and we figured Indians might of holed up in the cave at one time. Preacher Dob spoke a prayer that the Indians was not still nearby nor heading our way.

We settled in, and things become tense. The storm picked up. I am not sure I ever heard thunder like that before nor after. It seemed like the spears overhead might come

loose on us from shaking. The wind come
tearing down the canyon, ripping at trees
and slinging the rain onto the ledge and
nearly into the cave. I wondered if we was
having a storm as bad as I read of in The
Whale. We shivered and rubbed our arms in
a attempt to keep warm. I ate what was left
of my pickles.

Preacher Dob become agitated about
Zechariah and kept hollering at him to
come in. However, the dog was worked up.
He run back and forth in the rain sweeping
onto the ledge before us. We seen him in
blazes of light. He barked at us and troubled
the horses even more than they was troubled
already on their own. My mare reared a
good bit and I feared she might tumble
down into the cedars. The pinto pawed the
ground and tossed his head, then faced the
wind and bore it the best he could.

We watched the dog race past the entry
going one direction then the other and moving fast. He was such a bad looking dog,
soaking wet and smelly, and between you
and me, I was not displeased he was outside
instead of in the cave with us, except I did
not like the upheaval, on account of the
horses was upset, and on account of who
knew who might come looking to see what
all the fuss was about, if they could even

hear it over the storm. Maybe the law, maybe Comanches. Both was equally undesired.

Preacher Dob said, That dog would rather get struck by lightning than give up the hunt. If Hanlin hears him we're done for. He wants his hundred dollars.

Mr Pacheco was not bothered about that. He said Hanlin and the law was a bunch of gayeenas, which was chickens, and they was bound to be hid out from the storm. He told Preacher Dob to leave the dog be.

Preacher Dob went out for Zechariah. The rain that was blowing onto the ledge assailed him full in the face so hard I don't know how he could even see through his spectacles. It took some doing, but he got a rope off Mr Pacheco's saddle and got hold of Zechariah and tied him and made a attempt to drag him in with us. However, the dog fought back in a way that made us wonder if he might strangle hisself. I thought he might bite his own owner. His eye that looked like a egg was a frightful sight in the lightning. Preacher Dob give up and come sloshing back in without him.

Mr Pacheco gone out and got our shirts from under the saddles, as we was cold and miserable. They was damp but warm when we put them on. Sam still had on her shirt, which was mine outgrown, and soaked through, so I felt sorry for her. Pretty soon I felt sorry for us too, as our shirts did not stay warm. You might as well of put them on shards of ice stuck to a roof eave in the winter. The air whistled about outside and charged in through the entry. Therefore, what was the value of a jiffy of warmth. Not much.

Sam sat in the dirt a foot or two off from me and I heard her teeth hammering together in spite of all the noise going on. She sounded like a woodpecker. I regarded her in the flashes. She looked fierce. Her face was poorly and dripping wet. I figured if Comanches was to come along and peer in and have a glimpse of her they would wonder what kind of creature they had stumbled upon.

She said, The panther is not far off and me and the dog both know that for a fact.

I said, You have no more idea than I do where the panther is. He feasted on porcupine right over your head and you did not have a inkling he was anywhere near about.

I was asleep at the time, she said. I got a inkling now.

She was a one note song, as ever.

Preacher Dob pulled his shoe off and took a look at his hurt foot and leg. They was badly bruised and swole up. He sat holding his shoe whilst gazing out at the rain gushing down. He commenced to have something to say.

He said, I have doubts about this situation. There is a rough wind out there and water rising below us. There is a dirt floor under us, and sharp rocks above us, and wind wuthering at the entry, and bolts of lightning striking the canyon beneath us. We are hemmed by danger on every side. I have deserted my family at home and led two kids after a aging dog into a hostile wilderness that I do not know how to find my way out of. I am injured, I am humbled, and I am lost. I am in the company of a horse thief. My own horse is shot dead and laying in a hard rain at the edge of a canyon I can't name. I have got but half a gun. The law is in pursuit of us. I would prefer to part company with you, Mr Pacheco. However, you have been thoughtful to me, and without the stole horse in question I can't return these children to safety, as the boy and the girl and me can't all three mount up on one mare. My notion of honor and notions of pride and integrity are put to a hard test. Here I sit, a old man, half lame, liable for the lives of these kids and yet unable to take them home on account of the boy will not head back without his sister, and she will not head back without a panther that is gone off down the canyon. Therefore I find myself a accomplice to a horse thief. The Bible says blessed is the man that walketh not in the counsel of the ungodly. It says a man cannot take fire in his bosom and his clothes not be burned. But what other choice do I have. I am in need of you, Mr Pacheco, as much as you are in need of your stole horse. We are two humbled old sinners. I would tell you to go on and leave me here with the kids, as you have everything you need to escape the law. You might even hunt down the panther and claim the bounty yourself. You have a good horse and a good pistol and balls and dry powder. And yet you also have a considerable conscience to burden you if you was to take such a flight. And the both of us know, and these young ones among us will someday learn for theirselves, if the Lord should choose to give them such foresight, that a conscience can drag a man down, and hold a man back, more than a dead horse or a hurt leg. It is a heavy burden.

Preacher Dob finished having his say and I looked to see what Mr Pacheco might think about what he had said. Mr Pacheco was squatted on his heels. He held his hat.

His hair dripped and hung straight down. He stared out at the dog dashing about in the rain, barking in flashes around the horses that was worked up.

Did you not hear what I said, Preacher Dob asked him.

Mr Pacheco answered him in a solemn voice that got my attention. Your dog knows something we do not, he said.

Preacher Dob said, What might that be.

Mr Pacheco said, When he tracks the panther he howls. When he trees the panther, he barks. At no other time does he bark. Why is he barking at this cave.

Judge, I have told you how cold we was in that cave, but there was a different coldness, a greater one, that come over me when I heard them words spoke in the proper way Mr Pacheco spoke them. It was like the north wind decided to hole up in that place with us. It blew in and settled upon us, and the hair on the back of my neck rose up. A crash of thunder come down. In a blaze of light I seen Sam lift up her face at them words and Mr Pacheco turn to Preacher Dob, and Preacher Dob turn to him. And a air of evil washed over us.

We looked to the back of the cave and cast our eyes on the tunnels.

Preacher Dob said, Little girl, stay where

you are.

Sam's ears was deaf to such orders. She rose to her feet and was off to the back of the cave and squatted down peering into the tunnels.

Outside, the dark was like evening on account of the storm. About us, inside, the dark was like night. Deep into the tunnels where Sam was looking the dark was like deep water in the dead of a night with no moon.

Then come a flicker of lightning from the entry that spread itself through the cave and into the tunnels, and by it I seen a movement in the tunnel off to the left. A shape stirred there. Sam seen it, too. It appeared like a spirit crouched in the dark at one moment, and then in our midst, in a blaze of light, at the next. It swatted Sam out of its way. It made a snarling noise and come at me with its ears laid flat back. I threw myself to the ground and felt the heat of the cat pass over. I smelled the cat more than I seen it. I lifted my face from the dirt and seen Mr Pacheco rush at Sam and lay hisself over her, and Preacher Dob crawl my direction to care for me, and the panther go flying out into the dark as if it had not been in our midst at all. I might of thought we had dreamed it up, had it not left us toppled over and laying about the floor of the cave, in the way the wind lays down the grass.

Zechariah launched hisself onto the panther as it went out. I seen them fly off in a bolt of lightning like one creature, not two. They tumbled down the side of the canyon together. We heard the fight commence over the clamoring noise of the storm.

Preacher Dob seen I was all right, and rose up to his full height. He must of forgot his hurt leg, and the lightning, and forgot Comanches, and whatever the Lord might say, and forgot his nephew that was after us and no good. I think he must of forgot he had left his daughter-in-law and the kids at home. He took off down the wall of the canyon after his dog, hollering, Zechariah! Zechariah! and carrying his half rifle and the pepperbox full of wet powder.

Dear Judge,

Thank you for the spectacles. I did not even ask you for them like for the pen. The pen was the best gift anyone ever given to me but these spectacles is almost better. I am hesitant to say so, as I am fond of the pen. Mr Hildebrand said he got word from you to purchase the spectacles and you was to reimburse him. It was a handy way to do it. He did not get hold of first-hand ones, but a woman sold him a pair that was her husband's who passed. His face was injured on passing, on account of it was a rough death that come upon him, and she did not think it a good idea to put his spectacles on it after that. She said her husband would like knowing they was being made use of by a young fellow and not laid to waste in the grave.

They are in perfect shape. I do not see quite as good through them as through Preacher Dob's but a good bit better than on my own. I am bowled over, sir, as they now say. I do not know what I could give you in return that you might want.

The testament I am now sending concludes all the facts you requested me to tell you about Clarence Hanlin. The pages appeared to mount up.

I will write you another letter another time, as I do not care for this to be the last.

Yours kindly,
Benjamin Shreve

MY TESTAMENT

It was a doubtful case we had got ourselves in. Rain poured down, lightning crashed, thunder shook things, Preacher Dob went tearing down the wall of the canyon as if neither old nor injured, and even in spite of that din I heard the fight going on below. There was fierce snarling and growling that was hard to listen to on account of agony was being inflicted. The yelping and whimpering give the notion Zechariah was getting the worst of the fight.

However, we had troubles enough in the

cave that got our attention. It scared me a good bit that Sam was still laying where the panther had knocked her on the dirt floor. When I got to her I feared she was passed. Mr Pacheco and me tried to rouse her. I hollered at her to come around and sit up and tell us she was all right. Mr Pacheco attempted to coax her to open her eyes. She did not do so at once. When she done so, she was loopy and squinted a good bit in her fashion. She had scratches on her neck that was bleeding. Mr Pacheco took as close a look at the scratches as he could make out in the glimmers of light. He tore a sleeve off his shirt and got her to sit up and tied it around her neck.

She said, I smelled it when it come at me.

She seemed to get stuck on the fact of that smell, and went on about it. I guess that odor had recalled her recollections.

In haste, Mr Pacheco made his pistol ready with dry powder.

Sam said, Did Preacher Dob leave me the pepperbox.

Upon hearing her speak of the pepperbox we knew she was in her right mind again. Or rather, she was back in the mind she was born with.

Mr Pacheco took her out in the rain, un-tethered the horses, and put Sam on the pinto. Off we started down the route they had brought the horses up, Mr Pacheco leading the pinto with Sam atop, me leading the mare, and the rain dumping buckets on us. We heard nor seen nothing from Preacher Dob until we got down there and found him in despair at the side of the canyon. The dog was nowhere in sight.

We had to shout to make Preacher Dob hear us, on account of the storm. We asked him, Where's Zechariah! Is he alive!

Preacher Dob hollered, He's hurt and he's gone after the panther!

We mounted, two and two as before, Sam clinging behind Mr Pacheco, and set off down the canyon after the dog, traveling in the direction the water was running. We did not have a easy go. We thought we heard Zechariah bawling a time or two, but none of us was sure. The center of the canyon was by now a stream about half thigh deep, nearly up to the horses' bellies. Therefore we was compelled to ride on the slopes, where the mud sucked at the horses' hooves and rocks give way beneath them. The horses was not happy and stumbled a good bit. We was traveling the direction the water was flowing. The pinto was willing and well trained and my mare was faithful to the core, but it was a lot to ask of them and they was not pretending to like it.

Preacher Dob said he could not tell which way we was even heading.

Mr Pacheco said he thought we was about to strike the Medina River.

We traveled maybe half a hour down the canyon. It was getting toward night by then. However, it had felt like night nearly all day long, so the time was not of great importance to us. We kept on until the canyon run headlong into a good sized river out of its banks and moving at a clip, which Mr Pacheco knew to be the Medina.

Where the canyon struck the river we come across Zechariah holed up under a wide overhang of rock that faced the river. He did not show a great deal of life other than the feeble barking he attempted to do. He was wet through, shaking, whimpering, laying on his side, and pretty well done with it all. He thumped his tail a time or two, to say he was glad to see us.

Preacher Dob was sure glad to see him. He got him in his arms despite that the skunk odor was no better for him being sopping wet. I think he must of always been fond of the dog but now had a added respect. He said he believed the dog was barking just to hear hisself bark and prove to hisself he was still vital. He said he had seen people mumble theirselves right up to the pearly gates to prove to theirselves, word by word, that they was not yet entered.

The dog had sure done his best. The panther had tore him up. His neck was sliced up in a way that made the fur not hang right. The water dripping off him was red on account of being so bloody. Also the pads of his feet was cut up and practically wore off. I have seen chunks of meat that looked less worse than that. He was a pitiful sight.

Mr Pacheco said it might be a kindness to put a end to his suffering.

Preacher Dob declined to do such a thing just yet.

Mr Pacheco offered to do it if it become necessary.

Preacher Dob looked like he might break down at that thought. However, he held up all right. He said, I already lost my horse and I am not going to give up on Zechariah. We have been together too long. He said he would do right by Zechariah hisself, if the time should come.

We secured the horses and sheltered under the ledge of rock with the dog, because where was we supposed to go. We sat staring at the river through the rain. It was muddy and moving at such a pace there was eddies and waves. Mr Pacheco ventured a short distance and studied our whereabouts, looking upriver and down and calculating what he was able to figure from what light there was left in the day. He come back and said he thought we was downriver from Bandera a good ways.

We did what we could for the dog and tired to figure a course of action, but did not triumph in either regard. Mr Pacheco discovered the last of his powder was wet, so we had no hope even of shooting a rabbit. Preacher Dob was cheered that the wet powder forestalled any chance of having to shoot his dog.

Sam was looking more poorly by the minute. She sat beside me hunched over in a woeful, gloomy manner with her clawed up neck wrapped up in Mr Pacheco's shirt sleeve. Mr Pacheco was not wearing his poncho, as it was wool, soaked wet, and more trouble than it was worth. Therefore he had a bare arm. We was all shaking cold.

You would of thought Sam might feel a calling to at least own up to the fact that none of us would of even been there by that river if not for her being so willful. For six whole years she had talked of nearly nothing but killing the panther, and now here we was, having followed her inclinations, all of us doing her bidding, perhaps each for our own purpose, I will grant you that, but swayed by her wishful thinking and dire need. We was not in a respectable situation. We was wet through, shivering cold, and hungry. We was lost but for knowing we was somewhere on the river.

Considering where we was and thinking how she had got us here, I commenced to fume. I said, Did you never even stop to think how bad a panther's hide might stink nailed up and drying out. Did you never stop to think of nothing that is real. You have put yourself on a single track, heading but one way, and here is where it has brought you. And where is here. You don't even know. It is a cold miserable place and you have got your neck wrapped up in Mr Pacheco's shirt sleeve and leaving him with a bare arm in the freezing cold. I would not care one thing about you being here if I did not have to be here with you.

They was rude things to say to her and I should not of laid it on her as thick as I done. I might of stopped there, but she give me a look like Juda, as if she cared nothing for me or my thoughts, and turned her face from me and looked at the water, and said, Talk all you want, I ain't listening.

My feelings come boiling up then. I said,

All these years you been saying you had powers to know that panther was coming around, and we was just now in a cave with it and you was dumb to the fact. You know nothing. You can't do nothing without me making it happen for you. You been saying I ain't your boss. Well you ain't mine neither. I am tired of being trod on. I have fed you, clothed you, and done for you, whilst you have not lifted a finger. You might be more clever than me, but you are littler than me, and a girl, and a half nigger, and I have been long suffering long enough. When we get out of this place and get you home, I will see things become different.

Judge, they was hard and thoughtless words, the evilest I ever said that I remember. I am sorry to this day. Sam did not so much as turn to look at me. It was even the case that Preacher Dob and Mr Pacheco felt no need to remark upon what I said, as I guess they figured I had a point about some, if not the worst, of it, and I guess they also figured it was not the time for me to of made it. I did not feel much relieved for having done so.

Sam sat and said nothing. She watched the water. As wrong as I felt for my words, I was still mad and nearly wished I could shove her into the flow.

It was a long, long, long night that come upon us then. I will not go into a lot about it, as what is the point of that. Also there is not a lot about it to tell you, as it was all of one piece, like the flow of the river, just time going by. It was dark, cold, hungry, miserable time that gone by, and the sole comfort I took in it was knowing that every minute got me closer to having it over.

Mr Pacheco did manage to build us a small fire with wood of a old dead tree that had kept dry enough under the ledge, and to keep it going. However, it was the coldest fire I ever knew, as the wood was not much and the rain run down before us in sheets off the wall of rock we was sheltered under, and splattered in upon us.

Preacher Dob borrowed me his spectacles again, but what was there to see. A sputtering fire alongside me and a sheet of rain before me, was all. There was nothing to listen to, neither, just the loud water. We could hear nothing else. No night birds, no crickets nor frogs, no coyotes nor wolves howling nor any varmints rustling about. There was no thunder now, neither. There was just the never ending sound of the water spilling down off the wall we was tucked under, and rushing by alongside in the canyon we come out of, and running fast in the river before us. There was just these sounds and the smell of cold smoke and wet dog, and blood, and skunk.

Preacher Dob said a prayer over Zechariah.

Sam said, Will the Lord answer.

Preacher Dob said we would have to wait and see.

Sam said, He's a wait and see Lord, ain't he.

Preacher Dob said she was right about that.

He's a hide and seek, wait and see Lord, she said.

Preacher Dob was forlorn. He hunched over Zechariah in his lap and dozed as best as he was able.

The dog shivered and panted. He licked his lips as sick dogs do. On occasion he growled or barked like he was dreaming about the panther.

Mr Pacheco kept going along under the overhang to cut more dry wood out of the dead tree. The rest of the time he sat staring at the rain. He was a fine looking man the day before in his good looking outfit, but now he looked no better than Preacher Dob. They both was unshaved and dripping. They was old enough to start with and had gone downhill.

We none of us talked much nor made a attempt to work out a plan of what to do next. What kind of a plan could we even do. We wanted nothing but out of where we was and to have dry clothes, and food, and a better fire. I could of spit on our fire and put it out, it was so puny. Also, the incline we was on was such that if we would of stretched out we would of rolled down into the river, so we had to watch out for ourselves. The river was not more than thirty feet down. I guess Mr Pacheco was the only one amongst us who did not want to go home, as he did not have one to go to.

Sam leaned on me and slept. There was a sharp rock under me and I could not get comfortable without waking her, so I had to let her be. I begrudged her the comfort but my father would not of been proud of me if I had shoved her off me whilst she was sleeping when she was hurt and might roll into a river. So I let her be.

That is what happened in the night. It was not much. It was no fun. The horses did not like the time, neither. They shifted about and stood the rain pouring on them the best they could.

Toward daylight the rain ceased. Dawn come along gray as a wolf.

And who should come along with it but

Clarence Hanlin.

You can bet I was not too happy to blink and see him. It was like he sprung up out of the mud. Our horses stomped and shifted, I looked up, and there he stood, not ten feet off, on the incline between us and the river, evil as ever and aiming his pistol up at us. He had snuck up. He had his pistol in his left hand on account of his right was wrapped in a filthy bandage nearly as big as his head. But no matter, he terrified me, pistol nor none, in right hand or left. He was not as wet as us, on account of he had on a poncho made of black India rubber. He wore a mean look on his face, with a haversack over his shoulder, and did not appear to of suffered the kind of night we had bore.

He said, Well, well. Top of the morning to you four fine people.

Sam and Preacher Dob woke up at hearing his voice.

Zechariah seen Hanlin despite that his good eye was looking the other direction. He growled.

Mr Pacheco had been in the act of laying twigs on the fire. He now sat there looking at Hanlin and holding them twigs.

Hanlin slogged up the hill and come close to us. He said, Fancy this. I was idly walking along down this river and I happened across sight of you four having a see-esta here and recollected that one of you owed me a hundred dollars. Might that be you, Pacheco.

Mr Pacheco stood up but did not answer one way or another, as we all knew it was him that owed it, and answering nonsense such as that would give it credence.

Hanlin said, So I come up to see if I might collect. Also, I am scratching my head here, but I seem to recall that one of you has my pistol. It ain't you, Pacheco. I see that's your own that you have. And mine is no pepperbox like what my Uncle Dob's got. So the one belonging to me must be the pistol the boy has got tucked in his belt. Might that be true, Benjamin.

I said, Yes sir, it is.

Hand it over, said he. Get it out of your belt. Lay it here at my feet.

I done so and sat back down.

Preacher Dob rose to his feet. He was wobbly on account of our hard couple of days and nights. He said, Clarence, none of us needs your show. Quit acting the smart ass. You shot my horse. You bothered these kids. You was in on hanging innocent men, despite that you deny it. Have you not

312

brought enough shame on your family already.

Hanlin took a moment with that. He squinted his droopy eye and looked Preacher Dob over. He said in a way to prove he was boss, Uncle Dob, give me the pepperbox and what's left of that rifle. Shove it over here.

Preacher Dob appeared disgusted, but done so.

Hanlin picked up the pistols and tucked them into his belt. He said, Now give me yours too, Pacheco. If you don't, I think I'll just tug on my trigger and shoot you in the face.

He aimed his pistol at Mr Pacheco and we all of us thought he might shoot him. I guess it was not the first time Mr Pacheco seen a gun close up pointed at him, as he already had powder marks deep on his face, as I have before told you. He did not flinch nor draw back. It was a long minute that passed that way before Hanlin raised up the gun and shot into the sky, knocking down branches.

Is there no bottom to your meanness, nephew, Preacher Dob said.

Hanlin owned there was not. He said his friends that was coming along was no nicer. I'll have your pistol, Pacheco, he said. Wet

313

or not. Holster and all. Flask as well.

Mr Pacheco taken the rig off and laid it all down and shoved it forward to him.

Preacher Dob said, Clarence, if you harm these kids you're going to hell.

Hanlin picked up the rig and hung the belt over a branch. He pulled the pistol out and stuck it in his own belt. He now had our three pistols with mucky powder, along with his own that was dry and worked fine. He had a large hack knife in his belt too. He looked in a pointed way at the pinto. It appears like one of you might have something else that don't belong to you, he said. And if I ain't wrong, the owner is heading this way. It's a patch of bad luck you are having, Pacheco. I am having a lucky day, and you are not. I have got all these pistols with me, whilst all you got with you is a long winded preacher, a stinking dog, a boy too big for his britches, and a ugly little wee nigger.

Mr Pacheco appeared to ponder that. He said, The day is even more lucky for you than you know. Today you can make a fortune.

Hanlin looked askance at him and said, How might that happen.

Sam figured what Mr Pacheco was fixing to say, and sprung to her feet like a grasshopper. It is my right to shoot the panther! she hollered at Mr Pacheco. Don't you go egging him on to do it!

Mr Pacheco told her to hush. He commenced to tell Hanlin about the bounty for the panther. He said, However, you will need me to tell you who is offering the bounty, where it is, and how to collect it.

Hanlin said, Bounty, my ass. That panther is gone. I come for my pistol, my hundred dollars, and that horse.

Mr Pacheco give him a nod. He said if this was the case, Hanlin's luck had run thin, as the only dollars he had on him was not real ones and there was not nearly a hundred of them, and what there was of them was wet and likely coming to pieces in his saddlebags, as counterfeit was not sturdy.

You goddamn son of a bitch! Hanlin hollered. You owe me a reliable hundred dollars! Unless you got the panther tied to a tree or penned somewhere that I can shoot him, I am not interested in your two thousand dollars that is somewhere you won't tell me. I will shoot you in the face, you son of a bitch. You better come up with a offer I want, or I'll string up these kids! Don't think I won't. I strung up grown men on the Julian and watched them jerk. There's a rope on your saddle there long enough to hang these kids with no problem. I'll do it. I'll watch their necks pop.

Those was his words that he spoke in just that order, Judge. That is the true admission he made. He stood in a arrogant stance under wet branches that dripped on him whilst the river flowed reckless behind him out of banks at a pace that would make you dizzy to watch for too long. He confessed it all in more detail than we wanted to hear. He told us he and some of the other soldiers in his command walked the captives off from the place they was encamped in the dead of the night and hanged them one after another whilst the others looked on. He said the noose was tied around their necks and tossed over a sturdy limb, the other end of the rope was tied to a saddle, and the horse spurred forward. All the prisoners was strung up that way but the last. He asked to be shot, and mercy was taken on him.

It weren't me that taken the mercy, Hanlin boasted.

Preacher Dob looked like he might break down from hearing the spiteful nature of these words. He said aloud, I will not tell my sister. I will not breathe a word of what I just heard. Any of you who live may do so, but I will not shatter my sister's heart.

Hanlin got a biscuit and salt meat out of

his haversack and made a show of partaking. He said, This meal is sure tasty. Too bad there is none for any of you. However, you all did have a considerable breakfast two days past in your stinking house, when I was allowed none and suffering over my finger.

He smacked his lips and took a firm look at the horses. He approached the pinto and patted him down. He said, Uncle Dob, did you call me a idiot yesterday. How do you think I found you, if I'm a idiot. The fact is, I'm a genius. I figured you'd follow that canyon you took off for, and end up right about here. So I rode ahead of my companions, tied my horse yonder at a creek he was having a hard time with, come across on a log jam, and walked on down this way. And sure enough, here you are. It looks to me like you're the idiot, Uncle Dob. Not me.

He continued to feed hisself the salt meat and biscuits and he waved the pistol about and made a show of giving the mare a pat on her rump.

I have told you, Judge, how much the mare liked a pat on her rump. What happened was faster than I can tell you about it. The mare wheeled about and got a firm grip within her teeth on the hand he patted her with. It was the one within the bandage.

When she got hold of it, Hanlin hollered and part of his biscuit come flying out of his mouth. He knocked the mare over the head with his pistol. But she did not turn loose of the bandage. I think he could of beat her brains out and she would not of turned loose of it. He commenced to scream in a terrible manner. I think he thought he might wind up short of another finger. I thought he might find hisself short a whole hand. The mare yanked his arm and tossed him hither and yon like he was a rag doll that come to life and learned to scream. It might of been only a second or two but it seemed a lot longer. It was a hubbub I will not forget. Preacher Dob and Mr Pacheco pounced on Hanlin and wrestled him out of the pistols. They whacked him and socked him about. Before long, the pistols was all in the hands of Mr Pacheco whilst Preacher Dob had hold of the knife. There stood the mare, stamping her feet and snorting and swinging the empty bandage like she was having a fun time with it. There stood Mr Pacheco with the loaded pistol aimed at Hanlin. There laid Hanlin upon the ground in his rubber poncho, howling about his hand. His head was gory and his mouth crumbly with biscuit and bleeding and missing a tooth.

Preacher Dob and me got a rope off the pinto and tied up Hanlin's legs and bound his arms behind his back. It was no fun binding his arms, as his hand commenced to bleed like before. It was blue and twice the size of the other and oozed in a ugly fashion. He hollered about the pain. Mr Pacheco said he would shoot him if he did not quiet down. We stood and eyed him whilst he laid on his side on the wet ground and cussed us and spit out more blood than you would think even a mouth of that size could hold.

Preacher Dob said, Nephew, you have undergone the will of the Lord.

Sam squatted beside Hanlin's face and said, You got what you had coming.

Preacher Dob told her, Little girl, the Lord is having his way and it is not for you to comment upon it.

We was short of a clear idea of what to do next and commenced to debate our choices.

Mr Pacheco was not in favor of worrying over the fate of Hanlin. He said he wanted to shoot him. He said if we turned him loose, no good would come from that. He said he could shoot him and throw him into the river, and the current would take him off.

Sam was in favor of doing that.

Preacher Dob sat on a rock and give things thought.

Mr Pacheco shored up his argument. He said, a snake will not grow legs and get up and walk like a respectable animal. To the contrary it will always crawl.

Hanlin laid curled up like a grub and spit a great deal of blood. He said, Don't shoot me. I am sorry. I did not help hang nobody. I was just trying to scare you all.

Preacher Dob said, You done it, and you know it. You cannot take back such words. I think there is no hope for you.

Hanlin said, Give me some time to come around, Uncle Dob. I need help and mercy. Don't let the Mexican kill me, please.

Sam expressed she would like to have Hanlin's poncho.

Mr Pacheco give Hanlin a kick and rolled him about and took the poncho off him and give it to her. It was quite large on her when she put it on.

Preacher Dob told Mr Pacheco, If we kill my nephew we're no better than him and his cohort on the Julian stringing men up without a proper trial. I got enough sins to atone for in my life without giving a nod toward you shooting my sister's boy.

Mr Pacheco inquired of Hanlin how far

off the lawman and the fat man might be in pursuit.

Hanlin said the lawman had turned back on account of he thought well of Preacher Dob when he known who he was. He said only the fat man was coming, and he was a ways back.

Mr Pacheco give him another kick and said, That is not what you told us before.

Hanlin allowed he had lied about it before.

Mr Pacheco inquired how far back Hanlin had left his horse.

Hanlin said his horse had got loose of its tether and run off spooked in the storm in the night.

Mr Pacheco said, That is not what you told us. Where is he.

Hanlin said, I swear to God, I don't know. Why would I not tell you. My chances are better if there is a horse to put me on, and there ain't.

Sam helped herself to biscuits out of Hanlin's haversack and give one to me and offered a share to Zechariah, although he laid there and did not eat it.

Preacher Dob said, What kind of lessons would we be giving to these young kids if we was to kill a man without a fair trial.

Mr Pacheco said justice would not get done in a trial by the Sesesh. Hanlin would get turned loose and cause more trouble to Sam and me, he said, and he did not see that as a good end nor even what God would say was right.

Preacher Dob argued that a good portion of Sesesh was fair people and he thought justice might get done, however he could not guarantee it.

We was in a quandary then about what to do. There was no hope left of finding the panther, as we did not have a viable dog and there was no tracks. Therefore chasing the panther was not considered. Preacher Dob would not agree Hanlin aught to be outright shot, though he did agree he deserved it. Mr Pacheco come around to that too. However, what else aught to be done with him was a puzzle.

At long last, Preacher Dob declared that Sam and me and him was to escort Hanlin to Bandera. He said Mr Pacheco was not to go along with us, but to head south, on account of the law was looking for him. He said the task would not be a easy prospect, on account of the mare would not be friendly to having Hanlin laid over the saddle, and how else was we to get Hanlin anywhere, for if we was to cut his legs loose and allow him to ride or walk he would run off. There was none of us willing to shoot him if he done that other than Sam, who we would not allow to. Also, Preacher Dob could not walk far on his hurt leg. He would not leave Zechariah behind, and I did not like the thought of having to carry Zechariah, as it was a task I figured would fall to me.

We sat to ponder it out.

Mr Pacheco noted the horses was in need of grazing and said he would take them up top to the mesa and let them graze whilst we considered. He stood and took the reins of both horses.

Sam sat on a rock and looked at Hanlin. She said in a bossy manner, Lord, give us a sign if he is to live or die.

Preacher Dob told her, The Lord will answer questions or requests that is made in a polite way but will not answer demands.

She become tetchy and said, Well, then, Lord, my question is, will you not hurry up and give us a sign.

There was pecan trees between us and the river, and I started down to fetch pecans for breakfast. I was nearly to the trees when a deep rumbling come from upriver. The ground shook under my feet and there was yelling behind me. Sam screeched my name. I turned about and looked up to where I had come from, and seen these four things.

I seen Mr Pacheco grab hold of Sam and toss her onto the pinto. I seen her jump down from the pinto and come running at me in Hanlin's big poncho that was dragging about her, hollering for me to run, which caused me to figure Indians was coming. I seen Hanlin get to his feet, which was bound, and stand hunched over with his hands tied at his back, shouting Cut me loose! Cut me loose! And I seen Preacher Dob look at him, and take up the knife as if to cut him loose, and hold back, and drop the knife, and lean down to pick up the dog.

Then I turned back to the river to check if Indians might be coming, and a mountain of water crashed down on top of me. The water knocked me so hard I was not in my right mind nor the master to my own fate. The river become the master. It said what I might do, and where I might go. There was no more deciding about going this way or that, or turning back, or tracking the panther or not, or which way the panther might be. There was just going with the river whilst not knowing where it might take me and not giving a lot of thought as to where that was, but just trying to keep my head above water.

It is a strange matter how a person's need can come down to just air. Before the waters come over me I had a great deal of difficulties in my life. I had Sam and her ornery nature, and the panther's whereabouts, and being lost, and a sorry house to go home to, and winter coming, and work I aught to get back to, and goats and chickens waiting on me to be fed. I had a future I had to think over. I had a stinking dog I thought I might have to carry, and a risk of Comanches and snakes and other things, and problems I felt I should think on. However, when the water come over me, my whole struggle in life become for air. Hunger meant nothing to me then. Cold meant nothing. They was small potatoes compared to what I needed.

I come to the surface, kicking and scratching. I do not know if my eyes was open or closed, as I seen nothing but dark about me until I got my head out of the water. The river hauled me off at a speed I had not traveled before in my life, neither on foot nor horseback. I think it might of been carrying me as fast as a train. My head was above water and then it was under, by turns. At times when it was above, I heard roaring water and screeching noises of things clashing and breaking. At times when it was under, I heard deep rumbling of things in a reckless jumble knocking me about. There was branches and creatures caught up.

There was antlers and thrashing hooves churning. There was turtles and weeds and fish and items I can't put a name to, as they was moving too fast to make out. They moved swift in the water whilst things on the ground and above seemed like they come to a stand still, as I seen them only in short hints when I could get air. There was gray clouds in the sky and bright leaves in the trees and a gang of geese overhead, but I was never above water long enough to see the clouds move nor the leaves drop nor the geese so much as flap their wings. There was nothing above the water but still pictures and nothing within it but things soaring past and coming apart.

One picture I recall above water is Mr Pacheco. I seen him every time I come up for air. He was atop the canyon, against the sky, mounted upon the pinto and headed fast in the same direction the water was taking me and keeping abreast.

Another thing I seen when I was up for air was Hanlin in the river and going around the bend. I was working to get myself to the bank, where the current was not so lively, and he come alongside me in the dead center of the river and passed me in a tangle of river trash, neither thrashing nor kicking but laying on his back, nearly as flat as if laid out on a table, his eyes open like they was staring up at the sky. If he had not of been moving so fast he might of looked like he was enjoying a float atop the water on a summer day. However, he was in a stanch current. His face had a waxy look and he did not appear to be vital. He was moving head first in the water as the river took a turn. The fact he did not put up a fight against being swept at such a rate might of been sign enough he was passed, except the fact his legs was tied and his arms bound at his back meant he could not of put up a struggle no matter if he was vital or not. For that reason, I can't swear to you he was dead when he went flying by me. But I can tell you it was the last I ever seen of him. And I can assure you, on account of I was in that roaring water myself, and tumbled about and beat up by sharp branches and whatnot at that time, there was nothing besides a merciful act of God that might of saved him, bound as he was, and it seemed to me like the act of God was that of sending the flood that done him in.

That is my own opinion. At the time I did not have a opinion. I was too busy scrambling for air, as you might think, and for the bank, and casting about for Sam, as I figured the water had taken her up same as it done me. It is a strange thing to say, but I had a inkling where in the water she was, even whilst I could not see her. My mind appeared to keep track of her. She had taken a chance with her own life to come running to me and warn me, and now I feared she was lost in the terrible mess of the frothy water, jammed in a tangle of branches or knocked out by wayward rubble, when instead she might of been riding atop the ridge on the pinto with Mr Pacheco if she had not been loyal to me.

I have told you that Sam is a bossy braggart, and will not work, and complains a great deal. It is all true. However, she risked herself for me, and even whilst the water carried me on, dragging me out of her sight and her out of mine, there was a pull on both of us that kept us close to each other in all the tumult.

It is a curious thing what a flood will bring together and what it will tear apart. It yanked trees out of the ground and ripped off their branches and skinned them of bark. It churned creatures under, and spit others out. It delivered some to the shore. It took my shoes and my shirt off. However, with all the taking it done, it give me a gift that was better than any of what it carried off from me, as it was a gift of hope. It was a large cypress tree pushed sideways up behind me and clogging a bunch of rubbish behind it. I got hold and pulled myself into the branches and climbed up out of the rushing water, and rode the river as it carried me full speed around the bend I just seen Hanlin pass through.

It was a perilous ride among needled branches that rocked and shifted and might of tumped over and dumped me at any minute, or penned me under. However, there was a thrill to it, sir. I would be deceiving you if I did not say so. I felt as if I was mounted upon the masthead of the Pequod and sailing out at top speed.

I looked up and seen Mr Pacheco at full gallop alongside on the mesa atop the bluff. My perch afforded a wide view of the gray sky, the birds flying, the water on either side flowing eight or nine feet out of banks. It was snatching up trees by the roots and hauling them off whilst swamping them that held fast.

I had on nothing but trousers, and they was frayed to mere shreds. The cold air hit me full on. It stung my flesh and tugged my hair. But I did enjoy the freedom of moving fast and having a view.

I might of enjoyed it longer if I had not been looking about for Sam. I was peering hard into the churning water when my gaze settled upon the most awful vision. It was the black poncho jammed in the thick rubble behind the tree. It floated in a eerie way amongst bubbles and branches. Fear seized my body and soul. I figured Sam was under the poncho and drowned, and fast as I could I made my way down through the branches to get to her.

I was nearly down to the roiling water when the weirdest sight of my life presented itself to me. There clung Sam, holding tight to the end of a long branch of the very cypress I rode in, her head above water, whilst right alongside her, his claws dug into the same branch, his back end underwater but his head above the surface, was the panther. Side by side, sir, they was riding that river, both hanging on for their lives.

I took stock of the sight and it come to me that perhaps it was not real. It come to me I was knocked out and dreaming. It come to me Sam and the panther was both passed and swept off and done in, and this was their ghosts come back to pester and haunt one another. I thought, They are dead and will ride this river together forever all the way to the sea, and there they will be tossed into the stormy depths with Captain Ahab and Moby Dick.

However, they did not look passed. They looked sopping wet and scared. Sam was out on nearly the end of the branch, and the panther was between her and me. The two of them was no more than three feet apart, but took no notice of each other, as they was working hard just to hold on. The panther had his ears laid flat and his claws dug into the branch and his hind legs twisting around for a hold. He looked smaller in the water than before. However, I noted the ear with the notch that I noted before, and the scars on his face, and I was certain he was Dos Dedos. Sam did not waste her vigor to talk to me, but latched her gaze on me in a way that left no doubt she was counting on me to save her.

We was rounding a bend at that time and our tree become lodged in a jam near the bank, jolting me nearly from my hold and forming a strong eddy that sucked at the wreckage around us. I seen we was tangled with a upright tree. It was rooted but half under water. If we could climb from our tree into the branches of that one, then we might wait out the flood without drowning.

However, the fact of Sam being on the far side of the panther was a hindrance to that. The branch they was both hanging on to was limber and skinny. Sam was doing her best to hold on, but it was a task. She was nearly sucked under the branch by the eddy. The way things was set, I would have to get past the panther to get to her. I could think of no other way to do so than to knock him off his hold. I was in need of a firm branch to poke and whack him with, and I give it my all to break one off. However, I could not break one big enough with my bare hands, so I finally give up and pulled one out of the water that was hardly more than a needled twig.

Whilst holding on to other branches I made my way onto the one the panther and Sam was hanging on to and jabbed at the panther. He snarled and hissed but did not swipe at me, as it would of obliged him to turn loose of his hold and get swept off. I feared the branch would not support us all three, as it was sustaining a good deal of tug from the eddy as well.

I commenced to poke at the panther's eyes. You could not of told me, at a erstwhile time, that I would one day find myself with the nerve to jab a stick at those eyes. When I done so, he must of got strength out of his dander, as he pulled with his forelegs and swung his hind legs up under him, and up he come onto the branch, snarling and swiping at me and causing me to lose my balance fending him back. I grabbed at branches about me but the tree tipped and dumped me into the drift that was bunched up in the eddy. I sank down under the tangle.

And here come the panther, tumbling in on top of me. I do not know if he attacked me then when he hit the water, or if he was purely trying to get a purchase on some solid thing and I was it, as he had been dumped in the eddy against his will, same as me. He thrashed and clawed and climbed on top of me, shoving me further under. I made a attempt to dive down deep to get away from him, but we was both practically drowned by the eddy with nothing else to get hold of but each other.

It was a strong suck down there. The panther and me was caught up amongst branches down deep. I cut myself nearly to pieces trying to get out of that cage of needled branches that locked me in. The water was thick with mud, and I could not open my eyes enough even to see which way was up. My chest begun to heave and I thought I might have to go ahead and breathe the water. I did not have a clear sight of the panther but I felt him thrashing about with me in the snare of branches. His hide that Sam had been so eager to walk upon writhed against me in the struggle.

I guess you are wondering what might of happened next, as it is apparent to you that I am amongst the living or I would not be writing this testament. You might be thinking the jam broke up by a miracle and set me free to rise to the surface. However, that is not what happened. What did happen was I felt somebody take hold of my arm and commence to yank and pry me out of the snarl. I did not know who it might be, nor even wonder, as beggars are not choosers, so goes the saying. I give myself up to the yank, and thereby got untangled and dragged to the surface even whilst the panther twisted and tossed about in the snag.

I think you will not be surprised, Judge, to hear it was Mr Pacheco that had hold of me. He hauled me onto the bank and left me there on my belly, spitting mud and coughing water, whilst he climbed out onto the branch that Sam was still clinging to. He hollered at her over the roaring of the river to get hold of the branches and move toward him. He shouted that he could not go out to the end where she was, as the branch was at risk of breaking and she would go with it. He told her where to put her feet, where to grab hold, and how quick to move. He kept her coming.

I did not hear a peep out of her the whole time. She locked her eyes on him and done just what he said.

He said, Neenya, you are almost here now.

The next thing I knew he was dumping her onto the ground beside me. She was shaking so hard her teeth clanked. I guess we was a pitiful sight together. I had no shoes. Sam's shirt was nowhere about. She had Mr Pacheco's sleeve tied around her neck, and had on her trousers, but nothing other than that. He took off what remained of his shirt and covered her up. His boots was on the bank, as he must of thrown them off before going into the water. He squatted on his bare feet, wearing nothing but his black trousers and huffing and puffing beside the pinto. Twigs and cypress needles dangled out of his hair, his skin looked white from being cold, the powder that was burned into his face looked blacker than before, on account of his face looked whiter, and his hands was bleeding, as was mine too.

He said, Deeos meeo.

I said, Did the water get Preacher Dob and my mare.

He said he believed they was all right, as Preacher Dob had got the mare and the dog up the slope before the water struck them.

The three of us huffed and puffed and wiped water out of our eyes. The pinto was breathing hard too. His head drooped. He was lathered from running so fast at the top of the bluff. He had outrun the river. Mr Pacheco stroked his head.

We heard a snapping and crackling over the roar of the river and seen the cypress tree break free and commence to move out into the current.

I said, The panther is snared in branches under there.

I guess Mr Pacheco knew that. I guess if he seen me topple into the water and get stuck in the branches, he seen the panther go in too.

He squinted his eyes as the tree headed off downriver and picked up speed, dragging beneath it my third of two thousand dollars, and his third of it too, and the future we might of had, and the hide Sam wanted to walk on. We watched it all go. Mr Pacheco shook his head and made a regretful sound. He patted Sam's leg and begun to say something, as if to raise our spirits. However, before he had got a word out we was surprised by a loud gunshot from upriver, and turned and seen the fat man come riding full speed in our direction.

Mr Pacheco give me a unsure look. I seen in his eyes he did not want to leave me and Sam there on the bank, cold as we was, without food nor shelter, still coughing water. But what choice did he have.

I said, Mr Pacheco, go.

He took a look at his boots beside him and tossed them at me. He took up the pistol he had laid aside, the one he had taken from Hanlin. He said a thing or two I did not make out about Deeos and ameegos, by which I think he called us his friends. Then he mounted the pinto barefoot and lit out into the cedars behind us and up the slope, riding toward the rim, firing Hanlin's pistol down at the fat man as he gone. We glimpsed them both in snatches amongst the trees whilst they made their way up, rocks tumbling down behind them. They was yelling and shooting at one another. We heard them feebly over the roar of the river.

We stood up and watched until they topped the canyon, and then we seen them no more. I have seen neither Mr Pacheco, nor the pinto, nor the fat man since then. However, Mr Pacheco was in the lead of the fat man, and mounted upon a nobler horse, and I believe he outrun him.

So ends my honest testament as to all I know of the deeds and death of Clarence

Hanlin and all things and folks related to my acquaintance with him.

Dear Judge,

You could of knocked me over with cotton fluff when Mr Hildebrand give me another parcel from you. I was not expecting such a thing but stopped for a visit, as I was in town and I had change in my pocket for strudel. I have determined to pay for the strudel now, as I have no more official business with Mr Hildebrand.

And there sat your parcel right on his desk. He said, Well, pick it up.

I could not believe how heavy it was. He wanted me to open it so he might see what was in it. However, I enjoyed pondering on that myself, so I packed it on my mare and come home with it and opened it when I could take the suspense no longer.

Sir, I was hoping it would be books,

and it looks like you read my mind. I have never heard of these books but I am excited to read them. I do not know who Tristram Shandy is and I am eager to learn about his opinions. I do know about Benjamin Franklin and it looks like he has told some good stories on hisself in this book. I will also enjoy knowing about the Roman Empire, as I have heard of it. The book on grammar will come in handy, as my grammar is not perfect and Sam could use a great deal of instruction. I will take you up on teaching her how to read. She has been interested to learn but I have not taught her, as I have been too busy to do so. Also, she has not done a great deal for me, and I have begrudged her that, as you know, but at your suggestion I will now take time. She is happy with the scarf you sent her and has put it on and wore it down to the creek in spite of it is not cold out and there is nobody she might show it off to but the sow. She has got it on down there as I write. Also the necklace with the glass beads. The socks for me will come in handy, as the ones of my father's I wore was done in. Thank you, sir. It was like a large number of Christmases come our way all at once, late and early too.

As to your letter, I will do what you think I aught to and write other accounts of events that befall me in my life as you suggested. However, I do not think they will be of as much interest to anybody as this account about Clarence Hanlin has been to you, as I have not seen any other people hanged nor looted since the day I seen Hanlin's unlawful actions on the Julian, and it could be I never do. However, maybe I will. I have been reading The Whale again, and I seen where Ishmael says that a most perilous and long voyage ended only begins a second, and a second ended only begins a third, and so on, for ever and for aye.

I did promise you that I would write another letter and I am sorry to of spent a month before doing it. The man I told you about whose place is next to the camp and whose cows got loose that time has purchased six uncommon long-haired goats and I been helping him stack rock walls and build more fences and am too tired at night to put pen to paper. But I do not have to work today and am eager to write you the letter, of which this is it. It is the last one you will need from me.

I am glad you asked about what happened to us after the flood and inquired of Preacher Dob. He was all right. After the fat man chased Mr Pacheco up the hill to get back the pinto he felt was rightfully his, which it might or might not of been, depending on factors that you have more knowledge about than I do, on account of you are a judge, Sam and me walked upriver in the direction of Bandera.

It was a miserable walk. I did not have shoes. I did not have a shirt, neither. I had Mr Pacheco's boots that he left me but I give them to Sam to wear. My father would of rose up out of his grave had I wore the boots and let her feet freeze. They was big for her puny feet though, and she stumbled a good bit. She had on Mr Pacheco's shirt with the one sleeve tore off and tied around her neck to cover the scratches the panther had made when he knocked her down in the cave. We was both lucky to have trousers.

The day was freezing and we was wet. A north wind blew. There was ice in Sam's hair. The sky was like flint, however there was no rain nor sleet. The river withdrawn back in its banks and there was a great deal of wreckage and ruin left behind, with trees tore up and driftwood piled high. Cypress trees that remained upright was skinned of their bark. Some was broke in half. The river had made shortcuts in places that was lower, and we was forced to walk through streams of freezing water, despite the fact we stayed on one side of the river.

Whilst we walked, Sam commenced to brood and then to complain and argue. She was having some trouble, as her teeth was clanking together and her lips was stiff from being so cold, but she managed to keep on talking. Things was building up inside her. She was trounced, body and soul, on account of killing the panther was likely a lost cause now that he was almost assuredly dead. She showed spite toward me and pestered and blamed me for how things was. She got in her head that the panther might still be vital and we should go back and look for him, as she would know the right cypress tree and we might look under it now that the water was down and see if the panther was stuck alive under there.

I told her that was a stupid idea and I

did not want to hear her talking about it. I told her there was no way a creature could live that long without drawing a breath. She argued that even if the panther was dead, we aught to go back for the hide. She was not thinking straight. I was not sure I was thinking straight neither by then, as I was so cold. However, I had wits enough not to turn around and head downriver to look for that tree and haul a dead panther out from under it and skin him and carry his waterlogged, beat up old hide back to wherever we might get to before freezing or starving to death in the task. Also, there was no way to skin him, even if I had chosen to make the effort. We did not have a knife, and I had no plans to try to shoulder the panther up and carry him whole. He would be stiff as a board by the time we got him anywhere we needed to be. It was not something I intended to do, nor even to hear suggested by the likes of her, who had got us into the bad situation we was in.

After I had my say about that, she become quiet and surly again. I seen a lot of anger was jammed up inside her and aching to bust loose. I did not feel she had a right to be spiteful with me, and yet I knew I would have no choice but to take on her anger, as there was nobody else to do so. We was in the middle of nowhere, and nearly froze to death, and it was up to me to take on whatever I had to take on, and get us home.

I will tell you, Judge, I was scared. I missed having Preacher Dob and Mr Pacheco alongside me to consider with and to make decisions on things. I wondered if Preacher Dob was looking after my mare and if Mr Pacheco had got away. Mostly I missed my father and wanted his counsel. I thought of our home and how it would be when we got there. It had not been the same place, empty of him. I thought of the camel's old carcass laying nearly on top of the old chief's grave, stiff and dripping icicles from the cold rains and pecked to pieces by buzzards and bothered by our pigs and half eaten by wolves and coyotes, as it would surely be. I thought of the bowl of bloody water leftover from Mr Pacheco cleaning up Hanlin's hand that would still be on our table, probably froze hard by now. I thought of having no food, and no warmth, and no powder nor balls, and how cold the winter was bound to

347

be. And I commenced to become nearly as gloomy as Ishmael whilst Sam harassed me about the way we was headed, and badgered me about turning back. It was a lot to put up with from her. Things was hazy, as I was so tired, and I was relieved when her chatter become a mere mumble that I did not have to answer to anymore. She did not seem to notice when I ceased to answer, but went on mumbling and making no sense at all about the panther, and about Juda, and other such things that had nothing to do with where we was, nor where we was trying to get to.

After a while, she sat down on a rock.

I said, Get up. We got to keep going.

I can't, she said. I need a rest.

I said, You can't have one. We can't stop here. We'll freeze to death. I ain't freezing to death with you.

I commenced to prod her. However, she would not get up, and I had to yank her up by her hair and nearly drag her.

We had gone some way like this, with her mumbling and falling down and fighting me off from shoving and pulling at her, when we seen a rider on horseback coming our way on our side of the river. Under other circumstances we might of hid in the cedars, as we could not make out who it might be, and we was in unknown territory. But I did not have the energy to haul Sam there. So we waited whilst the rider approached. It did not take us long to figure out that it was Preacher Dob, on account of he had a dog in his lap and was riding my mare.

He seen us, reined in, dismounted, and broke down crying. I thought Zechariah must be passed and that was the cause of the tears. I confess the dog did look dead. The smell of the skunk had not wore off, and the wounds looked like they was festered. However, Zechariah was alive and Preacher Dob was crying on account of he was so happy to see us and not on account of the dog being dead. He had rode our direction downriver in search of us instead of going upriver toward home, despite he was hurt and his dog was nearly done in.

He said, I thought you two was carried off to the Promised Land. Lord, look at you both. Oh, dear. Oh, Lord. You're nearly froze. We got to get you some warmth right away.

He rubbed our arms and tried to get color back into me, as he said I was blue.

Sam was not right in the head and was breathing fast and talking about things that made no sense, like where was our hogs. She seemed to think we was at our creek looking for the old sow. Preacher Dob had Hanlin's haversack, which held some matches, so he built us a quick fire. It was a small one, as things was soaked. He jammed me and Sam together and hauled Zechariah down off the mare and nestled him into our laps to try to feed us some of his warmth. The fact the dog stank so bad hardly mattered to me, as he was warmer than we was. His breath stank too, but it was warm, so I did not mind him breathing on me.

Preacher Dob went off in search of dry wood and come back with some, and got the fire going better. He made us take off our wet pants and said, Never mind that you're naked, nobody cares.

Sam had on Mr Pacheco's shirt, and it was fairly dry by now, so that was lucky.

Preacher Dob strung our pants on a limb by the fire and set Mr Pacheco's boots alongside to get toasty. He give us the rest of the biscuits in the haversack and boiled water in Hanlin's tin cup and made us drink it.

When Sam was warmed up some, and

back to her normal thinking, she told Preacher Dob the panther was down-river stuck under a tree.

He's dead, I said. Hanlin is too. I seen him float by. I told Preacher Dob that Mr Pacheco had rescued us from a tree and that I thought he was all right, but that the fat man taken off after him and they exchanged gunshots.

Preacher Dob become nearly speech-less upon hearing all that news. I guess he figured some of it was good news, and some bad, and some hard to decide about. He shook his head and said, My poor sister. Then he said, May the Lord deliver Mr Pacheco to safety. Then he said, It is a blessing at least to be rid of the panther. Now he can't hurt innocent folks.

Sam looked churlish at him and said, You might think it's a blessing, but it ain't. We did not kill him. If he's dead it's on account of he got stuck under a tree.

I did not like the fact that she give me no credit for my part in the matter. I said, You forget he got stuck under the tree on account of I poked his eyes with a stick and knocked him off the branch to save you.

She give me a look like Juda, and said, You had better not try to take the glory. It was not you that done it. He drowned on his own. You would not even of been there if I hadn't made you to come along. If he's dead, it's my glory.

If I could of foreseen how bad she would take it, I would of kept my mouth shut at that time. However, I was tired and hungry and cold and could not even wish I was home, because what kind of a home did I have. So I said, You was hanging on to a branch for your life. You would be dead if not for me. You get no glory at all. I have saved you three times. You owe me some thanks.

Judge, I will tell you what. It was like another flood took place on that river. Sam's face balled up in a wad and she put her head back and opened her mouth and out come the most horrible grieving wailing noise I ever heard out of a human being. She shoved the dog out of our lap and come up off the ground where she sat, and screamed that I was a liar. She pounced on me with her fists. I made a attempt to get hold of her arms to avoid taking a beating. Preacher Dob made a effort to help me but he was kept busy stopping my mare from rearing up and running away. I guess she had put up with more than her share of shrieking from Indians back in her day, and would not put up with that kind of senseless yelling from us.

I tussled Sam to the ground on her belly and sat on her. She stopped screeching but kept on crying into the mud. It had been a long time, if ever, since I seen her cry and it was a frightening thing to hear how loud she was at it.

All right, I told her, it's your glory. Maybe you did kill him. We wouldn't of been there if not for you.

However, Preacher Dob said, Hush and let her cry. Get off her, and let her cry.

I done so, and she laid howling in the rocks and mud.

He said, She has had a terrible disappointment. Her whole life, she has wanted to kill the panther, and now it's likely dead, and downriver, and taken its hide along with it, and she is left with nothing to show for her plans and none of those plans to look forward to anymore. They are washed off by the water and carried downstream. The Bible says where our treasure is, there will our heart be also. If the panther's hide should remain our little girl's treasure, her heart will lie under a uprooted tree, beyond the edge of all she has ever known in her life, and far out of reach of them that cares for her. We do not want that to happen. She is now called on to leave the hide behind. She is called on to walk off from this river and take nothing that she brought to it. That is a hard thing to do. I would fear for her soul if she did not shed a tear about that. Loss is a bitter pill to swallow. Them that don't taste it are not our kind. It's better to let her cry.

She laid there and wailed aloud, and cursed the panther, and cursed his hide, saying, He killed my mama! He ruined my face! It was my right! It was my right!

She yanked at her hair, and broke her heart right there in the mud, and spent her grief whilst we watched her.

After a time, Preacher Dob told her, Little girl, we need to get going. We need to start back. The Bible tells us the Lord is close to the brokenhearted and saves them that are crushed in spirit. It is time for you to stand up and come on.

She got hold of herself, and we put our pants on, and I shouldered up Zechariah, and Preacher Dob mounted, on account of his leg was still hurt and he could not walk, and Sam mounted behind him, and we started off at a slow pace to make our way upriver.

At nightfall we come to a cluster of houses below Bandera that Preacher Dob knew. They was part of the camp the Mormons had moved on from, and now was lived in by Poles that did not speak English. We knocked on a door and was taken in.

The next day Sam and me rode the mare home, whilst a Polish man eighty or ninety years old carried Preacher Dob home in a wagon with Zechariah.

You might wonder about Zechariah, sir. He has been doing all right in the time since all this happened. I seen him not long ago and he was like a young dog. That hunt did him good.

Preacher Dob has stopped by on occasion to look in on us. He has been good to us and tried to help our situation but does not have means to do so. After his leg got fixed he come to our house and fetched Sam to live with him and his family. She went, but lasted there only a day. She would not agree that Preacher Dob's Mexican boy named Jackson, that had got away from the Indians and come starving to Preacher Dob's corn field, was not a actual Indian posed as a Mexican. She feared he would do them all in. She run off, and I found her back home, and we been here together since then.

Thank you again for your effort to find her a home that would take her. She will not do chores around here, and has nothing of interest to do, and I do worry about her. I am sorry it did not work out. And thank you for the gifts you give us. It is a odd thing how a event like that on the Julian, that had no justice nor kindness to it and cost eight decent men their lives, has somehow, by the way things turned, earned me books, and spectacles, and a steel nib pen.

I promise to make good use of them.

Yours kindly,
Benjamin Shreve

Alfred R. Pittman
Attorney-at-Law
35 Eberly Building
215 South High Street
Columbus, Ohio
April 9, 1925
The Reverend Jackson Beck
First Methodist Episcopal Church
Third Street and Lead Avenue
Albuquerque, New Mexico

Dear Reverend Beck,
  I fear you may have received from me
a batch of papers sent to you without
adequate explanation. This is entirely my
fault. At my age I am not as orderly as I
used to be, and apparently I mislaid the
introductory letter when I gave the
papers to my secretary to post. I have
just come across it here on my desk,
dated a month ago.

Presumably by now you have discovered the nature of the papers. I feel, however, that I should tell you how they came into my custody and why I sent them to you. They were originally in the possession of Judge Edward H. Carlton as he presided, at the close of the War Between the States, over a judicial district that extended from Kimble County, Texas, to the Mexican border. This was during a fractious era when the law was devoted to the arduous and often unpopular task of locating and bringing to justice those individuals guilty of crimes against civilians during the war. The judge conducted interviews with many individuals pertaining to the case of Clarence Hanlin, but it was Benjamin Shreve's testimony, the pages of which you received from me, that most assisted him in rendering to the grand jury his recommendations.

I served as assistant and traveling companion to the judge during the time he was receiving Benjamin's letters and written testimony. Shortly afterward, he left Texas and returned to his hometown of Cincinnati to care for his aging mother. I accompanied him on this move. We took with us the file containing Benjamin's papers, as files were known to disappear from county courthouses and the judge intended to see to its preservation.

Some two years after our departure from Texas, I finished my law studies in Cincinnati and was admitted to the Ohio bar. At that time Judge Carlton and I returned to Texas for a visit. While we were there, we inquired of Benjamin and Samantha in the towns of Bandera and Comfort. We were told that Samantha's whereabouts were unknown and that Benjamin had departed the state with an outfit out of San Antonio to transport cattle to Kansas and had not, as of that time, returned. We stopped at the location on Verde Creek that we presumed to have been their home, but we found the house deserted and uninhabitable. The judge was especially regretful at having lost touch with the boy. Being unmarried and having no children of his own, he had experienced during Benjamin's testimony something akin to a fatherly feeling. He intended to make a further search for Benjamin in the future and see to his welfare and that of Samantha, but on our journey back to Cincinnati by train he was afflicted with a minor chill that quickly progressed into influenza. After we reached his mother's home, the condition settled into his lungs. He passed away a few days later.

After his death the judge's papers came into my possession and have remained in my care for the ensuing decades.

I am now approaching my ninetieth year. My health remains vigorous, but I have felt the ever more pressing need to set my affairs in order. As well I have carried an increasing regret for having failed to search further for Benjamin and Samantha in the nearly sixty intervening years. The judge's death was as great an emotional crisis as I have faced, and I fear that any lingering responsibility I felt toward the children became a casualty of my grief, in that I felt the necessity to cast my mind ruthlessly forward in time and not back. I departed the country for almost a decade of life abroad and on my return settled near my family in Columbus, built a law practice, and lost myself in it and in other scholarly work. Over time the great wound caused by my companion's death healed, but by then, in the complexities of a new life, I had all but forgotten Benjamin's papers and the sense of responsibility I should have felt toward them.

It was a few months ago that my omission began to weigh heavily on my conscience. I wrote to a friend who resides in the area of Comfort and asked what he might know of Benjamin and Samantha Shreve, or possibly of you or other members of your family, who I hoped might have information about them. When he told me of your ministry in Albuquerque, I felt that you would appreciate Benjamin's letters and the testimony involving your father, whose wisdom and compassion pervades throughout, and that you might be kind enough to inform me of anything you know of Benjamin or Samantha.

It has been a happy occasion and great pleasure for me to read Benjamin's pages once again, as they brought back those times on the circuit when the judge shared them with me alongside campfires or on porches in towns where we stopped and received the mail. I recall how he anticipated the postal stops and how he would often rapidly sift through envelopes, even before exchanging proper pleasantries with the postmaster, and hand me all other papers so that he might come upon Benjamin's envelope and open it at once.

Concurrent with sending the original pages to you, I have placed photostats in the Bandera County Courthouse and the archives held by the Texas State Historical Association at the University of Texas. It was vastly important to Judge Carlton, as he stated to me shortly before his demise, that Benjamin's testimony find its way to an appropriate archive.

I leave the destiny of the original pages to your discretion.

Respectfully yours,
Alfred R. Pittman

Reverend Jackson Beck
First Methodist Episcopal Church
Third Street and Lead Avenue
Albuquerque, New Mexico
August 19, 1925
Alfred R. Pittman
Attorney-at-Law
35 Eberly Building
215 South High Street
Columbus, Ohio

Dear Sir,

I hope you will accept my deep and sincere apology for this belated response to your kindness in having sent me Benjamin Shreve's testimony and your letter that followed, which I received, respectively, three and four months ago. I read the testimony immediately upon receiving it but delayed responding to your letter because I lacked adequate words to describe the impact of Benjamin's tale on my thoughts. My wife speculated that I was thrown into a deep emotional well. If so, it has taken me these months to find my way out. The story seemed to resurrect in me a buried longing for an element of my past that has been long lost to me and that I had thought was gone forever.

I will try to describe to you the journey that I subsequently embarked upon. To explain from the beginning my memories of Benjamin I will need to explain to you my own uncomfortable beginnings, or what little I know of them. I hope not to try your patience but rather to supplement the record Benjamin has left.

It is presumed I was born in Mexico to Mexican parents. At about the age of four or five I was taken from my family by Indians. I suppose they were the Comanche, who were prevalent in the area, although I cannot be certain, as they spoke primarily their own language and did not refer to themselves as such. I recall playing beneath large trees near a stream with other children when the Indians appeared on horseback, charged through the water toward us, and chased us as we ran through a field. I do not know the fate of the other children and recall only that I was pulled onto a horse by an Indian and carried away from my home at a great rate of speed. I have explicit memories of the harsh treatment I received at the hands of these Indians, over what period of time I do not exactly know, but I have long since ceased to dwell on these things.

My escape from them, some months or perhaps a year later, happened as the result of a surprise attack by other Indians — I do not know of which tribe. It occurred in the dark of night while we slept. At that time I believe I was partially, and perhaps wholly, assimilated into the tribe's way of life, as I was sleeping freely among them beside a woman who treated me as her child. I remember sudden noise and chaos and a great deal of gunfire, from which I fled. After this I recall being utterly alone and feeling deep disquiet and extreme hunger. I wandered in the wilderness, for how long I don't know, and would be a wanderer still had the Lord not guided me to the cornfield of Dobson Beck, known as Preacher Dob, who would become my father.

As muddled as most of my recollections of that time are, I recall with clarity the moment Dobson Beck discovered me in the cornfield, starving, naked, and retching up his raw corn, having made myself sick by eating my fill. I was overcome with fear upon seeing a human shape appear at the end of a row of stalks, pass by, and then instantly return, having seen me also. He approached me with the late sun of a winter afternoon glinting through his white hair. I attempted to escape him, but he dragged my sick weight into his arms and held on to me even as I, from habit or instinct, struck at him and attempted to claw my way out of his grasp.

That moment in his arms was the beginning of my salvation. I am alive because of him. I am a Christian because of him. I have a name because of him.

I am supposing it was less than a year later when I first saw Benjamin Shreve and his sister, Samantha. I believe this was the timing, as I remember that I had not yet learned to speak adequate English. By that time I was fully situated in the family as one of three children in the home, the other two being the grandson and granddaughter of Preacher Dob, whom I refer to as my father although

368

he was never legally so.

The story of that initial visit paid to us by Benjamin and Samantha, in the company of Lorenzo Pacheco and my father's nephew, Clarence Hanlin, is thoroughly described by Benjamin in his testimony. I will not burden you with my own memories of it except to tell you that I was instantly and acutely drawn to, as well as repelled by, Samantha. Her scars were even more disfiguring than Benjamin has described them, and I was compulsive in my need to look at them and to try to make sense of what had caused them. I had numerous scars of my own from wounds incurred during my captivity, as you may recall from Benjamin's testimony. While my scars could be easily hidden and Samantha's were stretched across her face in the most obvious placement, creating a situation for her that I presume was more difficult to bear, I remember nevertheless feeling a kinship based on the scars and perhaps also based on the implicit suffering. Most vividly, I am still able to evoke the deep and instinctive need I felt to connect or communicate with her.

Samantha's need, in contrast, was for isolation. She refused, in the way Benjamin has explained, to be looked at. I was therefore a threat and even a terror to her, and I have been saddened to learn from reading Benjamin's testament that it was largely her distrust of me that caused her to flee from our house after my father attempted to take her in.

It was likely the same impulse, coupled with her insatiable craving for revenge on the panther, that eventually caused her to take the flight of which I am about to tell you. Nothing of this part of Benjamin's story is included in the materials you sent, as it happened later, perhaps a year after Benjamin wrote his testament to the judge.

I was ten or eleven years old. Benjamin must have been eighteen by then. He came pounding at our door late at night, in a frantic state, and told my father the panther was not dead, as they had believed him to be, but alive, and had preyed upon them once again. He said that on coming home after dark he had found the chickens slaughtered, the panther's two-toed tracks leading down to the creek, and Samantha gone. She had taken a pony Benjamin had recently acquired, had taken with her the hunting gun, and had left behind a note composed using the writing skills that Benjamin had been teaching her. He pulled the note from his pocket and showed it to my father in the light of a lamp on the table. I do not know the exact content but presume it said she was going after the panther.

At that time my father had been anticipating the inevitable passing of his dog, Zechariah, who despite his state of relative decrepitude, as described by Benjamin in his testimony, had nevertheless managed to live through the intervening four years. Although the dog had grown increasingly feeble, when my father held Samantha's note to the lamplight and took full stock of the desperation in Benjamin's face, he declared that Zechariah would appreciate nothing better than to track a panther for one last time and even to die in the attempt. He said that he and the dog would join Benjamin and go in search of Samantha and the panther.

I begged my father and persuaded him to let me come along. He sent me to fetch the dog. I took the lantern and searched every row of the cornfield as well as the sheds and the smokehouse but could not find Zechariah. When I returned to the house and told my father, he shared a look with Benjamin that acknowledged what I think they both at once suspected, which was that Samantha had come and taken the dog herself. I remember the stricken look and the words of my father: "She has beat us to him."

My father and I then accompanied Benjamin to his house on horseback, taking the trail Samantha was most likely to have taken in case we might come across her. When we reached the house we found the panther's tracks and attempted to follow them by the light of our lanterns. However, they were muddied and intermingled with the pony's, and we lost every trace of them in Verde Creek. In some places, near the water, we discovered the tracks of what appeared to be a dog alongside, but we could not distinguish these with any certainty from the tracks of the wolves and coyotes that Benjamin said were known to frequent the creek, and we could only guess if they belonged to Zechariah.

I was told to wait at the cabin in case Samantha might return there while Benjamin and my father searched for her. I can still hear, echoing in my mind, Benjamin calling her name, throughout the night, from across the dark canyons. The sound was heartrending and unfathomable to me, greeted as it was by silence. When Benjamin and my father arrived back at the cabin before daylight, hoping beyond reason to find Samantha there with me, Benjamin's anguish and grief when he saw me there alone were evident to me, even at my young age, in spite of his attempt to remain stoic.

In the morning my father sent me home while he remained with Benjamin for several days and they continued to search the canyons. For at least a month afterward, Benjamin persisted in the search alone, riding from town to town, inquiring if Samantha had been seen. He returned, each time, defeated.

It was only a few years after this that my father passed away, suffering a hard death of what I now believe must have been a cancer of the stomach. I was but thirteen or fourteen years old at the time and unaware of the specific cause of his death, but I recall Ida's desperate and prolonged efforts to relieve his pain. His son had been killed in the war, and I remember that he called out for him shortly before passing.

At this time, Benjamin had left the area to drive cattle out of state and therefore was not in attendance at the funeral.

That is everything I knew of Benjamin prior to reading his testimony and prior to the journey I took this year. I remained with Ida and her children, whom I considered then, and still consider, my brother and sister, until the age of eighteen, when I left to attend Baylor University, in Independence, at the generosity of a benefactor whom my father, before his death, had convinced I was worthy of education. My visits to the hill country were infrequent after that, as I married young and moved with my wife to New Mexico to raise our two children and carry forth my father's service to those in need.

I have mentioned already that reading Benjamin's pages cast me into a time of deep thought. In reflecting on the family that had cared for me with such innate generosity of spirit, I then began to reflect, with more emotion than I had previously allowed myself to feel, on the family I had been taken from as a child.

I had long planned to search someday

for the parents I was born to in Mexico, but knowing I would have so little information to guide the search, I had procrastinated, not fully considering the disappointment I would feel at the end of my life if I did not at least make the attempt. The Gospel of Luke instructs us to put our hands to the plow and look only forward, not back. And yet, now in the vicinity of my seventieth year, I began to feel the impending sorrow of future regrets and to wonder if my parents might still, by the grace of God, be living and if I might have siblings and other living relatives in Mexico.

With only a vague notion, then, of what I hoped to discover but doubted I would, and uncertain if I was acting on the will of the Lord or merely on a simple and fruitless wish that I had held since I was a boy — to reunite with my family — I drove south across the border and began my search, traveling eastward through the states of Chihuahua, Coahuila, and Nuevo Leon.

I will not burden you with details of the journey or of the rise and fall of my hopes. I met a great number of fine people at border ranches who had long ago lost family members to Indian raids, but I was unable to discover anyone who knew of a boy taken in about the year when I suppose myself to have been.

I would consider this futile search a failure and disappointment, misguided and unblessed by God, if it were not for the fact that in the course of these extensive inquiries I happened across a curious piece of intelligence in Nuevo Leon, in the village of Santiago, that resulted in a provocative discovery toward which only the Lord could have guided me.

With the knowledge of this discovery, I traveled directly to Texas in search of Benjamin, going first to the town of Comfort, where I was greeted warmly by many old acquaintances and by my sister, who still resides there. I located Herman Hildebrand, the son of the postmaster Bernard Hildebrand, whom Benjamin had known. You can imagine my happiness when Herman told me that there existed a series of notes Benjamin had sent to the elder Mr. Hildebrand over several years, to inform him of his various locations so that Samantha might be told where he was if she should come looking for him, and that these notes were in the care of the current postmaster, who kept them stored in a box at the post office.

I called on the postmaster, who on hearing my purpose was delighted to open the box and allow me to read the notes.

The most recent was dated forty years ago. It relayed the simple information from Benjamin that he had married and purchased a small piece of property ten miles from the town of Cometa, Texas, in Zavala County, and that Samantha might find him there if she were to come looking. He said his wife's family, with the surname of Valdez, was well known in the area and it would be no trouble to find him.

After spending the night in my sister's home, I rose early and drove in the summer heat a hundred and fifty miles south to the town of Cometa, where I had only to speak the name Benjamin Shreve to the first person I encountered — a woman walking alongside the road — to be told, in a mixture of Spanish and English, directions to Benjamin's house.

It stood at the end of a long road in the midst of vast pastures of cattle. Two cars and several trucks were parked in the yard, and I encountered small children and a number of chickens and dogs as I pulled in beside them. The house was nicely painted and well kept. An elderly man, seated on the porch, set aside a stack of papers and rose from his chair as I got out of my car. I knew him almost at once. He did not recognize me at first, as I was hardly more than a boy when he had last seen me. He seemed to think I had come for directions to some other place, but when I told him my name he knew me without hesitation and came down the steps to welcome me with a look of boundless warmth and a mighty handshake.

My visit lasted throughout the hot afternoon and well into the evening. It is enough to say that Benjamin's wife, Estela, treated me as family, and that numerous of their kin came throughout the day to meet me. Two of Benjamin's sons live on the property and help him manage his cattle, and one of his three daughters still lives in the home. A number of grandchildren were present and other people besides, including one young man who told me he had come to Zavala County thirteen years ago in flight from the Mexican Revolution and that Benjamin had taken him in and taught him English and how to read.

At dusk, after a long dinner with many members of the household, Benjamin and I sat alone on the porch remembering old times in the hill country and talking about my father and what he had meant in our lives. When I felt the time was appropriate I asked about Samantha and inquired if he had heard anything of her.

He was slow to answer and finally said, in a thoughtful manner, that he was grateful to have me ask about her, as he had not heard her name spoken in a while and had not seen anyone in many years who had known her. He then spoke of her with great feeling for some time. I recalled how she had shouted at me to get away from the windows when I first saw her and how my father had told his grandchildren and me to turn our faces to the wall. The memory brought a smile to Benjamin's face. He said it was good to remember how cantankerous Samantha could be. He said his memories of her have grown increasingly dim but only weighed more heavily on his heart, and he continues to hold out hope that she might one day appear at his door.

It was then I told him of reading the testimony he had written to Judge Carlton. He was astounded and overwhelmed to know that it had been preserved. I told him of your letter and of how you said the judge had treasured his testament and thought of him with fatherly affection.

Last of all I told him what I will now tell you — that I discovered, in Santiago, the story of a young woman who stayed in that village for a brief time in the early 1870s. She had worked at a shabby cantina on the edge of town and lived in the quarters in the back. By all descriptions, she was a mulatto with a face scarred by the claws of a panther. She was said to have been disagreeable to the owner of the cantina and to have fled the town one night after a violent altercation when a customer insulted her face and she spit in his food. According to the story, which has become something of a local legend in the ensuing half century, she bolted from the cantina, pursued by angry customers, and escaped through the streets of Santiago into the dark of night, never to be seen in the town again. On the morning after her flight, the owner of the establishment entered her unkempt room and took possession of her effects.

As long as I live I will not forget Benjamin's astonished inquiries, his rapt attention, and most of all his expressions of grief and gratitude, and ultimately of joy, when I told him that I had been to the small cantina, which still stands at the edge of the town. There I had seen, behind the rustic bar, nailed to the boards of the wall, the hide of a great panther. Beyond a doubt, I can verify that it was the hide of El Demonio de Dos Dedos. I saw for myself the right hind paw. It was not, like the rest of the hide, deprived of its skeletal structure but displayed the full array of the bones, intact but for two missing toes.

After I had finished relating to Benjamin what I had heard that day in Santiago, and what I had seen in the cantina, he and I sat for a long time on his porch in the warmth of the evening, listening to the pulsing chirp of the crickets and the lowing of cattle. We were quiet in our companionship much of the time. I reminded him of what my father had said on the riverbank when Samantha lay crying in the mud, believing that the hide was downriver and gone forever.

He had said she would have to forsake the hide as her treasure, because where her treasure was, there would her heart be also, beyond the reach of those who loved her. He had called on her to take courage and to walk on.

We pondered the unanswered questions while darkness settled. Why had Samantha never returned to Santiago for the hide? Perhaps it had not given her the satisfaction she was seeking and she had been lost without the sustenance of longing. Perhaps she had gone in search of another elusive thing. I thought of my own journey through life, and where it had brought me, and how the hard wanderings of my childhood had led me into the keeping of Preacher Dob and eventually, through the avenues of time, to the life I now had. It was possible Samantha might have found a similar blessing.

As the night deepened, Benjamin spoke of his struggle between hope for her and despair for her. His face was placid, his manner reserved, and his eyes held a calm and steady gaze as he looked out over his cattle grazing in the pasture. But now and then his voice could not hold back his emotion, and he paused to gather his words.

Where had she gone? To the mountains, to the ocean, to the desert — who could say? I shared with him my belief that she is all right in the way God intended her to be, for we are told in Hebrews 10:35: Cast not away therefore your confidence, which hath great recompense of reward.

I apologize again for my delayed response to your very great kindness in sending Benjamin's testimony to me. It was a thoughtfulness that I will appreciate for the remainder of my days. You will perhaps be pleased to know that before parting with Benjamin I promised to return for another visit and to bring to him the original letters and testament that he posted from the Comfort postal office fifty-nine years ago. Without your care, and that of Judge Carlton, Benjamin's tale would have disappeared alongside countless other tales of old times in Texas that have been forgotten and vanished into the host of days gone by.

Sincerely yours,
Jackson Beck

ACKNOWLEDGMENTS

For the story of *The Which Way Tree* I owe thanks to the following people.

Kenneth Groesbeck advised me on everything from bee bush and possumhaw to the necessary height of a goat pen, the heft of an 1860s Colt six-shooter, and the mechanics of how a rainstorm from the south can precede a cold front from the north and drop temperatures in the hill country down to freezing within hours. Thank you for your patience, Kenneth.

Stephen Harrigan, brainstormer extraordinaire, helped me find my way into the story and all the way through it, his off-the-cuff notions often opening paths out of what seemed to be box canyons. For thirty years Steve and I have been passing our manuscripts back and forth, swapping ideas, sharing research, and scribbling our thoughts in the margins of each other's drafts. When I was puzzling over what sort of character might own a panther dog, it was Steve who said, "How about a preacher?" Steve, thank you for everything except all those snide comments about my spelling.

Jeff Long, invaluable reader and dear friend whom I've known even longer than thirty years, was in this case also a great wrangling partner. Thank you for believing so passionately in this book from the beginning, Jeff.

By an unforeseen happy circumstance an early draft of the manuscript found its way into the hands of Robert Duvall, who has been my favorite actor since he played Captain Augustus "Gus" McCrae in the 1989 miniseries *Lonesome Dove.* I'm beholden to him, as well as to Eric Williams, Salli Newman, Alberto Arvelo, and Ed Johnston for embracing the story with so much passion and for their indispensable insights. It was Bob Duvall who first loved the title *The Which Way Tree* and persuaded me to settle on it.

Randolph B. Campbell and the Honorable Thomas R. Phillips allowed me to pester them with numerous questions about the nature of judicial districts and circuit courts in Texas in the years after the Civil War. My sincere thanks to both for being so generous with their time.

My literary agent, Gail Hochman, with her perfect instincts, submitted the manuscript to Ben George at Little, Brown, who took Sam and Benjamin into his care with as much attention, and what seemed to me like real affection, as if they had been real children. I can hardly believe my good fortune in having this book with the team at Little, Brown and with an editor as meticulous and discerning as Ben.

Family and friends were my earliest readers, as always. I owe the usual heap of thanks to my mother, Eleanor Crook, my sister, Noel Crook, my brother, Bill Crook, my husband, Marc Lewis, my uncle Charles Butt, and my friends Marco Uribe and Sarah Bird for spurring me on from the get-go.

My most heartfelt gratitude is forever to Marc and our kids, Joseph and Lizzie, who during the time I was writing this book somehow managed to keep me happily grounded in the twenty-first century even while my thoughts were rolling back to the nineteenth.

Joseph especially deserves thanks for planting the seeds of this story on a night in the canyons in Bandera County when he was fourteen years old. He and a friend overshot the cabin where they intended to camp — easy to do in that terrain — and became lost in a web of narrow ravines. Our discovery, on driving out to check on the boys at dark, that they had never arrived at the cabin led to nine harrowing hours of driving the rocky roads in search of them, shouting into dark gullies, making our way along stream banks by flashlight, and watching the searchlights of a helicopter fan over the hills as we prayed for the pilots to see something. Sometime after midnight the chief deputy of Bandera and two companions searching with him on the ground radioed that they had seen an enormous mountain lion, known in the old days and in this book as a panther, trailing, quiet and ghostlike, through the canyon into which the boys had disappeared.

Not until we had searched for several more hours did the pilots finally spot, deep in a tight ravine, the glint of a small, smoky campfire with two figures beside it. They landed to pick up the chief deputy and transported him to the bluff above the campsite, from where he hiked down into the canyon, found the boys, and hiked them out. They were flown to a landing spot in a pasture, where we met them. The helicopter was lifting off and the boys safely guzzling water when the deputy turned to me and shouted over the wind noise of the rotor blades, his face lit by the flashing lights, "I don't mean to scare you, ma'am, but when I got there that cat had its eyes on your boys."

Most likely, the cat was simply curious about the unusual invasion of his canyons and the boys at their campfire. The boys, for their part, were not aware he was there until they were told afterward. For Joseph the night was no more than a childhood adventure during which he was thirsty, lost, a little nervous, and subsisting on a shared bag of marshmallows and a few prickly pear fruits he managed to dethorn. It faded quickly from his thoughts. But a writer can never anticipate where stories will come from. The eyes of that mountain lion held me for years.

Finally, I would like to express my abiding gratitude to my grandparents Howard Edward Butt and Mary Elizabeth Holdsworth Butt, to whom this book is dedicated. They grew up in the heart of the Texas hill country, in Kerrville — originally known as Kerrsville — not far from Camp Verde. After they married, they moved to south Texas and finally settled in Corpus Christi, but their roots remained deep in the hills of Kerr and Bandera Counties. Their property near Camp Verde has been the gathering place for our family since long before I was born, and is still in family hands, profoundly loved by all of us down to the fifth generation.

I would be negligent here not to mention a liberty I've taken with the history of Prison Canyon. The last of the prisoners were marched out of there in July of 1862, while in this story they remain into 1863.

I would also be remiss not to state my appreciation for James Wilson Nichols, who came to Texas in 1836 at the age of sixteen and remained until his death in 1891. I've read many firsthand accounts of early days in Texas, but none more thoroughly captivating than Mr. Nichols's journal, published after his death with the title *Now You Hear My Horn.* I was stalled in the early stages of thinking about the story of Sam and Benjamin, in need of finding Benjamin's way of speaking, when I stumbled across the book in a library corner in the home where my grandmother was born, on the property near Camp Verde that I've mentioned. It was signed from my grandmother to my grandfather and dated Christmas 1968.

Reading Mr. Nichols's writing, I perceived the first faint intonations of Benjamin's voice. The manner of speech eventually gained clarity and settled into its own, but a vague semblance of Mr. Nichols's sentence structure, and possibly a phrase or two, have found their way into the telling of *The Which Way Tree.* I wish my grandmother could have known how her gift to her husband would one day, half a century later, be a gift to her granddaughter, too.

ABOUT THE AUTHOR

Elizabeth Crook has published four previous novels, including *The Night Journal*, which received the Spur Award from Western Writers of America, and *Monday, Monday*, a *Kirkus Reviews* Best Book of 2014 and winner of the Jesse H. Jones Award from the Texas Institute of Letters. She lives in Austin with her family.